THE WRONG KEY

AJ CAMPBELL

The Wrong Key

by AJ Campbell

For Edward
Thank you for the inspiration to write this novel
Mum x

ALSO BY AJ CAMPBELL

Leave Well Alone

Don't Come Looking

Search No Further

The Phone Call

ELLIE

All my energy is spent screaming. Desperate cries for help as the glorious lunchtime sun disappears unannounced. I'm shrouded in darkness as if clouds have rolled in and blackened the scene, and a kerosene-like odour replaces the flowery smell of summer. Unadulterated terror rakes through my body, my stomach turning as I digest the gravity of the situation. 'Help! Jack, help me!' My cries are muffled. 'You're hurting me.'

'Stop struggling.' The voice is gruff. It's not Jack, though. Jack's American accent is softer. I feel a clenched fist pressing painfully into the centre of my back. There is another one. Man Two. His heavy footsteps stomp beside me. Man One is pushing me too quickly. I stumble, unable to keep my balance. He drags me effortlessly into an upright position, like I'm a rag doll. My hands curve into claws as I try to attack him, but Man Two is quick to respond. He wrestles with my thrashing hands and binds them behind my back with cable ties, I think. So tightly, I can feel the plastic cutting into my wrists. I stumble again

against the force of Man One's fist pressing into my back. One of them yanks at the rough material of the bag covering my head to keep me vertical. 'Just do as you're told, and you've a chance of surviving this.' He pushes me again. 'Move.' His voice is as fiery and nasty as the bile burning the back of my throat.

I try to scream again, but fear silences me. My muddled thoughts wander inexplicably. Where's Jack? Has he abandoned me, or is he part of this? Have I been tricked? Did he lure me to this park on the outskirts of New York with his sweet talk and irresistible boyish smile? One minute we were lying on the grass, his faithful dog, Teddy, by his side. We were holding hands, staring up at the sky. A cobalt blue so perfect, he said, it looked photoshopped. The sun was beating against our flushed skin, the gentle breeze making it bearable, and birds were chirping, overriding the distant hum of passing traffic. We were discussing the most devastating memories of our lives: that mealtime when my parents announced they were splitting up. The morning his sister died.

Then what happened?

I can't think. The bag pulls rigidly against my nose and mouth. It's suffocating me. I can't breathe.

I have the same wild mop of hair as his sister had. I remember now. That's what Jack said as he unhooked his hand from mine and propped himself up on one elbow, lacing his fingers through my long, dark strands. Before the chemo stripped her head as bald as an egg. And the same eyes, he said. Dark blue, like sapphires. 'I'm so glad I met you, Ellie Knight,' he said, kissing the tip of my nose.

'Me too,' I replied. Never before had I meant two words more.

'I need to pee,' he said, comically ruining the moment. He smiled. 'Don't go anywhere. I'll be right back.' His lips moved down to meet mine.

I was in heaven.

And now I'm in hell.

PART ONE

1

STEPH

It's only seven am, and I've made good time. Leaving my small Victorian cottage some twenty miles out of London, it has taken barely an hour to get into the city: the drive from my village to the station traffic-free at such an early hour, and a train on time for once. So I stop at Costa on the walk from the station to my office. Back-to-back meetings pack my diary from eight until mid-afternoon, so this will be the only chance to get my morning coffee fix. The sun is shining. London is starting to wake up as commuters rush to start another day.

It's the one-thirty meeting that has been on my mind since Charles slotted it in late last night. The message titled *Catch-up* flashed in the corner of my screen as I cleared my inbox of the couple hundred or so emails that had flooded in since Friday evening. I need to find time to unsubscribe to some of these industry news bulletins, but spare moments in this place are like gold dust. Besides, I might miss one of those golden nuggets that has raised me to Charles's number two this year.

Dropping my bag under my desk, I log in to my computer, staring out at the Thames. It glistens a tangerine hue bouncing off the water in the early morning sunshine. As far as office views go – with Tower Bridge and the Shard among the many London landmarks in sight – this one sure takes a beating.

An email pings. A phone rings. And so the day begins.

'You eaten?' Charles mouths, as he stops at my desk at midday. Charles is partial to working lunches, as he is to any meal so long as it involves a business discussion on some level or other.

I shake my head, holding a forefinger in the air. 'I'll read the report and get back to you by the end of the day,' I say to my colleague in Hong Kong before removing my headset.

Charles mimics biting into a sandwich, appearing stressed. 'I thought I'd arrange a bite to eat for our one-thirty. Usual?'

'Sounds good to me. I'm intrigued. What's this meeting about?' I call after him as he walks away. 'We only had a catch-up on Friday.'

He turns around briefly. 'I can't talk now.' He gives a tight-lipped smile and strides off, his tall, broad frame carrying him with the confidence he deserves as the Global Head of Audit and Compliance.

. . .

Charles's glass-walled office shares the same stunning views as mine. He guides me to a leather sofa by the floor-to-ceiling window. After presenting me with a brown paper bag containing a tuna niçoise salad and a black coffee, he tells me about a deal one of our New York traders has structured. He takes a bite from his prawn on granary sandwich. 'Do your thing. Dig deep into the detail,' he says munching. 'Report back to me in the morning.'

I inwardly sigh. There goes my evening.

I like Charles. A lot. Most people do. He is highly regarded at Crayhorne. A great communicator, a motivator, and the first to dish out the compliments for a job well done; most of the time, he is the near-perfect boss. Tough but fair, you know where you stand with him. I can relate to that trait. He can just be too heavy-handed with his deadlines on occasion. Crayhorne prides itself on its commitment to promoting a healthy work-life balance. Charles recently admitted to me at one of our monthly team meals that his last year-end 360-evaluation highly questioned his contribution to this commitment. Not that he seems to have taken steps to do anything about it.

I watch his prominent Adam's apple bob up and down as he makes small talk about a team member's untimely maternity leave that Human Resources has extended and his recent knee surgery following a hapless skiing accident during the Easter break. What a waste of time. Such an inconvenience.

'So, what is the real purpose of this meeting, Charles?'

3

I ask, knowing full well he didn't summon me here today for such confabulation.

He runs a hand over his bald head. Always clean-shaven, the only hair on his head is two greying eyebrows. He sits straight and steeples his fingers, tapping his joining forefingers against his chin. 'I want you to go to New York.'

I wasn't expecting this. 'OK. Interesting. How long for?'

'We're looking at a few weeks, maybe a little longer. I need cover for Melissa.'

I stop eating. 'Has anyone spoken with her?' Melissa is my equivalent in the New York office. She hasn't been with Crayhorne long, a year or so. But in that year, we've become close friends. 'I've tried to contact her, but her phone is off.'

'From what I've heard, she's not in a fit state to talk to anyone. HR has been talking to her mother. Things are pretty serious, I gather. I'm unsure when she'll be back.'

'It's dreadful. Do we know what happened?'

'Rolled her car. Hit a tree.' He shrugs. 'That's all I know. Bad timing. Really bad. No disrespect to Melissa, but this is not what I need when we're due a visit from the external auditors in September. I need someone out there.'

'Poor Melissa. I'll keep trying her. So, why me?'

Charles looks me in the eye. 'I'd go myself, but you know I'm off to Florida with the kids the week after next. If Melissa isn't back by September, I'll cover off with the external auditors, but for now I need someone on the ground who I can trust. You've got the right credentials we need... I need.'

The grave look on his face piques my interest. 'Sounds a bit cloak and dagger. Enlighten me.'

'Steph, I need to know if you're interested before I go any further. I don't want to involve you in this unless it's something you can give serious consideration to.'

'When would you want me to go?'

'Tomorrow.'

I give him the look. The head dropped to one side, deep frown, and scrunched up nose look that I've developed especially for the increasing occasions when I need to ask him if he realises how utterly unrealistic he sounds.

He laughs. 'It'd be good to have you in place by the end of the month.'

'This month? Eight days, you mean?'

He nods.

'Are you crazy?'

He laughs. 'Very.'

'What about the Stenson project? It's due on the first.'

'You can finish it there.'

'This is sounding more than simply keeping Melissa's seat warm.'

'You interested?'

'There's Ellie to consider.'

'I know. My boys would bite my arm off for the opportunity of a few weeks in New York, but we all know eighteen-year-olds can be tricky customers.'

'She's got plans for the summer.'

'What kind of plans?'

'A girls' trip to Majorca for starters.' I hope he doesn't

notice the tone of envy in my voice. Although I don't begrudge my daughter anything, it's events like this that dredge up my regrets for getting pregnant at her age and making the biggest mistake of my life by marrying her father. 'She won't be back by the end of the month.' I make a quick calculation in my head. 'I'd need to be back mid-August. I've got her eighteenth party *on* the eighteenth, don't forget. Plus, her A-level results. Then there's Reading.' I wince at the thought of my daughter's first festival. 'She hasn't stopped talking about it since her new boyfriend got them tickets.'

'I could buy you a couple more weeks so you can go after her holiday. I'll get her flight covered. And I promise to have you back here by mid-August.'

His offer comes as no surprise. Although I'm not as overprotective of Ellie as I used to be, he knows I won't leave her behind, so the deal has to include her. Her dad has always accused me of being a helicopter parent. I hovered over our daughter so much, I propelled him into the arms of other women, he told me after I discovered what a cheating rat he was. He's never understood. When you hold your five-year-old daughter's hand for seventy-two hours straight while she lies in a hospital bed on life support and you've been told she may not make it through the night, it changes you. As a person, and as a parent, I've never been the same. The crushing fear that Ellie could have another serious attack at any time has remained a threat ever since. Her asthma is now mostly under control. We had a scare last year, but thankfully it wasn't as severe.

And after her piano teacher told me how gifted she was, I did everything to help Ellie find the bows to perfect that gift, which has paid off. Her future is very bright. So, I wouldn't call myself overprotective. I just want the best for my child. Doesn't every parent?

'It could work out perfectly,' says Charles.

He's keen.

'OK. Let's assume we can make this work. Cut to the chase, Charles. Tell me what's involved in this clandestine operation.' No longer hungry, I close the box of my salad and remove the lid from my cup of coffee, inhaling the strong arabica scent of the freshly ground beans.

'Steph, this is highly confidential. So not a word to anyone. Agreed?'

'Agreed.'

'There are a number of projects Melissa was working on that I need you to look into, but the main reason is Austin Cunningham.'

I raise an eyebrow. Austin Cunningham, the engineer of the Kingston set of trades who single-handedly launched our company into an uncharted stratosphere. I met him last year when he made a fleeting visit to London on his way to our Luxembourg office. Charles wasn't in that afternoon. He had taken a rare half-day annual leave to celebrate his and his wife's joint fiftieth birthdays and asked me to step in for him.

As far as first impressions go, Austin Cunningham has it all. He knew my name for starters, even though we'd never met. My colleague from Legal said this was one of his traits. Austin Cunningham knows everyone's name. He's the type of person who commands an audience. You find yourself taking what he says as read, even though it hasn't been fact-checked. I understand why people are drawn to him, but as the meeting progressed, I found his arrogance irritating. A smooth operator, he reminded me of my ex-husband. And I never like being reminded of him.

'Without putting too fine a point on it, the recent trading structure he masterminded – between you and me – earned the company and him a shedload of money.'

'That's good news, isn't it?'

'You know when something is too good to be true?'

'Come on, Legal and Compliance would've been all over each one of those trades.'

'I know, and I checked it all out at the time, but some-thing about it is keeping me awake at night. And you know how much I like my sleep. Jennifer tends to agree with me.'

Jennifer Penderson works in the New York office. Another one of Crayhorne's devoted partners who joined straight out of college. She worked in Controllers, the accounting engine room of the organisation, for a large chunk of her career, and had a close working relationship with Charles during her time in London. Rumour has it they had a fling, but not one to gossip, I'm not sure how much truth there is in that tittle-tattle. Charles is not the type, in my opinion. And neither is Jennifer. They are both happily married. But what do I know?

'Austin has his fingers in so many pies, he'll soon need to start using his toes. I don't like it. On the face of it, everything looks kosher. But I don't like the way he operates. I need some reassurance.'

'Which is why you want someone out there as soon as.'

'You got it. I've been in this game long enough to know when I smell a rat that needs catching and slaughtering.'

'And you want me to confirm your senses are correct?'

'I'll make it worth your while, of course: nice apartment, attractive boost to your end-of-year bonus, plus think of the promotion prospects. This will give you the push to get that promotion you're after. If all goes well, I can secure you VP out of this.'

He's got me there. After my ex-husband crushed my self-esteem, I've been hankering for the Vice President title. It's the goal I set myself. To prove that I'm better than he ever gave me credit for. Charles knows I've paid my dues: completed the endless exams, worked my fair share of weekends, and pulled an impressive number of all-nighters to meet the numerous Charles-imposed over-zealous deadlines. But he can't help dangling that final bright orange carrot of promotion to persuade me that New York is the place for me to go this summer.

'I also thought, perhaps, personally, it'll give you an opportunity to get away. I know how difficult this past year has been for you, Steph.'

He can say that again. Finding out the man I had a daughter with, and who I thought I would grow old with, had been cheating on me, destroyed me. For a long time, I felt like I was a contender for the ugliest woman alive award as he kept me dangling on the scraps of his empty promises that he would never do it again. It was soul-crushing. He tore me into a thousand pieces, and I still don't know if I'll ever be able to put myself wholly back together again.

'What do you think, then?'

'I'll discuss it with Ellie tonight.'

2

Once we've passed through the frustrating rigmarole of customs, the letting agent I've been in constant contact with since agreeing to this trip almost three weeks ago greets us. She is smartly dressed in white trousers, a navy jacket, and heels. 'Welcome to New York. Wonderful to meet you two at last. Smart move coming on a Friday. Means you have the weekend to settle in and to enjoy a few of the sights.'

Ellie follows along quietly as the letting agent escorts us to a black Lincoln, and I chatter about the mid-flight turbulence. The sun is blazing, as if it's opening its arms to welcome us to this city. I can't help a sideways glance at Ellie to see how impressed she is as a chauffeur loads our four suitcases into the luxurious limousine and commences the drive from JFK to our Upper East Side apartment, home for the next few weeks.

'You're in for such a treat with Bridgewood Plaza. Such a grand complex.' The letting agent fiddles with a gold pendant charm hanging below her chest. 'Crayhorne sure looks after its employees. What do you trade?'

I laugh. 'I don't. I'm an auditor.'

She raises her eyebrows, the corners of her mouth turning down as she nods. 'Impressive. Impressive. Crayhorne would usually only put partners or senior traders in these types of apartments. Or important clients when they're in town. You must be very good at your job.'

I smile modestly. 'I like to think so.'

The glum face Ellie has been wearing breaks into the slightest of smirks. I'm sure she will remind me of that self-gratifying comment at some point. She pulls her headphones out of her leather backpack and, inserting the cable into her phone, zones out.

'You're going to adore it. There's the most spectacular gym too.' The agent looks me up and down. 'You work out, I take it?'

I nod. I never used to. Not until a few months ago when, reaching the wrong side of thirty-five, I decided enough was enough. The unwanted excess wobbling around my middle had to go. Taking advantage of the executive membership of an exclusive gym a few streets away from the Crayhorne London office, I spent weeks swearing my way through a tri-weekly personal training program or recovering on the sofa, moaning profusely about how much my muscles ached. Along with a strict diet, I started digging myself out of the deep, depressing rut I'd fallen into.

'They've all the latest machines. I prefer Pilates myself.'

The agent cocks her head in my direction, the flicks of her lacquered hair not moving. 'Gentler at my age.'

We pull up outside Bridgewood Plaza. She wasn't lying. It's a grand limestone tower block with a twenty-four-hour concierge and plump beige sofas in the reception area.

The apartment is breathtaking. Light and modern, with a minimalist design and the bonus of an en suite bathroom in each double bedroom. No more screaming and shouting because Ellie's hour-long morning shower makes for a stressful start to my day.

After the letting agent has given us a quick tour and briefed me on how to deal with the trash and the entry system, she leaves us in peace. Ellie and I wander from room to room again, looking at each other with dropped jaws as we point to the impressive range of appliances in the kitchen and the top-notch coffee machine.

'Mum, come here,' Ellie shouts from one of the two bedrooms. I dash to see her lying flat on the mattress, her slight figure lost in the vastness of the bed. Her long dark hair fans the pillow. 'This is the most comfortable mattress ever.'

I laugh. Ellie always has been fond of her sleep. I jump on the bed and lie down next to her. 'Ells, listen to me. He's not worth it.' I take her hand and turn to look at her. I know how she feels. I've walked in the shoes of infidelity and it's a truly painful experience. 'I know you're hurting now, but before you know it, Toby will be a bad memory.'

She involuntarily takes a large gulp of air.

I squeeze her hand. I hate to see her hurting. Her pain

is my pain. 'Please don't waste any more tears over that loser.'

'I still can't believe he was two-timing me all the time I was in Majorca.'

'Ells, you'd only been seeing him for, what, six weeks?' I don't need to ask her this. I can precisely recall the day she began seeing her first proper boyfriend. She came home from a night out with friends with flushed cheeks and the coy smile of new love. I was disappointed and worried she'd started walking on this path so close to her exams. She'd never shown any interest in the opposite sex other than on a friendship level. She has always been far too committed to her studies and devoted to her music. A place at the Guildhall School of Music & Drama is practically a given. And then, only weeks before starting her A-level exams, she had to go and meet Toby.

'It was seven weeks and three days.' She turns to look at me, and we both laugh.

'You're going to have the best summer ever here.'

'I was so looking forward to Reading.'

I could remind her she has always explicitly expressed her aversion to festivals – spend a fortune to sleep in a field, get all muddy, and wee in a stinky portable toilet. No thanks! – but I've learned, especially over the past year, when trying to negotiate with my teenage daughter, it's best to bite the tongue of confrontation. I can't complain, though. She's mainly been a good kid and a beautiful person. A straight-A student, she hasn't given me anywhere near the grief some of my friends have experienced with their kids. And although the past year has had its ups and downs with the divorce, and the stress of A levels, uni applications and a few decisions she has made that have bewildered me, on the whole, I'm coming out of the parenting experience with a caring, lifelong friend. There's still a little way to go. At times, she can be difficult. And extremely unreliable. She has a terrible habit of forgetting things, and timekeeping is not her forte. It's the creative side of her character. Being an analytical and logical person myself, it's where we differ. 'I tell you what. I'll get tickets for Reading. I'll go with you.' She wrinkles her nose and looks at me as if I've just suggested we strip naked and dance in the street. 'What do you want to do tonight?'

'Nothing.'

'How about we go out for dinner?'

'Not tonight, Mum. I'm tired.'

'How about coming with me to check out the gym?'

Another look of horror. She gets up. 'I'm going for a shower.'

The agent was right. The rooftop gym is striking, with views over Manhattan. I bet it's even better up here at night with the city lights. With a vast array of fitness machines, a free weights area, a separate exercise studio and most importantly, six treadmills, there will be no waiting for equipment here. I can see myself keeping up with my routine for sure. I might even be able to get Ellie to join me. I laugh to myself. Who am I trying to kid?

MTV is playing from an imposing flatscreen. Inserting

my EarPods, I hop onto one of the treadmills facing floor-to-ceiling mirrors and set the machine off until I'm in my zone. The place where I can turn the volume up loud and get lost in the heavy beat of my Spotify workout playlist.

After running for half an hour, I head to the drinks fountain, catching my breath. I'm filling a plastic cup with water when a slim guy approaches me. 'That was inspiring,' he says in a cultured English accent. Tall and dark, with a trimmed beard, he is distinguished-looking with muscles well-toned for a man his age. Not that I'd call him old, but he's older than me. 'You must do a lot of running.'

'Most days,' I reply, glad for cheeks still flushed from the exertion.

'A Brit.'

I glance at him warily.

'Your accent, you're British.' He helps himself to a cup of water. 'Where from?' He places an elbow on the drinks fountain and leans into it.

'Just outside London.'

'Been here long? I've not seen you in here before.' He pauses. 'Sorry... I mean... not that I go looking for strangers.'

I smile. 'I arrived this afternoon with my daughter.'

He raises his eyebrows. 'You have a daughter? You don't look old enough.'

I laugh. 'She's eighteen in a few weeks' time.'

His eyebrows stay raised. 'Are you on holiday?'

'Work trip. Well, I'm working. My daughter is on holiday.'

'Who do you work for?'

'Crayhorne. It's a small, private British bank.'

'Where're they based?'

'Just off Times Square.' Awkwardly, I excuse myself. 'Nice to meet you. I'm off to have a shower.'

'I didn't catch your name.'

'Stephanie, but most people call me Steph.'

'Nice to meet you too, Steph. I'm Edward, which is what most people call me. For some reason it's never been shortened. If you've any questions or need help, I'm in apartment nine-two-seven.'

Damn, he must be on the same floor as me. I wipe my forehead on my towel, alarmed at the warm feeling passing through me, knowing it's not from my half-hour workout. 'Thank you. I'll be sure to call if I need any help.'

He waves and smiles. It's a warm, friendly smile. Why, then, do I feel incredibly uncomfortable?

3

A voice startles me as I wait for the lift back to my apartment. It's the guy from the gym, Edward. 'Hey, Steph. I was wondering... I'm not sure if this is being too forward, but would you like to have dinner? I cook a mean stir-fry.' He pauses. I don't answer. He slaps a hand on his forehead. 'What am I saying? Stupid me. You're in New York. You should be out and about. I know a great Irish bar and restaurant not far from here – the Palace Bar. It's very popular with locals.'

There's an awkward pause.

'Please feel free to say no. I know you've had a long flight. It's just I know what it's like when you first arrive in this city and don't know anyone. Perhaps another night?'

The words blurt out of my mouth. 'I would love to, but I have my daughter with me.'

'Bring her along.'

'Is she allowed in bars?'

'Some are OK with it. We can go straight to the restaurant.'

'I'll ask her.'

'Really?' He looks as surprised as me at my response, which in turn surprises me even more. A guy as good-looking as him can't be turned down often. I nod. There's another awkward pause as we stand staring at each other, sweaty in our gym kits. 'What's your phone number?' I say. 'I'll ask her and let you know.' This seems my best get-out clause.

He reels off a number. 'Will you remember that?' I relay the number back to him. 'Impressive.'

'I'm an accountant. Well, an auditor.' I cringe. 'Numbers are my thing.' How boring I sound.

As the lift bell pings and the doors open, he steps backwards towards the gym, waving. 'Hope to see you both later.'

The doors close. I stare at myself in the mirrored wall. On my first night in New York, I've been asked out on a date. I haven't dated anyone since I met Ellie's father twenty years ago. Panic sets in. Then I tell myself not to be so stupid. It's not like I'm going to his apartment.

'No way, I'm not playing gooseberry.' Ellie pulls a serious face. 'Anyway, I'm too tired, and I want to call my friends. You go on your own. I'll be fine here.'

'I can't leave you alone. We've only just arrived.'

'What's the problem? Lock the door. I have my phone. There's a concierge downstairs.'

'I'm not going without you.'

'Look, Mum. I'll be eighteen next month. You've got to stop treating me like a kid.'

Her father's words ring in my head: "You've got to let go."

Opposite a smokehouse restaurant sits the Palace Bar, a family-run establishment along a side street roughly a ten-minute walk from Bridgewood Plaza. A buzzing bar occupies the front section of the building, and a restaurant serving American classics is in the back. The aroma of buttery melted cheddar of mac and cheese plays with my senses. Ellie would love it here.

Pulling out a stool from the end of the carved mahogany bar, Edward guides me to take a seat and perches on the one next to me. His smell is alluring – the cleanliness of freshly laundered clothes mixed with an oaky aftershave. I check my phone, relieved to see I've got a signal. If Ellie needs me, she can call me. A bartender appears, sliding two drink mats in front of us. The young guy is dressed in jeans and a branded T-shirt with 'Palace Bar' emblazoned across the chest. 'Hi, Edward, how's it going?' He nods and smiles at me. For some reason, I think of Ellie. He has her dark hair and striking blue eyes. It's a powerful contrast.

'Hey, Jack. Good to see you,' Edward replies. 'Not seen you in here for a few weeks.'

'I've been busy with my exams.'

'Of course. I remember you telling me.' Edward

touches my hand. A spark of electricity jolts me. I pull my hand away. 'Steph, meet Jack – the best bartender in the whole of New York.' Jack coyly smiles and nods at me.

Edward recommends the Irish Manhattan, and I go with his suggestion. Anything to calm my nerves. We watch Jack as he swipes two Martini glasses off a shelf along the back wall, which holds every type of glass for any occasion. Slick with his movements, he picks up a bottle of Jameson from the shelf above. A smooth operator: it suits his rugged looks. A tattoo inked into his smooth skin dominates the inside of his right wrist. It resembles a pink and blue feather with the top left-hand side partially missing, and looks like it has a meaning of some sort.

'So how did your exams go?' Edward asks him.

Jack crosses his fingers and shakes his hand. 'All good, thanks.'

'What're you studying?' I ask.

Edward chips in. 'He's a brainbox, this one.'

Jack's lips form another coy smile. There's something about him that's particularly endearing. I can't place it. 'I'm halfway through a post-grad in bioethics at Columbia. Finished for the summer now, though.'

'What's bioethics?' I ask, intrigued. 'I've heard the term, but I'm not sure what it involves as a career.'

'It's the study of the ethical issues arising from the advances in medicine, biology, and technology.'

'What's morally right, you mean?'

He nods. 'You've got it. I always give the example of gene editing. There's a tool that can alter our DNA by cutting out the bad genes in our cells and replacing them with good ones.' What's charming about his voice registers: it's full of excitement. This young man loves life. The same as my Ellie. When she isn't nursing a broken heart.

I'm intrigued. 'Where's the ethical issue in that?'

'One of the biggest is that any such editing will be passed down to future generations. Also, for minors, who gives consent?'

'Sounds fascinating. So what're you doing with your summer?'

'Working to repay my debts.' He circles his head, glancing around the bar. 'I can always get hours here, and I've a few other odd jobs lined up.' Picking up a cocktail strainer, he pours the mixture into the glasses. He finishes mixing our drinks and places them on the mats in front of us. 'Enjoy,' he says, before stepping sideways to greet the group of four who have walked in. Edward's phone rings. He apologises profusely and excuses himself to slip outside to answer the call.

I lift the sleeve of my white shirt. It's nine o'clock. I drop Ellie a text, asking if she is OK. She swiftly replies.

Concentrate on your date. I'm going to sleep. See you in the morning. x

Edward rejoins me. I wave my phone at him. 'Just checking up on Ellie.' I laugh. 'I've been told to leave her alone.'

'Typical teenager, then. It's a shame she didn't want to come along.'

'She's not herself at the moment.'

'What's up?'

'Before we left England, she discovered her boyfriend had been cheating on her. Or ex-boyfriend, I should say.'

He winces. 'Ouch.'

'I know. Big ouch. Her first real love. I hope you don't mind, but I won't stay out late. I don't want to leave her alone too long.'

'No problem. I understand. We can always skip food if you want. It's what?' He glances at his watch. 'Two am UK time.'

'I'm wide awake. I'll head back straight after dinner, though.'

'Sure. So how long are you two here?'

'A month at the most. It's Ellie's eighteenth birthday next month.' I slap my hand against my forehead and give a mock grimace. 'Stupid me agreed with her dad to host a birthday party. We've arranged a marquee in his garden, and she's invited over one hundred people. What about you? Do you have children?'

He shakes his head. 'You're close to your daughter, then?'

'Like sisters. Her dad and I split up last year, so it's only the two of us. But if I'm honest, he worked so much it's like it has always been just the two of us.'

'Are they close?'

'So-so.' Since the separation, I've done everything possible to preserve their relationship. They were close all through Ellie's childhood. And, although it pains me to admit it, what he lacked in the husband department, to his credit, he made up for in the fathering one. I didn't want my bitter feelings towards him to ruin what they had. Even though I found him an onerous puzzle I couldn't solve, it didn't make him any less of a father. But despite my very best efforts, not even I can conceal his innate ability to be an absolute dick at times.

'What does he do?'

'He's in the Met police. And he deals watches on the side.'

Jack appears and asks if we would like another drink. Edward looks at me. I nod. Why not?

We chat about New York and the places Edward recommends I visit during my time here. 'Do you have plans for tomorrow? I could take you sightseeing. Ellie is welcome too.' He bites his lower lip. 'I'm sorry. I'm not normally this forward.'

'I'm heading out to Queens tomorrow. Do you know that area?'

'I've only been over there once to a party a friend invited me to. What's in Queens?'

'The reason my company assigned me here is because my counterpart in New York was in a car accident. We're very good friends, so I've arranged to go and see her.'

'Was she badly hurt?'

'Apparently so. I haven't spoken to her, only her mother. Anyway, less about me. What do you do?'

'I'm a lawyer.'

'Who do you work for?'

'Pembrooke Cross International. You heard of them?'

That's a strange question. Everyone has heard of PCI. They are a private bank with offices across the globe. A competitor, of sorts. 'I sure have. You're English, though. What're you doing in New York?'

'I was sent out here two years ago to help out for a month, and...' He smiles. There's something about his smile – unassuming, and vulnerable, somehow. 'I'm still here. So watch out. It may happen to you.'

'I'm only meant to be here for a few weeks.'

'That's what my boss at PCI told me.'

'Where're you from?'

'I grew up in Salcombe in Devon but moved to London for uni and never went back. Except to visit my parents, that is. Until they died.'

'I'm sorry to hear that. Nice part of the country. We used to go to Salcombe every year when I was a kid.'

'Small world.'

I excuse myself to go to the bathroom before we head into the restaurant. Not that I need to use the toilet. More so to check that I haven't got a speck of black olive stuck between my teeth from the Irish Manhattan or a blob of mascara beneath my eyes.

When I return, Edward is deep in conversation with Jack. They stop talking when I approach. Jack wishes us an enjoyable evening and turns his attention to a young bartender who appears to be struggling with the till.

The meal is enjoyable. Nothing fancy, but wholesome food, which I welcome as the alcohol has gone to my head.

Conversation flows smoothly, assisted by the bottle of white wine Edward orders.

As the evening progresses, I realise I like him quite a lot. He is good company, and he has a great sense of humour. But when we part ways at the lift at the end of the evening, I feel like I've told him my life story, and yet, apart from him being a corporate lawyer, originally from Devon, I know very little about him.

4

The following morning, Ellie and I take a walk in Central Park. It's a warm day, and the atmosphere is relaxed, cocooned from the noise of the traffic outside the park, which is dampened by the thick masses of American elms. Saturday cyclists and rollerbladers are out, and walkers are strolling across the grass, some stopping to sit down and rest. It seems incredible that the chaos of the city is never too far away, and yet this feels so tranquil. I could get used to this.

We chat about my evening last night, and the pain of Ellie's broken heart. 'I know now how you felt when you found out Dad was cheating on you,' she says.

I put my arm around her. I want to tell her she doesn't know. She couldn't possibly. A seven-week teenage romance can't compare to an eighteen-year adult relationship. 'You'll get over it.' I kiss the top of her head. 'I promise you. We need to get you out and about. Edward offered to take us sightseeing tomorrow. Please come.'

'I'll think about it.'

The smell of straight-from-the-oven cookies tempts us into a bakery on the way back to the apartment, and we buy a freshly baked loaf for lunch. At the store on the corner of the road to Bridgewood Plaza, we stock up on groceries, and I buy a bouquet of flowers to take to Melissa.

After lunch, I take an Uber to Queens, while Ellie catches up with her friends back in England over FaceTime. 'Nice part of town, Fresh Meadows,' says the driver, as he slows to exit the interstate. 'New York's safest neighbourhood, did you know that?' I catch his eye in the rear-view mirror and give him a quick nod.

My phone beeps. There's a text from Edward thanking me for an enjoyable evening, adding that the offer to take Ellie and me sightseeing tomorrow is still there. My stomach flutters. A feeling I haven't had for a very long time. I reply to tell him I'll let him know. I catch up on a few work emails from yesterday and then click on Instagram, checking to see if Melissa has answered any of the messages I've sent recently. We follow each other and always comment on each other's feeds. She is a keen amateur photographer. My photos are a shoddy attempt compared to artistic shots of her and her son hanging out in New York. It takes less than a minute to discover that either Melissa has closed down her account or she has blocked me. Why would she do either?

Melissa has been over to our London office twice since

she started working for Crayhorne. Once when she first joined to meet the team and for training, which I mainly delivered. Then again, at Easter time, to work on an IT project we are jointly heading up. As soon as we met, we hit it off. Like me, she is a single mother. Her husband ran off with her best friend when she fell pregnant with their son. Little did she know the affair had been going on for months. She thought he was working overtime, saving for the deposit for their dream house. By the second time she came over, our friendship had grown enough for me to invite her to stay for the Easter weekend while Ellie was at her dad's. Melissa and I spent a few drunken evenings putting the world of cheating exes to rights.

The driver proceeds under a bridge and turns into a road surrounded by greenery. It's a typical suburban neighbourhood: kids playing softball in the park, joggers running along the sidewalk, and a father teaching his son to ride a bike. Turning left, we arrive at Melissa's road where the well-maintained lawns of family homes line one side, and a tree-rich park the other.

I get out of the car to a wave of heat, and I feel a sweat coming on as I approach Melissa's semi-detached house, partly shaded by a large maple tree. Black grilles cover the windows, upstairs and down, which I find strange because, as far as I can see, this is the only house in the vicinity to have them. A red awning hangs over the downstairs window. I take a deep breath and knock on the door. After a while, a skinny, older woman with pink hair and a weathered face appears, wearing an apron. She frowns at me. 'I'm here to see Melissa,' I say, wondering if she is a cleaner, but then think it's strange to have a cleaner in your home on a Saturday. Perhaps they do over here. The woman squints and looks me up and down before pointing to a small placard to the side of the door that I hadn't noticed. It's worn, but I can just about make out the numbers 7329 #1. She nods her head towards the back of the building. 'Around the side,' she says in the husky voice of a chain smoker, and promptly closes the door.

Ignoring her lack of social charm, I follow her order to find another door with 7329 #2 lettering fixed to the front. I ring the bell. There's no answer. I'm about to ring it again when Melissa opens the door. I should be prepared, but seeing her chokes me. She is wearing a neck brace, and her right arm is in plaster from her elbow to her fingers. 'Steph, what're you doing here?' Her tone is hostile, as if I'm the last person she wants to see. She touches her nose. It looks as if it has been broken, and although it's healing, a gash splits her bottom lip in two.

I hand her the flowers – a summer mix of roses and gerberas – and the gifts I brought over from London. Some English breakfast tea and a Union Jack T-shirt I know she'll love. Melissa adores all things British. 'I've been trying to contact you, and then your mum called me before I left London. She invited me to come here today. She said you gave her my number. I thought you knew I was coming.'

Her stern expression tells me otherwise. She looks wiped out. Her head of generous tight black curls that she normally wears free are scraped into a bun, and her usually radiant complexion is discoloured in places and spotted with blemishes where it looks as if shattered glass has pierced the skin. 'My mom was wrong to do that.' She grabs the gifts as if she resents my generosity. 'Thank you.'

It's her vacant look that is most troubling, as if she is physically standing in front of me, but her soul is somewhere else. We've been close since we met. I'd go as far as to say, she's one of my closest friends, and typically, when we meet outside of work, we hug, but today there's an awkwardness I've never experienced in her company. Where do I go from here? 'Can I use your toilet, please?'

She looks at me, confused.

'Bathroom. Can I use your bathroom, please?'

Understanding dawns, but she pauses before stepping backwards. 'Through the lounge, first on the right.'

Her home smells musty as if the windows haven't been opened for a long time. I pass the kitchen on my left – a large room with patio doors to the rear. It looks bare. As if she has swiped her arm along the worktops and swept everything into the plastic storage boxes stacked in the corner.

When I come out of the bathroom, she is standing in the doorway to the lounge. 'Are you moving?' I ask, nodding in the direction of the kitchen.

She shakes her head. 'I'm cleaning my cupboards. When I'm up to it, I want to decorate.' The awkwardness between us is disconcerting. A mutual discomfiture that betrays our friendship.

'I've missed you. Work's not the same without our daily chats.' It's true. Even if we have nothing to discuss work-wise, we share the same warped sense of humour, and she brightens my day with the memes, jokes and funny videos she clutters my inbox with.

She hesitates, staring at the floor, before begrudgingly offering me a drink.

'I wouldn't say no to a glass of water.' I peer around the small, gloomy lounge with its smeared coffee table and pulled curtains. This whole place reminds me of our family house when I was preparing to leave Ellie's dad. A home I'd once adored but had fallen out of love with. It's so far from what I imagined Melissa's home to be like.

She appears with a glass of water. 'How did you get here?'

'Uber.' I nod towards the sofa. 'Can I sit down?'

She digs the knuckle of her good hand in her hip. 'Look, Steph. I appreciate you coming all this way to see me, but I'm not up to visitors. You need to go.' Her abruptness is so out of character. 'My mom is bringing Leo home any minute. I'd prefer it if you weren't here when they get back.'

'What's happened to your Instagram account? I've been messaging you, and now I can't find you.'

She runs her tongue over her lower lip. 'I've left social media.'

'Why? You love your Instagram account. What's happened, Melissa? You can talk to me.'

'I don't want to get you involved,' she says quietly, as if it's an afterthought.

'Involved in what? Melissa, whatever's going on?' I can't let this lie. I reach out and touch her arm. 'Why won't you talk to me? I thought we were good friends.'

'That's exactly why I don't want to involve you.'

'But I am involved. I'm here in New York. Talk to me. What *has* gone on?'

She sighs and, with the sweep of her good arm, invites me to take a seat. Sitting beside me, she picks up one of the turquoise cushions strewn across the sofa and squeezes it tightly against her chest. Her eyes close. She looks like half the woman I know. The bubbly, but private, person, who is always out to help anyone and everyone, seems trapped behind a screen of misery. She opens her eyes. 'You must promise me.'

'Promise you what?'

'Not to say a word about this to anyone.'

'Go on.'

She pats the neck brace with her shaking hand, then circles a finger around her face. 'This was no accident, Steph. Someone tried to kill me.'

5

My jaw drops. 'What do you mean? What happened?'

Her nostrils flare as she takes a deep breath, and her cheeks puff out as she slowly pushes out a stream of air. 'I went on a date.' Her eyes close momentarily, and her face grimaces. 'It was a guy I met online. My friends had been hounding me for so long, telling me it was time I started dating again. And to be honest, I've been lonely. Once I've put Leo to bed, I often spend my evenings logging into work and not logging out for hours. You must know how it is.'

I nod my understanding. I can recall noting the time stamp on many of Melissa's emails flowing into my inbox in what would be her early hours. When I look back, I was lonely even when I was married. Endless evenings spent alone because my ex was apparently working on yet another major case, the lack of love and communication making my existence hollow. There was of course Ellie to help fill the void, but with her busy music schedule, she was often out playing in various orchestras and bands or singing in the school choir.

Melissa clears her throat. 'I signed up to this dating site a couple of months ago.' She glances upwards. The light catches the emotion in her eyes. 'What a big mistake. I'd been chatting to this guy for a few weeks.' She looks back at me. 'He seemed different to the others on there. More mature, worldly. He told me he was a lawyer. But it was a set up.'

'What do you mean?'

'The guy who turned up was nothing like his profile. OK, he had dark hair, but that was about as far as it went. He had a beard too. The guy in the profile picture didn't.'

'He could've grown it.'

'Maybe.' She rubs her chest. 'As soon as we'd had one drink, I knew I had to get out of there. There was something about the way he looked at me, or should I say looked through me. Call it a sixth sense, I don't know, but he creeped me out. So when he asked if I wanted another drink, I apologised and told him I suffered from terrible migraines, and I could feel one coming on.'

'He didn't spike your drink, did he?'

She shakes her head. 'I don't think so. When we left the bar, I remember him walking me to my car.' She looks at me. The fear in her eyes is palpable. 'He stopped me. Grabbed my arm real tight and spun me around. His face was this close.' Melissa holds her hand an inch from her face. 'I was so scared. He said if I knew what was good for my son and me, I needed to stop sticking my nose in where it wasn't wanted. He said I knew exactly what he was talking about.'

'Did you... know what he was talking about?'

'I couldn't get away fast enough. All I wanted to do was get home to Leo. I'd left him with a new sitter, and I was terrified she was part of the plot. I managed to shake myself free and tell him to keep away from me.'

I want to reach out and hug her. 'This is awful, Melissa. I'm so sorry you've had to go through this.'

'As I was driving home, I noticed a car following me. At first, I thought I was imagining it, but of course I wasn't. It was driving far too close.' Her voice weakens. 'I tried to convince myself it was kids, but in my heart, I knew it was him. It was terrifying.'

Throwing the cushion aside, she supports her plastered arm with her good hand. 'Admittedly, I should've slowed down. I took a bend too fast.' Her body rocks backwards and forwards. 'But I'm telling you, he was determined. Nearing a corner, he nudged the rear of my car, and I skidded and flipped it. Over and over it rolled. I thought I was going to die. I can remember heading for this tree.'

'This is awful.' I reach across and touch her knee.

'Before I passed out, I saw the bottom half of that monster standing by my car. I recognised his trousers and shoes, before he casually walked off.'

'Let me guess who it was.'

'That's right. The guy I'd been on a date with.' She tuts, rubbing her creased forehead. 'I think it was, anyway. Oh, I don't know. Perhaps he was on my mind when I was driving.'

'Can you describe him?'

She shrugs. 'Early fifties. And I hate to say it, but he was good-looking. A real charmer... at first. Until he turned, and man did he turn. No wonder I felt uneasy from the start.'

'Why haven't you reported all this to the police?'

She lowers her voice to a whisper. 'Because the last thing he said as I was getting in my car was that if I said anything about ever having met him to the police – or anyone else for that matter – then I'd never see my Leo again. I've had a look since. His profile has been removed from the dating site. Disappeared.'

'I can see why you're scared.'

'That's an understatement.'

'So what was his beef?'

'What do you mean?'

'You said he told you that you knew exactly what he was warning you against.'

She stares into my eyes, her lips sealed.

'It's work-related, isn't it?'

She remains silent.

Ignoring her reluctance to talk, I press her for answers. 'Is it to do with Austin Cunningham?'

'I don't know what you're talking about.'

'But you do.'

Her voice is barely a whisper. 'I'm too scared to say anything. Scared for me, for Leo, for you. Go home, Steph.

Get on a flight back to England. You don't want to be involved in all of this.' She shrugs. 'Whatever all this is.'

She's talking to the wrong person. It's not in my nature to avoid things. I'm a solver, not an ignorer, of problems. 'But I'm already involved. Now you've told me all of this. I can't ignore it. Neither can you. You don't want to spend your life looking over your shoulder.' I pick up my glass and take a sip of water.

She runs her finger along a cut above her left eyebrow. It looks like it has been stitched, but it's still screaming red with anger. She takes a deep breath. 'There's this fund. The Harvey-Bowen fund. One of their trades came up on an exception report. You could call it a coincidence, but it caught my attention because it was one of Austin Cunningham's trades.'

I consider telling her about Charles asking me to look into Austin's trades while I'm here but decide to hold tight.

'It led me to a set of transactions that weren't stacking up for me. Singularly, they weren't massive deals, but collectively they added up to a sizeable sum. The more I dug, the muddier the water became. A significant number of sub-accounts are linked to the fund, all with a similar trading pattern. All the traits of large-scale corruption.'

'Money laundering?'

'Exactly.'

'Did you tell Charles?'

She shakes her head.

'How did anyone know you were looking at it, then?'

'Someone has been accessing my computer system.'

'What do you mean?'

'On two separate occasions leading up to the accident, I noticed my system had been accessed. At first, I thought I was mistaken and thought nothing more of it, but the second time, alarm bells rang. You're an auditor. What's the first thing you do when you leave your desk?'

I know where she's going with this. 'Lock my computer.'

'It's second nature, isn't it? We don't even think about it. We do it. A couple of weeks before the accident, I'd gone out to lunch one day. And when I came back, it wasn't locked. That's never happened before. I changed my password. But it happened again.'

Had suspicion got the better of her? Did she just forget? 'Who do you think it was?'

She shrugs her shoulders. 'It stinks of layering to me.' She tells me that all regulatory checks are in place and up to date. 'I doubled-checked,' she continues. 'But those accounts are masking something.'

'Who runs this fund?'

'Chris Smith. I've always found him easy to talk to. When I asked him questions about it, he was helpful, but I got the feeling he wasn't happy.' She sighs heavily. 'Oh, I don't know. I could've been wrong.'

I'm about to ask her more about Austin when the sound of a car beeping its horn makes her jump up. She winces in pain. 'That'll be my mom and Leo. You must go.'

'I'd love to meet your mum.'

'No, you must go. I don't want Leo to see anyone here. He's been unsettled enough lately.'

Reluctantly, I follow her into the kitchen where she

opens a patio door and before I know it, she has ushered me into a small tumbledown garden. The front doorbell rings.

'Don't you think it's time to tell Charles? Or Jennifer?' I say, before I leave.

She shakes her head, vigorously to start with, slowing considerably when she realises this is not something she can do wearing a neck brace.

'Why not?'

'Because, in all honesty, I don't know who to trust.'

On the way back to the apartment, I ponder everything Melissa has told me. When her mum called me, and arranged for me to come over here today, she said she was concerned for Melissa's mental health after the accident. She felt Melissa kept having fits of what she described as "psychotic outbursts", where Melissa's versions of events were distorted and far from reality. Searching the web, I find an article about the accident. It took firefighters over fifteen minutes to pull Melissa from the mangled Mini Cooper after she lost control, spun off the road, and ploughed into a tree. It mentions nothing about the car Melissa told me caused the accident or the driver who left her to die.

6

I tug at the duvet covering Ellie's head. 'I need to get going. I'll be late for work.'

Moaning and groaning, she pulls the cover back over her head. 'Leave me alone.'

'It's a beautiful day.' I walk to the window to open the blinds, side-stepping her unpacked suitcase and the pile of clothes she was wearing yesterday. 'Perhaps we could meet for lunch?'

Another groan. 'I'm busy.'

'Come on. You need to forget about Toby and get on with your life.'

Her head pops out from the top of the duvet. 'He's forgotten.' Her eyes sparkle in the rays of glorious sunshine beaming into the room. She holds up her phone. 'We've been texting all night.' The kittenish smile of new love radiates from her flushed face.

My head jerks back. 'With Jack?'

After I returned from Melissa's on Saturday, Ellie

agreed to come out with me to the restaurant Edward took me to on Friday night. I knew she'd love their mac and cheese. Two waitresses had called in sick, so the barman, Jack, was waiting tables. To say there was an instant attraction between him and Ellie would be an understatement. And despite how uneasy it made me feel, he took her rollerblading in Central Park yesterday afternoon and then out to dinner, while I embarked on a sightseeing tour.

Edward proved himself the perfect tourist guide as we walked, bussed and boated our way around New York City. 'How you see this city reminds me of when I first got here,' he said later, in the bustling steakhouse in SoHo where we ordered prime rib-eyes and drank too much wine. 'When you've been here a while, you start to see it differently. You'll stop noticing the smell of cardboard and black bags of rubbish lining the residential streets. And it won't be long before you start calling your mobile your cell phone and chips French fries. Oh, and the lift, the elevator.'

Ellie waves at me, interrupting my thoughts. 'Mum, are you listening? Jack's cute, isn't he?'

I slip my hands into my suit jacket, a sense of unease growing within me. 'I could tell you liked him.'

'We're meeting up today.'

'Where're you going?' I ask, guarded. I'm unsure I like this. She hardly knows the guy. Nor do I. And he's a lot older than her.

'He's taking me to the Rockefeller Center, and then tonight to a concert at Radio City. I told him I wanted to go there. He's got a friend who can get us tickets.'

'What time will you be back?'

'Late. So don't wait up for me.'

'Ellie, I'm not sure about this. You're in a strange city, and you hardly know the guy.'

She has always been a sensible girl, but this doesn't sit comfortably with me. She's only seventeen. But then my ex's words ring in my head. "Helicopter parent. Stop hovering. She'll be eighteen in a few weeks, and she's leaving home very soon. Let her spread her wings."

'You've met him. It's not like I'm meeting up with a complete stranger. He's a nice guy. You said so yourself.'

She's right. He did seem a decent enough guy. But what do I know? With a performance history well below average, I'll never win any accolades in the dating department. 'How old is he?'

'Twenty-three.'

I go to tell her that he is five years older than her. The age gap is far too big. But then I think back to when I was her age. My mother could never have stopped me seeing her dad. Unfortunately. But then again, I wouldn't have Ellie if I hadn't met her dad.

'I'll text you. I promise. Stop worrying, Mum.'

That's an impossibility for a mother, I want to say. 'Make sure you do,' I say instead, knowing how unreliable she can be at times when she gets carried away in what she's doing. 'I've left you a spare key in the blue dish on the table by the front door. Make sure you take your inhaler.'

She rolls her eyes.

'And make sure you do text me. I'll wait up for you.'

'No need.'

. . .

The New York branch of Crayhorne is located in a quieter street off the ever-bustling Times Square tourist location with its billboards, neon lights, and constant stream of sightseers. I think back to everything Melissa told me on Saturday as I enter the lobby. Her troubled face hasn't left me since my visit.

I check in with one of the two receptionists sitting behind a desk which is made entirely from an elegant, curved piece of marble. The receptionist has big hair and a velvet-like complexion. 'Take the bank of elevators on the right to the ninth floor. Ms Penderson will be waiting for you.' Her voice is as velvety as her dark skin. She gives me an energetic smile and hands me a lanyard. It's personalised with the Crayhorne corporate logo and has a security pass attached. All very efficient. All very Crayhorne.

The doors open onto a luxurious entrance hall, where a two-metre high Crayhorne midnight blue logo is embossed on the wood panelling of three of the walls. The fourth wall is glazed with a set of double doors which must lead into the main offices. Jennifer greets me with her usual dazzling smile and blonde hair she wears short in a slinky bob that is marginally longer at the front. 'Good to see you, Steph.'

Jennifer is a woman who radiates elegance, which no doubt comes at a cost both to her bank balance and in the blood, sweat and tears of her senior position at Crayhorne. Good luck to her, I know how hard she has worked to achieve it all. I like her. She has non-identical twin boys Ellie's age, and we forged a good working relationship when she worked in the London office.

She is carrying a set of files. 'Welcome to New York.' Having grown up in Texas, there's a hint of a southern twang in her accent, even though she has lived in New York since graduating high school. 'At last, we've finally managed to get you over here. I knew it'd happen one day.'

She leads me through the double doors, the expensive material of her flared trousers sashaying around her legs, and into the hubbub of an open-plan office, a working home to roughly sixty employees. In a similar fashion to London, Crayhorne spared no expense when kitting out this branch as it underwent a major overhaul of all its offices a few years ago. Glass screens section off one corner of the floor that houses ten or so traders; the remainder is for support staff. In the middle is a small common space used for casual meetings. There's a coffee bar and a line of fridges with see-through doors stacked with bottles and cans of soft drinks.

'Some of the offices are temporarily out of action. Damn air conditioning's not working,' she says, pointing over to the lines of glass-fronted offices for the partners, Legal, and HR executives that fringe the entire floor space. 'I've reserved the studio for half an hour to run through a few matters with you. I hope you don't mind, but I've had my PA arrange your day. She can be your point of contact while you're here.' She hands me a sheet of paper detailing meetings for me for today. 'I've arranged a drop-in lunch in the dining hall. Everyone in the office is invited, not that everyone will be able to make it, but we're a social bunch here. Most will try.'

'Sounds great.' I inwardly cringe but find a smile of

gratitude. Being the centre of attention has never been my thing. I prefer to get on with the job, but as Charles often reminds me, I need to network. 'Your work ethic is exceptional, you're thorough in your approach, and your attention to detail is like no other member of staff I've ever employed, but you need to engage with people more, Steph,' he said in my last quarterly personal development meeting. 'It's all bloody politics in my mind, but a must in the corporate world, I'm afraid. You need to build more of a rapport with your colleagues and, more importantly, the partners. After all, they're the ones who will vote on your promotion. Do you know what one of the partners said when I put you forward in the last round? "Who is Stephanie Knight?" You must put yourself out there more. There needs to be no doubt in anyone's mind, who *the* Stephanie Knight is.'

Jennifer guides me to a door with a placard saying STUDIO, where she taps the screen of a large tablet fixed to the wall to the right of the door with her perfectly manicured forefinger and enters a code. I catch a floral scent of her delicious-smelling perfume that I can't place. The door swishes open. 'If you ever need private space or a confidential meeting, this is the best room. You can use it whenever you want. Ask my PA, and she'll book it for you via our central reservation system. Failing that, the library is always good. But it's a bit more formal in here.'

I follow her into the studio. A sofa and two armchairs frame the room, positioned around a low glass table. 'Coffee?' she asks from the drinks machine in the corner of the room, shuffling a disposable paper cup from a plastic holder. She stops and gives a mock frown. 'Or are you going to do the Brit thing and tell me you only drink tea from china cups?'

I laugh. 'Coffee is good. Black, no sugar.'

'You're looking well.' She places the cup under the nozzle and presses a button. The machine springs into action, humming as it prepares our drinks. 'Very trim. What's your secret?'

This is not a question she needs to ask. She looks as if her own secret is working exceedingly well, but I tell her about my fixation with the gym since we last met in the London office. What I keep from her though, is that she was the person who motivated me to do something about the depressing slump of apathy I'd fallen into. We were in a meeting. There must have been about ten people sitting around the large conference table, and she was commanding the limelight detailing the finer points of a new trading structure. Her presentation was flawless. She was wearing a smart jumper dress that clung to her body like a second skin, and there were no unsightly lumps and bumps that would have been on show if I'd dared to wear such an outfit. Her hair shone, and her skin glowed, and I remember thinking, it's time for change, Stephanie Knight.

We make small talk about fitness and the weather in New York which has seen a rollercoaster of cool and hot spells this year. 'Before I forget. You have kept Saturday free, haven't you? My annual barbecue. Everyone from Crayhorne will be there.'

'Sounds fun. I remember Charles telling me he went when he was over here last year. He said you put on a spread to impress, and he got rather tipsy. I've never seen Charles drunk. He usually goes for fizzy water with a quarter of lime.'

'He sure got drunk that day. How's Ellie?'

I smile. 'Beautiful, lovely, interesting, the best company, but difficult at times. Her timekeeping sometimes drives me bonkers. And it would be good if she answered her phone once in a while.'

Jennifer laughs. Her teeth are perfectly straight, with the white brightness that only comes with regular whitening treatment. 'A bit like my boys then, but we'll swap the beautiful with handsome, replace the lovely with frequently insufferable, and add smelly.'

'Her father bought her some noise-cancelling head-phones for Christmas. I can't get them off of her.'

'How frustrating are those things? My boys have them.'

'Drives me potty calling her all the time and being ignored.'

She laughs. 'I can relate.' She passes my drink to me and strides to the sofa, gesturing for me to take a seat. Her eyebrows rise as she drops the pile of files onto the glass table from a height higher than necessary. 'Let's not beat around the bush, Steph.' Holding her cup of coffee, she sits next to me. 'I know Charles has already briefed you, but I want you to hear it from me. I want your main focus of attention to be on...' She leans forwards and opens the top file. 'Austin Cunningham.' She pauses until I look at her. 'I want every transaction he has ever engineered investigated.'

I feign a pained expression. 'That's a lot of deals.' I can't help but feel a little indignant at her request. After all, although she is a partner, Charles is my boss. Furthermore, Audit are independent and report only to the CEO. I let it go, though. I've always admired Jennifer's forthright approach. She can be ruthless but is always fair – a good balance.

Jennifer nods and sips her coffee. 'That's right – picked apart and taken back to their roots.' She straightens out creases in her trousers that aren't there. 'As Charles has told you, there must be no stone left unturned when it comes to this man.'

7

Melissa's desk, which I'm using in her absence, is at the end of a bank of six next to a guy named Cody and opposite a woman called Rhonda who, in total contrast to Cody, talks a lot. The other desks are vacated. One team member is currently working from home after breaking a leg, and another is on their honeymoon. The other desk is used by visitors to the office when needed.

My first meeting is with HR followed by Jennifer's PA who hands me a company mobile to use while I'm here. I then spend time with Legal and Compliance followed by Cody, a guy with old-fashioned slicked back hair and currants for eyes, who manages the post-trade team. It's an uncomfortable hour as he walks me through the US systems. With his Spanish accent I have to concentrate hard to pick up every word. His leg bounces continuously against the underside of the desktop making the computer screen constantly jiggle, and he jumps from screen to screen, clicking his fingers, expecting me to keep up. 'Hang on a sec. Could you go back, please? I didn't get that.' I need him to slow down this whirlwind of activity.

He gives a nonchalant nod. 'Sure.' Clicking back to the previous screen, he beats his short, thick fingers on the desktop with one hand. The other he uses to press the hair on the top of his head that is flattened down with far too much hair gel.

I point to an entry on the screen. 'Which account does this get posted to?'

'I'll show you.' He flits through further screens to answer my question. He is one of those people I have met during my career, gabbling on, who bounces from one transaction to another, assuming their audience is keeping up. If you don't have confidence in your own intelligence, these types make you feel inferior. I'm sure he is good at his job, and he likes to show it, but you could walk away from a conversation with this guy, having learnt nothing. 'You see, the problem we have is that the trading, settlement and accounting systems were all developed separately and often they have trouble talking to each other.' He presses his palm on the textured hair on the top of his head as if he is checking it's still there.

Now that is something I can relate to. 'Tell me about it. It's the same in London.' Our systems need a complete overhaul. They weren't built for the size and complexity of the modern trading structures that the likes of Austin Cunningham and his peers have engineered in recent times. It's a project Charles, Melissa and I are working on, but it's a massive undertaking still in the planning stage that will take time to implement throughout the organisation.

His breath smells so strongly of garlic every time he reaches over to point to the screen, I have to lean away. We are deep in the detail when Jennifer appears, tapping the back of my chair. I glance at my watch and gasp. 'Is it that time already?'

'I'm pleased we're keeping you entertained. Time for lunch.'

It's only as Cody stands that I realise I'm at least a foot taller than him. He shuffles into his jacket and straightens the collar as Rhonda joins us, chatting non-stop, and the three of us follow Jennifer upstairs. 'I won't be staying long.' Jennifer glances at her watch. 'I have a meeting in fifteen minutes. But you won't miss me.'

In contrast to the modern office area, the conservative dining hall on the floor above is more traditional with its high vaulted ceiling and giant oak tables. The tables have been moved aside to the outer walls and hold a sumptuous Asian-themed buffet of sushi platters, teriyaki chicken, breaded prawns, and tempura vegetables.

It's like the lion's den of the corporate world. A cage of rampant people hunting down the Brit in town to introduce themselves. There's no chance I'll remember all their names. I'm unsure if it was pre-arranged, or if Rhonda has taken it upon herself to be my chaperone for the hour, but she doesn't leave my side. Thankfully, her ability to talk non-stop allows me to digest the enormity of the situation. I've never met so many people in one sitting. Is this really all necessary? My conversation with Melissa remains in my mind as it has since I visited her. Every time someone introduces themselves, I question if they could be part of anything corrupt. My guard remains up. Before I know it, I glance at a large gold clock on the wall and realise an hour has passed. At this point, there's a shift in the mood. An unnatural lull in the chitter-chatter that has filled the room for the past hour as the door opens and Austin Cunningham enters.

He strides straight towards me with a sense of entitlement. Staff step aside, as if they are clearing the way for the mayor of New York City. 'Welcome to the Big Apple, Steph.' He extends an arm and offers me his hand. It's large and smooth, and his nails are manicured, his aftershave expensive. There's a waft of sensual sophistication about him. We shake hands. A teacup handshake, my mother would say. Our palms don't connect. This type of person is either shy or they are trying to hide something. And let's face it; shyness is at the bottom of the list of words to describe a man like Austin Cunningham.

He doesn't waste time beating around the bush of pleasantries. As appears to be the norm around here, I've noticed. 'I hear you have some questions for me.'

I swallow my nerves and hold back my shoulders. Stand tall. That's what the guy from Hybrid House – a consultancy firm that specialises in personal development for executives – advised about appearing more confident when you are quaking in your boots. Charles organised a course of one-to-one sessions for me last year when he said I needed to work on asserting myself more. The words reverberate in my ears. Stand tall, point your feet facing the person you are talking to and make eye contact. I look Austin in the eye. 'I'll be speaking to many people during my visit. I need to get to grips with all of Melissa's good work.'

'Anything I can do to help our friends from across the pond.' He steps closer to me. Another millimetre more, and he'll be encroaching on my personal space. 'Email me a few possible times, and I'll book a slot in my diary.' He places a hand on my shoulder.

I freeze, acutely aware of his fingers moving down my arm. He is quick to sense my discomfiture and withdraws his hand. We chat about how I'm settling into the apartment and my flight over here. He stares at me intently, as if I'm the only person in the room, and as if he is genuinely interested in the turbulence the flight encountered midway across the Atlantic. The more the conversation continues, the more I'm aware of how people have gravitated towards us. It's him, not me. Austin is like a magnet, pulling everyone in his direction.

I gather from the Crayhorne grapevine in the short period before I flew out here, that Austin Cunningham makes his mind up about people very quickly. If he respects you and thinks you have something worthy to offer, then you'll have no problem with him. If he thinks you are intellectually inferior, then you'll be in for a rocky ride. I suspect the people gathering around us are keen to watch the hostilities unfold. I will disappoint them. When I met him briefly in London, he was charming, however I guess he is now on his own patch. He catches the arm of a short man with an ashy appearance and grey eyes of different sizes, and introduces us.

'Steph, meet Chris Smith. One of our account managers. What he doesn't know about Crayhorne isn't worth knowing. He's one of your own. A Brit, but has been here for years.'

Chris is the guy Melissa told me about who runs the Harvey-Bowen fund. He gives me a friendly nod, running his fingers through his thinning hair which is combed across his high forehead.

'How long have you been here?' I ask.

'Seven years,' he says in a clipped, privileged accent, unaffected by his time living in this city. 'My wife is American.' He scratches his neatly trimmed goatee beard.

Interested in understanding more about this Chris Smith, I try to draw him into a conversation. 'Have you ever thought about returning to the UK?'

'Not really.'

This is going to be tough. 'What advice can you give me? A rookie here in New York.'

'Play by the rules, and you can't go far wrong.'

'And what rules might they be?'

'Well, New York is truly the land of opportunity; that's why you're here, yes? To further your career?'

'I've a job to do, supporting Melissa and Charles. I wouldn't want anyone thinking I'm an opportunist.'

'Quite.'

'And the rules?'

'I think you may have misunderstood me. You'll find,

generally, the people in New York are very accepting. They're a diverse bunch.' He lowers his voice and adds with a smirk, 'Although they can be a tad loud.' His voice resumes its pitch. 'One word of advice. Don't cross anyone. People can turn very quickly.' He pats his protruding belly and chuckles. 'Oh, and don't eat too much. Or you'll end up like me.'

I laugh too. 'Thank you. I'll bear that in mind.'

'What do you think of this?' Austin explains the intricacies of a new deal he has constructed to Chris and me. He is so intense, so wrapped up in his passion for the job, it's mesmerising. The more the conversation progresses, the more uncomfortable I feel. Not because I can't contribute my tuppence worth, but because there's something entrancing about Austin Cunningham.

8

I spend my first week getting my teeth into the Crayhorne New York operation, meeting with people and filling my notebook. Charles always laughs fondly at my way of operating. I'm a stickler for detail, but that's me. After each meeting, I set up a catalogue of entries, screenshots, and files to aid my understanding of how things work out here. Much of this is new for me, so I go into full overkill mode with the finer points.

'So how have you found your first week with us?' Jennifer asks when we meet on Friday morning. Her office is small but personalised with photographs of her sons and aluminium sculptures of ballerinas. We've spoken daily, but this is the first time she has scheduled a meeting.

I give her a rundown on my activities since we last spoke, extracting certain aspects I need more time to harvest. I give an update on the audit Melissa was working on and a summary of my progress in the overall house-keeping I've carried out on the business. From my experience in meeting with her, Jennifer is a note-taker, but today she taps her pen on the pad in front of her, umming and ahhing, seemingly uninterested. As if she has other more pressing items to attend to. 'How much do you know about the Harvey-Bowen fund?' I ask.

She shuffles in her leather chair. 'It earns us a lot of money. Why do you ask?'

'Some of the trading activity on that account caught my attention. I don't like the look of it.'

Her phone rings. She answers it, unusually abrupt with the person on the other end. She hangs up and asks, 'What's with Austin, then?'

'In all honesty, I can't see what the problem is with Austin. He gave me a generous amount of his time and walked me through the structure of every deal I asked him about.' It's true, Austin has been forthcoming with information all week. I found the exception report that Melissa told me about and confronted him with it. He answered every question I had. All his trading appears in order; exemplary. I called Melissa to tell her and see if I could get any more information, but she didn't answer and has not called me back.

Can I sense a coolness in Jennifer's manner, or am I mistaken? 'Keep looking. I'm still not convinced.' She stands up. 'I have a meeting across town today, and then I'm heading home. I've got a ton of stuff to do for the barbecue tomorrow.' She picks up her handbag. 'You're still coming, aren't you?'

I stand up. 'How could I miss it? Can I bring a guest?'

'Ellie?'

'A guy, actually.'

'Tell me more.'

'I met this guy in the gym at my apartment block who I've been out to dinner with a few times. He's a lawyer, works for PCI.' My cheeks redden. I don't feel it appropriate to say exactly how much we have seen of each other – every night, apart from when I took Ellie to the Irish bar.

She stares at me. 'The more the merrier. Bring him along.'

'If you were me, where would you focus your attention?' I ask Cody at the end of our meeting. It's a tactic I often use to gauge how straight people are being with me. Auditors are not always the grim spectres they are labelled as. There are always process improvements to be found, frustrations to be shared. We can be instrumental in bringing about change to benefit everyone. He flashes me a look that asks me to explain what I mean, as he rubs his stubby thumbs along his fingers so fast I can hear the friction. 'I'm an internal auditor, Cody. From your point of view, if there's a problem waiting to be found, where would it be hiding?'

I can't make this guy out. He is helpful enough. To such an extent that he is a tad irritating. But then again, it could be more my problem than his. My frustration at not understanding the systems over here in as much detail as I'm used to in London. Also, I'm tired. While Ellie has spent all her time with Jack this week, I've spent every evening with Edward, staying up way later than I normally would. I like him. A lot.

'I don't think there are any problems hiding.' Cody shrugs his heavyset shoulders. 'Not to my knowledge, anyway.' His hand moves to his head, his palm pressing on his hair, as if ensuring there's not a strand out of place.

'Walk through these trades with me.' I produce a report detailing the recent trades for the Harvey-Bowen fund and point to the entries in question.

He does as I ask. All seems above board. When I thank him, he returns to ticking and tying items on a report against entries on his computer screen.

I stand up. 'Anyone for a drink?'

Cody shakes his head. His gelled hair doesn't move. Rhonda looks up from her screen. 'Coke Zero here, please,' she says. Rhonda is from Alabama. She moved to New York five years ago when her husband was offered a promotion. He works in marketing. He wasn't sure at first but now loves his job as much as she does hers at Crayhorne. She has three cats and over one thousand books stored on her Kindle. Her cousin got married last weekend, and she took three days' annual leave to combine with the weekend to travel back home. She has a son. He is nine years old. Her mother is an English teacher, and her father is a car mechanic. She has seven brothers. I learned all this, along with the occupation of each brother and that of her husband's family, in the short walk from the subway yesterday morning.

When I return with two Coke Zeros, I freeze. My computer is unlocked. 'Who's been at my desk?' I say.

Cody looks up from his screen and shrugs. Rhonda says, 'No one I noticed.'

I frown and pass Rhonda her drink. How careless of me. All the late nights I've had this week must be getting to me. I pull the tab on my can. Taking a sip, I go to ask her the same question I asked Cody earlier. But on second thoughts, I say, 'Do you have plans for lunch today?'

We head to a small park Rhonda recommends, grabbing jumbo shrimp salads from a sandwich bar on the way. 'It's well worth the ten-minute walk.' She takes her purse out of her bag. 'I often come here when I need a proper break. You know, a proper lunch hour, not the eat-at-your-desk Crayhorne-style lunch.'

It's far too hot to sit in the sun, so we find a bench in the shade of a giant elm tree. After she has told me about her trip home, how drunk one of her cousin's bridesmaids got at the wedding, and the new shoes she bought for the occasion, I ask, 'How well do you know Melissa?'

She stabs a fork into a shrimp and takes a bite. 'She has a kid, so she doesn't socialise much out of work. We used to go to lunch occasionally.' She consumes the rest of the shrimp, smacking her plump lips noisily. 'Like you and me are now.'

'Do you know what she was working on before her accident?'

'She was looking into Austin Cunningham's trades. Is that what they've sent you over here to do?'

'I'm here for several reasons. Why, is there something bothering you?' I feel this is my chance to push her. 'Tell me something. Some of these trading patterns are pretty complex. Do you think any of them could be a cause for concern?'

She looks at me blankly.

'If a problem is waiting to be found here, where would it be hiding?'

She flicks a clump of her braided hair over her shoulder. 'Not sure there are any problems.' Her eyes follow the path of a young couple strolling past.

'Do you have any dealings with the Harvey-Bowen fund?'

'Cody looks after that account,' she says bluntly.

Rhonda is silent. For once. She shakes her head and starts telling me about her and her husband's upcoming holiday to Cozumel. They are leaving their son with her parents, and they are going to learn to scuba dive because it's on her husband's bucket list, and he must do it before kid two comes along because her parents won't be able to cope with looking after two children. They're getting too old. If they can have another one, that is. 'Don't say anything to anyone in the office.' She prods her fingers against her closed lips. 'We've been trying for a while. Since our son was a baby, I've had five miscarriages. We've been saving up, and in the spring, we started IVF.'

It's six o'clock, way past an acceptable leaving time on a Friday night according to Crayhorne's work-life balance offering, but I'm still in the office waiting for Edward to text. We are meeting for dinner again. It's becoming a habit that something tells me is going to be unbearably hard to break. I did try to persuade Ellie to have dinner with me. I've barely seen her since we got here. She has spent all her time with Jack, and tonight, he is taking her to an outdoor movie at Brooklyn Bridge Park.

'You sure you don't want to come for drinks?' Rhonda says, staring into a compact mirror as she applies lipstick. She is off to meet her husband. As they do every Friday night, except for the last one of the month when they double-date with friends or when her parents want relieving from their babysitting duties.

'No, you're good. I have plans. But thanks for asking.'

She drops the lipstick in her handbag. With each hand, she grabs the front edges of her braided hair. She pulls each handful and ties them into a knot on the top of her head, as if she is tying shoelaces. 'Enjoy your evening. See you tomorrow at the barbecue.'

It's eerily quiet, the daily chit-chat and buzz of the office long gone where it rightly should have – home. I look up from my screen. Only a few people remain. Are they truly busy, or are they, like I often was in London, delaying the inevitable in going home to an empty house? Scanning the office, I do a quick calculation and work out that fourteen percent of the office are still here: eight lonely people. What happened to the work-life balance offering Crayhorne prides itself on?

A guy from the other side of the office pushes his chair away from the desk. Sliding his laptop into a black satchel, he gets up. He looks miserable. Maybe he doesn't want to go home? I know how he feels. Shortly after Ellie found forgiveness for her father, Friday night became the night she stayed with him. Craving the normality and security I once had, I often didn't want to leave work on a Friday either.

I shiver, as if the air conditioning has been ramped up. Goosebumps cover my arms. I slip my jacket from the back of the chair and shuffle into it. One more push, and I'll call it a day. I turn back to my screen and the Harvey-Bowen fund. Last year, they weren't even in Crayhorne's top one hundred clients. Now they are in the top twenty. I plough through the trading history of the fund and the numerous associated accounts. Admittedly, there are all the hallmarks of a money laundering operation, but as Melissa pointed out, all regulatory checks have been completed and everything looks squeaky clean. I've triple checked. Could Melissa have been mistaken? I need to dig further here. I throw my pen on the desk as my phone beeps with a text from Edward.

> I've got caught up with something. Could we meet at eight? E x

I decide to walk back to the apartment. With all the extra food that comes with not being in my usual environment, I'm starting to feel the impact; even though I've been here less than a week. I'll end up going home the size of a New York sightseeing bus if I carry on eating all the belt-busting portions this city serves. I join the crush of pedestrian traffic marching like soldiers towards the subway, hailing taxis home or heading to whatever's in store for the evening ahead.

It's when I'm standing at a crosswalk, waiting for the lights to change, that I first sense an uncomfortable presence near me. A disconcerting sensation that I can't understand. But it's there all the same. The inclination to look over my shoulder becomes too much. I turn my head and scan the immediate vicinity of mainly men, laptop bags slung over their shoulders or packs on their backs, and younger souls, earphones intact, oblivious to their surroundings, all invading my space.

But it's the stocky man, staring ahead, close, who makes it a first: the first time I've felt uncomfortable in this vast metropolis. When the lights turn, he thuds past me, knocking me off balance. I've had this feeling before, back in London. It was after my ex put a hardened criminal in prison, and I received a death threat. My ex said it was a fake; he had it tested by someone at work, but I've never forgotten the words in the letter that told me I'd better watch out. My ex said it was from a nutter rather than someone who knew the criminal. But for months afterwards, I thought someone was following me. It messed with my head whenever I stepped out of the front door. Convincing myself that my paranoia is in overdrive today, I brush this stocky man off as an impatient commuter and continue my journey home.

The crowds peter out as I make my way up past the designer shops and famous landmarks of Fifth Avenue, and it's not until I turn onto East 72nd Street and I peep over my shoulder that I know my intuition hasn't deceived me. There he is, either an innocent pedestrian, oblivious that he is freaking me out, or a madman enjoying pursuit of his prey. I'm not the sort of person to stick my head under the pillow. When I'm in my cottage at home and I hear a noise in the middle of the night, I get up to find out where it's coming from. So, not wanting him to see where I live, I throw a left onto Madison Avenue, then another left onto East 73rd Street.

Unless my stalker has a leaning to walk in circles, I should be able to tell whether he is following me. Sure enough, there he is, brazen, not even trying to hide his intent. He is quick, nimble on his feet, despite his size. The desire to get back to the apartment is all-consuming. I quicken my pace, hurdling humans, trying to lose myself in the obstacle course of commuters. But the next time I look back, he is nowhere to be seen. This is stupid. I need to get a grip.

In my haste, I've inadvertently wandered a couple of blocks and it seems to take an age to navigate my way back. Before I step foot into Bridgewood Plaza, I look around one final time, but there's no one there. Spooked, I nod good evening to the concierge, and rush to the safety of the lifts.

It's when I open the door to the apartment that I freeze. Ellie is out with Jack but there's a noise coming from one of the bedrooms. It sounds like the swooshing of a wardrobe door sliding closed and a drawer being opened.

Someone is inside my apartment.

9

I leave the front door open; it will be easier to get out if I need to.

'Ellie, is that you?' I can hear the trauma in my voice. There is no answer.

Someone is moving around in one of the bedrooms. I'm sweating, my blouse stuck to my skin. A drawer crashes closed. As I creep towards the bedrooms, I hear movement in Ellie's room.

'Ellie?'

I stop. Was it the person who was following me? This is terrifying. I dart around the corner that leads to the bedrooms. A door opens and slams shut. I think it's the door to Ellie's bedroom. Footsteps tread along the hallway. I prepare to fight or flee, my heart racing, when my daughter appears in her noise-cancelling headphone-wearing world and strides past me. We scream in unison. 'Ellie, you scared the hell out of me.'

She removes her headphones and laughs. 'Shit, Mum. Don't scare me like that.'

My shoulders drop. 'You shouldn't wear those things all the time. I thought you were catching a film?'

She rips a band from her wrist and scoops her long hair up into a bun on top of her head. 'We're not going to the movies. Change of plan. Jack had to meet someone about a job, and we're too late. We're going to Times Square. He's got a friend who works in a rooftop bar. It has stunning views of the Empire State Building at night, apparently. I just popped back here to get changed.' Her face is glowing. What a contrast to the betrayed girl I flew over here with nearly a week ago. 'And you'll never guess where he's taking me on Sunday.'

'Where?'

'The Oculus in Lower Manhattan.' Her smile is as big as her heart. 'He said it's got amazing architecture, and I'll love the shopping.'

'I know. It's next to the Freedom Tower and the 9/11 Memorial. You must go there too.'

'Yes, that's what Jack said.' She pecks me on the cheek. 'Gotta go. Love ya, Mum.'

I want to tell her not to go. She can stay in with me. I'll cancel my plans with Edward and run to the shops to buy the ingredients for fajitas, our favourite dinner. We could paint our nails and watch a film together. Instead, I push aside the uneasy thoughts of her out in this big city that have been plaguing me all week and remind myself she is almost eighteen after all. And in a month's time, she'll be leaving home to start her life without me. And as much as it is killing me, I need to let her have her independence. 'Love you too. I'll wait up for you.'

'You don't need to do that, Mum.'

Oh yes, I do.

I have an hour to spare before meeting Edward, so I take a quick shower and settle on the sofa with a glass of wine. I fire up my laptop and click on Google, typing Austin Cunningham into the search bar. I've spent more time with him as the week has progressed and as I've looked into the structure of many of his trading deals, I've come to realise that this man fascinates me. His intelligence is way off the scale.

Images of him fill the page, mostly of him collecting various industry awards he has won over the past decade or so. I click on the pictures and scan some of the associated articles. Several quote him as a young entrepreneur of the corporate world, a rising financial star. A picture of him graduating from university with a first-class degree in economics piques my attention. He had long hair back then. Dark waves touched his shoulders. It didn't suit him as much as the shorter styles he has adopted throughout his twenties. But he was still as striking. He didn't wear glasses then, either. They came much later. From what I can tell, only recently. The tortoiseshell round ones he wears today also suit him.

I click on Twitter and find his profile. He is active, posting daily about the markets and financial information, but nothing personal. People frequently interact with his account, commenting on his tweets and retweeting. He has over one hundred thousand followers.

I try to find him on Instagram but can't. He has a Facebook page, though. He posts frequently but not daily, and an abundance of his five thousand friends regularly leave comments. I scroll through his posts. Similar to his Twitter account, they are mostly business related. His page reveals very little about his private life other than his love of cycling. Various shots of him on his road bike add a touch of personality. And he often shares bike-related articles, from *Ten Best Cadence Tips* to *The Top Five Best Road Bikes Tested*.

His latest post shows him sitting on a plane, smiling at the camera. The single seats are wide and covered with white leather. It looks like some kind of private jet. I look at the date it was taken – last week. Stubble shadows his face. I can't tell if he ran out of time for a shave or if he was intentionally adopting the rogue look. A single line accompanies the photo: *An early Monday morning trip to Chicago for business. Enjoy your week, all.* I read the top comments.

Living the dream – good on you, Hammy.
  Always off somewhere, you jet-setter, you XOX
  Lucky Chicago! xox
  Luv you bruv take me next time. P

I click on P's profile and discover more about Austin Cunningham. The side he doesn't reveal to the world. And

I'm shocked to find myself welling up. His sister Polly has Down's syndrome, and, judging by the number of photos she posts of the two of them, it's fair to say, his love for her is all-consuming and vice versa. Exactly how I would describe my relationship with Ellie.

His financial position appears to have afforded Polly a wonderful life. She lives in the leafy suburb of Hastings-on-Hudson, about a forty-five-minute drive upstate, in a charming weatherboarded dwelling with a porch running the width of the house. A swing-set sits in the middle of a grassed area out the front, and from what I can gather, she lives there with three other young women with Down's syndrome and a team of carers. I flick through the photos. Polly has posted a picture of her and Austin watching a film, lounging on a giant beanbag that comfortably seats them both. It's as if it was designed especially for them. This doesn't look like a man who is involved in multimillion-pound scams. But as I well know, never judge a book by its cover.

I'm curled up on Edward's sofa with a large glass of Shiraz in my hand while he prepares a frittata. It won't take long, he promises. 'Twelve minutes, and I'll have it on the table.'

How precise, I think, taking a large sip of wine. It's going down too smoothly. I take another sip, absorbing the mellow sound of Louis Armstrong's 'What a Wonderful World' playing through speakers attached to the wall. 'Ellie loves this song. It's one of her favourites to play on the saxophone.'

'I didn't know she plays the sax.'

'She plays the violin too.'

'Wow! She's super musical. Which is her favourite instrument to play?'

'The piano without a doubt. She's been having lessons since she was six.' My eyes wander. It's the first time I've been inside his open-plan apartment. We've only had meals together in a restaurant. It mirrors mine in layout, but this is more homely rather than a functional place to stay. Interesting modern canvases painted in acrylic adorn the walls. Stick people of various shapes and sizes, ages and colours, in action – walking, running, pushing prams, riding bikes, walking their dogs – in front of different buildings I recognise from capital cities around the world: the Statue of Liberty, Buckingham Palace, the Sydney Opera House and the Gardens by the Bay in Singapore. They are an abstract infusion of colours – a modern-day take on Lowry – and a perfect match for the plain walls of the apartment.

'I love your artwork,' I say as Edward appears at my side, the near-empty bottle of Shiraz in one hand, a bowl of olives in the other. He refills my glass. 'Did you get them here, or did you bring them over from the UK?'

He coughs, clearing his throat.

I sense his awkwardness. 'Who's the artist?' I ask.

His cheeks turn as red as the wine. 'Me.'

'You painted these?' I uncurl my legs and place my glass on the table. 'They're fantastic.' I stand up and walk over to study the paintings in more detail. 'You have a real talent.'

'Thank you.' He shoves his hands into the pockets of his jeans.

'Do you sell any of them?'

'Don't be silly.'

'You should.' I stare at him, feeling for the first time since we met that I'm getting an insight into who the real Edward is.

'Come with me to the bedroom,' he says, pulling my hand.

'Steady on,' I laugh.

'Steph, really?'

We giggle like teenagers as he leads me to one of the bedrooms and pushes open the door. I gasp at the easels holding an array of completed paintings and some works in progress. 'You're a dark horse.' I pick up a tube of paint from the cluttered workbench. Phthalo green; turquoise to the layman. It reminds me of the colour of the cushions on Melissa's sofa.

'It's just a hobby. It helps me unwind.'

Picking up a palette knife caked with paint, I think of Melissa. I've left her several messages this week but heard nothing from her. 'It appears more than a hobby to me.' I replace the tube of paint and knife and run a finger along the half-finished canvas about two feet square on the easel nearest to me. I know I shouldn't. It's rude and ignorant, but I can't help myself. It's cold to the touch, thick and bumpy from layers of texture. 'This is striking.' I point to the kaleidoscope of hues of autumn reds, yellows and oranges intertwined and blended on the canvas.

'Thank you.' The appreciation in his voice is palpable.

I feel a strong desire to touch him. Run my fingers over him like I did the painting. I pick up a paint brush and chuckle. 'This is the first time I've picked up a paintbrush since my Art GCSE. I miss it.'

'You should give it a go.' He reaches underneath his workbench and enthusiastically pulls out a blank canvas. 'Here you are. Especially for you. Anytime you want, come and paint. I'll get you a key'

'That's kind of you,' I say, unsure I'd ever intrude on his space.

As if the appreciation of his work is too much, he gestures towards the door. 'Shall we?'

I follow him back to the kitchen. 'How did you get into painting?' I ask, sitting on a chair at the breakfast bar.

He checks on the frittata and empties the bottle of Shiraz into our glasses as he opens up like a flower that's just come into bloom. It's a beautiful, yet tragic, tale about him and his first wife who died from a respiratory disease shortly after they married. She was an artist and taught him all she could, encouraging him to develop the gift he had obviously overlooked. 'Only a few people know about it.'

'I'm touched you felt you could share your talent with me.'

'When I retire, I'm going to open a gallery for under-privileged artists. Kids with talent who won't get the break otherwise.' He opens a second bottle, fills our glasses and serves our food. 'Enough about me. How was your first week?'

Whether it's the wine or the snippet of his secret life he

has extended an invitation to join, I'm not sure, but I uncharacteristically spill too much about my meeting with Melissa.

'And you've checked all the *Know Your Client* and *Anti-Money Laundering* regs?'

'Yep. All regulatory checks are up to date.'

I jabber on and on until, finally, I manage to shut myself up, annoyed at my indiscretion and the apparent ease with which he has managed to extract everything there is to know about me. 'I've said too much. Forget everything I've told you. It was unprofessional of me. And then tonight, I thought someone was following me.' I give him an account of my journey home from work, and with each word, I think how crazy I sound.

'This city can play with your head.'

'You think I imagined it?'

'I'm not saying that.'

'You're right.' I pause. 'How well do you know Jack?'

He shrugs. 'I met him at the bar when I first arrived here. He's a nice guy. Why?'

'Ellie has spent practically the whole week with him.'

'You have a problem with that?'

'Only the normal, how a mother worries about her daughter. Anyway, tell me more about you.'

I think the wine gets to him. He reels off a compelling and engaging account of his existence to date, delivered in a clipped, matter-of-fact manner. 'My parents died ten years ago. They were rich, sent me to boarding school. Wanted me to be a corporate lawyer like my father. So here I am a corporate lawyer.' There's a quiet kindness about him, I notice. 'You won't hear me talk about my work. It's not my passion. It's a job.'

'I'm sorry.'

'What for?' He looks at me, frowning.

I shrug. We sit in silence, staring at each other. Desire overcomes me. Both of us. We reach for each other. As he leads me to his bedroom, I can't help wondering if I'm making the best decision of my life, or the worst.

10

'Thanks for agreeing to come along. And thanks for driving. Makes life a whole lot easier.' I turn to look at Ellie slumped in the back of Edward's Cadillac. Having not arrived home until the early hours, she is taking advantage of the chance to catch up on some sleep.

'Good to take the beast for a run,' Edward says.

'It's a nice car.'

'If I'm honest, I regret buying it. It was an indulgence. A present to myself when I first moved over here. But I don't use it nearly as much as I thought I would. With the traffic, it's easier to take the subway. Besides...' He presses his forefinger against his closed lips. 'Don't tell anyone, but I hadn't even had it a month, and I had an accident.'

'What happened?'

He scrunches up his face. 'Purely my fault, I turned the wrong way down a one-way street. No one was hurt. Not seriously, anyway. It put me off driving for months, and I got used to taking the subway. I should sell it. After the accident, the insurance went through the roof. I'm paying a small fortune for it to mostly sit in the garage. If you want to use it while you're here, feel free. I've got an any-driver policy.'

'Thanks for the offer, but I might just skip that one,' I say with a laugh.

'Listen, why don't I take you out next weekend? We'll go out of the city. Kingston isn't too far. There are some fantastic live music venues there. Or Beacon is lovely and quaint. There's a great art museum there – Dia Beacon – that I've been meaning to visit. There's great hiking around the area too.'

'Let's do it.'

'Look, I was thinking about what you told me last night about your assignment at Crayhorne. I have a contact in the business. A good friend I've known since school, Rupert. He owes me a favour.' He laughs. 'Several favours, in fact. He's well connected. I'll get him to ask around and give you a call. It can't hurt to try. He knows everyone.'

'You'd do that for me?'

'The way I feel,' he reaches over and squeezes my hand, 'I'd do anything for you.'

How can I have known this guy for only a week? It feels like years. 'Give him my mobile number.'

'I will. So, tell me. What are we to expect from today?'

'A gathering of grandness.' I laugh. 'According to Charles, she puts on a spectacular show. Typical Jennifer.'

'And what is typical Jennifer?'

'Stylish, lavish, bold, and as cool as a cucumber. She has held this event annually since she joined Crayhorne and invites the whole office. What started out as less than ten of them has grown to sixty-plus now. Most employees and their families are going.'

Jennifer lives in Dobbs Ferry. I couldn't resist a quick online search of the area after she gave me her address. It's a small village in Westchester County steeped in history and boarded on the west by the Hudson River. As I expected, it has an affluent population, ideal for NYC commuters who crave suburban life when not working.

As we leave the parkway, detached houses set the scene, but we've seen nothing yet. The houses seem to get bigger and bigger and spectacular is the only way to describe Jennifer's abode. The home of a high-flyer; the type you see in films. The winding driveway, flanked on one side by a rich green lawn, the other by a thick double line of pruned juniper trees, meanders up to an elegant colonial-style property painted a light slate grey with white shutters. Ellie emerges from her forty winks. 'Bloody hell, Mum. These people have some serious dosh.'

Edward nods at the gloss-white BMW and cherry-red Porsche convertibles parked in front of the garage. 'Nice motors.'

'The reward for being a partner. It's the same for all the partners at Crayhorne. I went to one of their flat-warming parties last year, around the Knightsbridge area. It was as spectacular as this, albeit on a smaller scale. The price,' I say, shaking my head, 'for countless sleepless nights. They all work their socks off. Jennifer's husband is loaded too. He's in IT. Sold one of his businesses and made a mint. That's when they had this house built.'

The smoky smell of meat fills the air before we've even got out of the car. Edward finds a parking space. 'Don't forget you're dropping me at Jack's afterwards,' Ellie pipes up from the back.

Edward lowers his voice, smiling at me. 'How could I forget?' He turns to her. 'Remind me of the address.' Ellie relays Jack's address on the west side of Central Park, and Edward plugs it into his satnav. 'There we are. All set for when we're done here.'

I laugh. 'Young love, eh?'

He squeezes my thigh. 'Quite enjoying the older love, myself.' He reaches over to kiss me, sending a delicious shiver shuddering through me.

The smell of the barbecued meat intensifies as we follow a couple up the steps to the covered doorway, where a uniformed waiter dressed in black and white greets us. 'That's out of tune,' Ellie whispers as we step into the entrance hall. Someone is singing to the accompaniment of a piano. I frown at her. She shrugs. 'Well, it is.' The waiter swings a silver tray on his splayed fingers before us, offering champagne in delicate crystal flutes. Ellie and I help ourselves. Edward requests a soda, and the waiter grabs a tumbler of water from another tray on a glass-topped console. 'Please, go through.' He gestures us along the hallway with a slight bow.

'Wow! Look at this. Beautiful.' Edward runs his hand along the handrail of the grand spiral staircase. It's made of light maple wood and matches that of the floorboards. We pass the vast lounge where a group of teenagers is huddled around a grand piano, and on to a kitchen bigger than the whole of the downstairs of my cottage. A hive of activity, it's buzzing with caterers rushing in and out of the room, unwrapping cellophane from dishes on the granite worktops and ferrying plates of food.

Working our way through the throng of people gathered on the covered porch, talking loudly as they eat and drink, I nod and say hello to those I've met since I've been in New York, as we admire the indulgent display of multi-coloured balloons arranged to spell out 'fifteen'.

'There were less than ten of us in the first year. I was single then, so I came alone,' one of the partners says. 'That was fifteen years ago.'

Edward shuffles close to me and whispers into my ear. 'Must say, I do find these affairs a little difficult.'

I look at him and laugh. 'You and me both. My boss in London tells me I need to network more, so here goes.'

Spotting Rhonda by her mass of braided hair wrapped around her head like a turban, I head for her. She's a safe bet to ease us into this gathering. But I couldn't be more wrong. We swap introductions for Ellie and our other halves. The guys hit it off with baseball talk like they've always been buddies, and I try and talk to Rhonda. 'Impressive show, isn't it?'

She nods, staring ahead blankly as she fiddles with the batwing sleeve of her multicoloured wraparound dress.

'Have you tried the food yet?'

'No.'

This is proving cumbersome. The more I try to converse with her, the more it's gin-clear I'm alone with this one-sided conversation. She pulls on her husband's arm, telling him it's time to check out the food.

'See you in a bit.' Her fake smile brims with insincerity. She steers her husband down the steps, following the aroma of the barbecue below. Curiously, I watch them walk over to the group of chefs who are wearing black and white striped aprons and checked skull caps staffing a mobile barbecue unit and a firepit. To the right stands a large gazebo housing a bar and a button-popping display of food. Rhonda rotates her body to look behind her. She catches my eye, but just as quickly, turns away. I know people tend to act differently when they are in the workplace to when they are with their other halves, but this is on a different level. Only the other day, this woman offered up her life story to me. What has got into her?

11

'This is a house designed for parties, that's for sure.' Edward nods at the kids playing on the vast manicured lawn that stretches down to a densely wooded area. 'There's something for everyone.'

'Steph!' Jennifer comes bounding towards us dressed in a body-hugging maxi dress with a thick textured belt accentuating her catwalk figure. She is arm-in-arm with a man who is stocky, like an American footballer. 'Meet Todd.' She presents her husband as if he is a trophy.

Todd is bald like Charles. He wears a pair of sunglasses perched on top of his head which match his designer look. He has a strong jawline and show-stopper brown eyes, and his skin is as flawless as his wife's. They suit each other. An American couple living the American Dream. He immediately sparks up a conversation, welcoming us to New York and asking how I'm finding it.

'I hope Jennifer is looking after you as much as you look after her when she's in London.' He's a friendly guy, energetic with his hand gestures, but the zesty smell of his aftershave would be unbearable if we were inside. 'She always comes home with fun stories.' He turns to Jennifer and kisses her shiny blonde hair. 'Don't you, honey?'

Jennifer nods her agreement before turning to Ellie. 'Pleased to finally meet you. I've heard so much about you.' Jennifer takes her hand. 'Come with me. I'll introduce you to my sons and their friends.'

Edward carries on talking to Todd, as one of the partner's wives latches onto me. A voluptuous woman, she is wearing a low-cut top and has teeth too large for her mouth. She tells me she is off to Europe tomorrow. 'London is my first stop. Can I ask you some questions?'

'Sure,' I say. 'Fire away.'

She asks question after question. Brash and loud, she is the type of woman deeply in love with the sound of her own voice.

'And I want to go to Stonehenge,' she says with a grin full of her oversized teeth. 'What's the best way to get there?'

Before I've finished answering each question, she asks the next as if she is only interested in listening to herself. I'm relieved when she rejoins her husband.

Edward slips a hand in the small of my back. 'Let's get some food,' he says. Warmth radiates through me like a ray of today's glorious sunshine. He feels it too. I'm sure of it – this is something deeper than a fling. We exchange knowing smiles. It feels good. Really good.

'What can I tempt you with?' the waiter asks, sweeping a hand along the spread on offer. 'We've grilled lobster tails, a butterflied boneless leg of lamb, chicken satay skewers.' His hand stops at a dish of bacon-wrapped new potatoes. 'Have a serving of these, because I'm telling you, they won't be around when you come back for more.' He proceeds to reel off the names of the range of salads in every colour of the rainbow. The smoke of the barbecue and the aromas of the fresh cuisine on display play havoc with my taste buds.

'What a spread. Where do we start?' Edward laughs.

We fill our plates, and a guy from Controllers calls me over. We join him and his wife for some easier conversation than I've experienced with Rhonda, and the partner's wife who is heading to London. I look around and spot Rhonda at the edge of the lawn. Her husband is talking to her as she stares blankly at the children playing tag on the grass.

I pick at my food while Edward tucks in. We chat about his artwork and us. The places he wants to take me. The plans he has to show me more of New York. There's a sudden lull in the chatter around us. I turn to see Austin stepping into the garden. His eyes meet mine. I turn away, but when I look back thirty seconds later, he is staring at me. He smiles. I look away. Before I know it, he has worked his way over to us and is introducing himself to Edward.

'Been painting?' I ask, pointing at the splodge of paint on Austin's elbow.

Austin laughs and turns to Edward. 'This lady misses nothing. I tell you. She's got us all jumpy in the office wondering where she'll strike next.'

Edward is quick to fill the disconcerting silence. 'Sign of a good auditor, that fear factor.'

'Of course. Wouldn't have it any other way.' He scratches at the strip of paint on his elbow. Small flakes like snow flutter to the grass. 'I've been staying at my sister's place while I wait for my new condo to complete, and I'm working on turning an outhouse in the garden into a movie and games room for her and her friends. They all have Down's syndrome and live together in a house not far from here.'

I refrain from saying, I know because I've stalked you on Facebook, your sister too. 'That's kind of you. I bet she'll love it.'

'She's not seen it yet. It's going to be a surprise, but there's still an awful lot to do. We're having a party when we've finished. You should come along.'

'Sounds fun.'

'I'll send you an invitation.'

Why does he make me feel so uncomfortable? I wish I hadn't come. These kinds of events are really not my thing. But then I hear Charles's voice and the ugly networking word. "If you want that promotion, Steph, you've gotta mingle with the bigwigs."

I excuse myself to go to the bathroom. It's in use, so I hover outside the lounge. Ellie is seated at the piano, playing a medley of Queen songs. Her peers crowd around her, singing and cheering her on. It's hard to believe she met these people today, but dropping her inhibitions is what her music allows her to do. Todd sees me waiting and signals to me to use the upstairs bathroom. It feels wrong, but he ushers me on, telling me it's the first door on the left.

Wandering up the large grand spiral staircase, my feet sink into the deep pile cream carpet with each step. I survey the array of photos, memorabilia and certificates decorating the walls. Photos of Jennifer and Todd and their sons at different holiday destinations frame a display, a tour de force, telling the tale of a family of achievers. Jennifer and Todd are black belts in tae kwon do. She has never mentioned this. As I reach the landing, I turn left but don't stop at the bathroom. A photo of Jennifer as a cheerleader in her teenage years, balancing one-legged on the two hands of a muscled baseball player, waving red, white and blue pompoms, keeps me walking. Her education certificates are numerous. She has carried on studying throughout her career. Her husband is the same. An entrepreneur in the tech industry, Todd owns several companies, and a collection of academic accomplishments. He was a keen ice-hockey player at some point too. What a family!

Before I know it, I've reached the end of the landing where a noise from one of the bedrooms stops me in my tracks. I should turn around. I know it would be the right thing to do, but my inquisitive nature gets the better of me. The door is ajar, and it sounds like two people arguing. But I couldn't be more wrong. As I step closer, I see through the gap, and I have to stifle a shocked gasp. Jennifer is in a passionate embrace with one of the catering staff. She has his face clasped in her hands, the front of her blonde bob brushing against her wrists, and he is pulling her towards his groin by her behind.

Not wanting to see where the carnal encounter is heading, I turn one-eighty and leave the scene of infidelity, my eyes open wide, staring at the carpet. I always thought Jennifer was happily married. Todd is a good man who she has been in love with since college, or so she has inferred. I head for the stairs, outraged at the wrongness of what I've witnessed. For goodness sake, her husband and children are downstairs, not to mention all her work colleagues. Is this how she gets her kicks?

I pass all the happy family photos covering the walls.

They say a camera never lies.

Oh yes, it does.

I find Edward engrossed in an animated conversation with Austin outside the lounge. Austin gives me a nod, smiles and excuses himself. If I wasn't in shock, I would've asked what they were discussing, but Edward starts talking first. 'Your daughter is truly gifted,' he says of the enchanting sound of Ellie's voice. It's impossible to keep the pride out of my smile. She slides her fingers along the piano keys, executing a glissando, artfully bringing the piece to an end.

'By the way, my friend Rupert texted. He said he's happy to help you out with your queries on that Harvey fund. He said he'll call you,' Edward says.

'Your turn,' I hear Ellie say in response to calls from her new-found friends along the lines of, 'How can we beat that?' They beg her to carry on.

The aroma of lemons makes me turn around. Todd is

standing behind us. His aftershave is something else. 'Your daughter is talented,' he says. 'How long has she been playing?'

Still shocked at what I witnessed upstairs, I find it difficult to look him in the eye. 'She started having lessons when she was six,' I reply.

'Same as our boys, but they both dropped out during high school. Shame. A real shame.' He extends an arm to greet his smiling wife as she comes down the stairs. 'Hey, honey.' He wraps an arm around her and kisses her. Jennifer appears her usual composed self. I can't look her in the eye either.

It's true. You never know what goes on behind the closed doors of a family home.

Todd engages us in a conversation about Ellie's aspirations. I can't talk to him, but Edward somehow senses my awkwardness and tells him she dreams of winning a Brit award one day.

Austin surprises me by joining the youngsters at the piano. He whispers something in Ellie's ear. She giggles, and they start playing a duet: Queen's 'Don't Stop Me Now'. He nudges her and leans over to say something else. Is he flirting with her? Within thirty seconds, they have the whole party singing. I smile. This is so Ellie. Quiet and unassuming until she gets behind a piano where she can bring any party to life. Todd leaves us and walks to the piano.

When the music has finished, Todd rounds everyone up outside where he delivers a speech. He articulates with authority, heaping praise and adulation upon Jennifer's mastery of yet another successful event. I stare at her, as she relishes his words. How can she do that? Act as if butter wouldn't melt in her cheating mouth. 'And I must congratulate the catering team on yet another fantastic spread.' He throws his hand out towards the guy I've just seen Jennifer in an embrace with. 'They excel themselves year after year.' The catering guy bows theatrically and smiles at Jennifer. I can't believe what I'm seeing.

Todd hands over to one of the senior partners who delves into Crayhorne's history. I zone out and absently gaze around the captivated workforce beguiled by the words of one of their masters. I recall my conversation with Melissa. Who can I trust in this gathering? My eye catches Ellie talking to Todd. I wonder what they are talking about. I look away, to see Austin standing on the edge of the crowd, staring at me. The hairs on my arms stand up. I whisper to Edward, 'Do you think it's too early to leave?'

When we get back into the car, I turn to Ellie. 'What was Todd saying to you?'

'What?'

'During the speech, you were talking to him.'

She shrugs, taking her headphones out of her bag. 'He was asking about my music.'

'And what about Austin? He nudged you while you were both playing the piano and whispered something to you.'

Her brow furrows. 'Mum.' Her tone sounds the same as

her father's when he tells me to give her a break. 'He was just saying that was one of his favourite songs.'

I turn back around and chat to Edward until the satnav tells us we've arrived at our destination.

Ellie sticks her face between the seats, clinging to the black leather headrests. 'This is it. Turn here. Jack's place is about halfway down.'

Edward steers right at a tapas bar, past a rent-a-car place, a parking garage and a Thai restaurant, to a building set back from the road behind a row of low, manicured bushes.

Edward peers out of his window. 'Nice place.'

'He is flat-sitting for a friend who's between jobs,' Ellie says. 'His friend has taken the summer out from his banking career and is travelling the world. Lucky for Jack. He could never afford to rent a place in this part of town.'

'I remember him telling me,' Edward says.

As I glance skywards at the tall 1930s building with ornate stone balconies and a black iron fire escape winding up to the roof, I can't help wondering whether he and Ellie would have had the chance to spend so much time together if he hadn't been so lucky.

12

'I'm sorry, Steph, I'm on a bit of a tight schedule,' Chris says in his privileged, English accent as he sits perched on the edge of the sofa in the studio, his protruding belly resting on his lap.

We've arranged and re-arranged meetings on several occasions this past week, and I have to resist the thought that he is trying to avoid me. 'Sure, this shouldn't take long.'

'Fire away.' He keeps touching the area around his mouth. It's distracting.

'I see you've lost the goatee.'

'Indeed. My wife hated it. I'm just getting used to it not being there. You know, I had one for the best part of two years. Then suddenly, on the way home from Jennifer's barbecue last weekend, she blurted out how much it repulsed her. I had no idea.' He glances at his watch. 'Anyway. Shoot.'

I've prepared well for this meeting and home straight

in on the Harvey-Bowen fund. He answers all my questions precisely, not embellishing the responses with any additional information that might be helpful. But certainly not avoiding any details I request. We've only been chatting for about fifteen minutes, when his assistant, a young, slim brunette, puts her head around the door. She announces there is an important call he needs to take as if it's been rehearsed.

'I apologise, Steph. I think we covered a decent amount of ground. If there are any other questions you have...'

I interrupt him. 'Here you are.' I pass him a piece of paper. 'I have the remaining questions here. I'll email you a copy.'

He takes the piece of paper. 'Right you are. I'll get on with them.'

As my time in New York gathers momentum, the more I begin to piece together the different workflows and trading structures on the Harvey-Bowen and other similar funds. But as I ask more questions of staff, I feel the original civility with which they first welcomed me diminishing by the day, leaving me doubting everyone. Rhonda continues to treat me with disdain, which irritates me. I'm used to people being guarded with me. It comes with the territory of being an auditor. It's my job to break down those barriers, but her open hostility makes it impossible. I've tried calling Melissa numerous times to gauge her opinion, and to see how she is, but she never answers her phone. I leave her messages to contact me, but she never does. I rarely say this about a new assignment, but I can't wait for it to end.

But of course, I don't want it to end. Because then I will have to say goodbye to Edward. And that's something I'm not ready to face.

'We need to slow down,' I say, taking a sip of the excellent Chardonnay Edward has ordered. Having met after work, we are in the salubrious Lower East Side, seated in an outdoor dining area on the cobbled streets of South Street Seaport. The view of the Brooklyn Bridge is striking, and I feel the tension from another day in the office subside. 'I can't keep up this pace.'

Edward waves his hand dismissively. 'Nonsense! You only live once. We must make the most of New York while you're here.'

'But it's been practically the same every night since I got here. I'm going to go home with liver damage.' I laugh. 'Not to mention bags the size of suitcases under my eyes from not getting to bed before midnight each night. And then not getting to sleep until much later.' We share a knowing smile.

'What's it to be at the weekend, then?' He takes a sip of his wine. 'Kingston or Beacon?'

'Where on earth do you get your energy?'

'Healthy living.' He raises his glass to me and smiles. 'Oh, I need to tell you that I got a message from Rupert. He has a contact for you. Said he'd get in touch with you once he had more information. All a bit garbled, but I'm afraid that's Rupert for you.'

'Sounds ominous.'

I relay my growing concerns about the Harvey-Bowen fund, discussing the large sum of money deposited into the main account that first attracted Melissa's attention. Our relationship has accelerated like a locomotive at full tilt. I feel like I can talk to him about anything. I know I've overstepped the borders of professionalism, but I've needed a confidant, and he has been my perfect guide.

Edward stares at me seriously, holding both my hands in his. 'Just be careful. You don't need to go upsetting the wrong people. It's above your pay grade.'

'Charles is coming over next week. I need to have a report for him.'

'And you trust him?'

I scoff. 'I don't trust anyone.'

'You can trust me.'

I smile, nodding. 'Charles has my back. Anyway, he was the one who sent me out here.'

'Enough about work. Kingston or Beacon on Saturday. What's it to be?'

'Beacon, I think. It sounds delightful.'

He pours us both another glass of Chardonnay. 'Don't forget I'm going to Boston on Sunday.'

The corners of my mouth drop. 'Don't remind me.'

'It'll only be four days. Sure I can't twist your arm to come with me?'

'I can't. Work is too busy.'

'We should go in the fall, then. You and me,' he says. 'It's meant to be beautiful there in the fall. There's a whale-watching tour I want to go on. Out to Stellwagen Bank. You'll see dolphins too.'

I sigh. 'I won't be here in the autumn.'

'Hold those words. Look at what happened to me. Two years later, and I'm still here.'

'It won't work like that for me.'

'You never know.'

'It won't. My job out here is almost complete.'

'Am I just hoping?' he says.

'We need to face reality, Edward. I'll be going home. Very soon. It's Ellie's eighteenth. She has her exam results, and I need to get her ready for university.'

He squeezes my hand. 'We'll work it out. Maybe it's time for me to call it a day here.'

'What? Go back to the UK, you mean?'

'Not straight away. But I've been thinking about it for a while. Until then, we can still visit each other. We can be a commuter couple.'

'A commuter couple?'

'I don't want to lose you, Steph.'

I share Edward's evident enthusiasm as we stroll around Beacon's galleries, admiring the abundance of works by emerging artists as well as the more established names. It's such a delightful town set in such a wonderful region. Who would have thought that being so close to the madness of New York City, you could find somewhere of such natural beauty.

'You see, this is what I want to do with my life,' he says. 'Offer the opportunity to less advantaged people to explore their passions. There's a wealth of talent going untapped, and it's a crying shame.'

'Then do something about it.'

Edward remains quiet, deep in thought, and I stay silent, enjoying his passion for art with him.

After a long lunch in a deli along Main Street, we explore a small park he knows that hugs the Hudson, admiring the paddleboarders and kayakers. He unloops his arm from mine and puts it around my shoulders, squeezing me into him. 'Steph, I've been meaning to say this.' He clears his throat. 'I want to choose my words carefully. I don't want to sound foolish.'

'What's on your mind?'

'I just want to say that I can't remember ever enjoying someone's company so much.'

'That's very nice of you to say so.'

'Don't mock me,' he says, smiling.

'I'm sorry. It sounded a bit formal, that's all.' I laugh nervously, anticipating his next words.

He stops and takes my face in his hands. 'What I mean to say is that I've fallen in love with you, and I want you to be quite clear about how I feel.'

'Me too,' I whisper.

13

The prime dry-aged porterhouse steak Charles orders is huge. Like all the food over here. I've settled for a Caesar salad. 'A steak at lunchtime, what a treat.' He slices into his piece of meat. Blood oozes out. 'This is delicious.'

I dig my fork into a generously sized crouton. 'How was Florida?'

'Hot. The kids loved it. As they always do.' He runs his hand over his tanned, bald head that shines in the ambient lighting. 'I don't think they'll ever grow too old for holidays there.'

'Aren't they annoyed you're not staying on with them?'

He shrugs. 'Not really. They know I had the conference booked in Toronto before we arranged the Florida trip. Besides two weeks was enough for me.' He draws his napkin to his mouth and dabs his lips. 'New York looks like it's suiting you. You look... different.'

I shrug off his comment, glancing around the restaurant. Vases of fresh flowers radiate a scent of luxury, complementing the establishment's exclusivity. Soft jazz plays in the background. Edward would like it here. We need to come before I go back to England.

'By the way, your work on the Stenson project was praised by several partners. Thanks for putting that to bed on top of everything else you've got going on out here. People are beginning to know who *the* Stephanie Knight is. So, you've been here almost three weeks. Brief me. How's Ellie?'

'I've hardly seen her.' I tell him how she arrived with her heart smashed into pieces and how, within twenty-four hours of stepping off the plane, she met a guy who miraculously managed to glue them all back together. 'She spends her evenings and nights with him and her days catching up on sleep when he's working. On the nights he works, I see her when she comes back for a change of clothes.'

He laughs. 'You don't look impressed.'

'She's fallen so heavily in love that I don't know how I'm going to get her home.' I don't add that the same goes for me. Since Edward left for his business trip to Boston on Sunday, I've missed him so much, it physically hurts. A feeling I've never experienced before.

'This new guy. He sounds exactly what Ellie needed.'

'I guess. It's just scary when your daughter has her first serious relationship.'

'Tell me about it.'

'Especially when it happens in a foreign city. My ex has always accused me of being overprotective. It's hard when your kid is young for their school year. Some of her friends turned eighteen last September. They are practically a year older than her.'

'You've got to let them grow up sometime, Steph. At least you're around. You won't be when she's at uni.'

'Guess not.'

'So, how have you found everyone here? Playing the game, I hope. What about our superstar, Austin?'

I knew it wouldn't be long before he broached this subject. Jennifer has been asking too. 'Let me say, first of all, I've been carrying out a health check across the business, as I would on any new assignment.'

'Naturally.'

A waitress clears our plates and asks if we would like dessert. 'Not for me,' I say.

'I'm tempted, but I'd better not.' Charles orders coffees for us instead. He waits until she is out of earshot, then asks, 'So what have you been able to find out about him so far?'

'Nothing.'

'Nothing?'

'Everything I've looked at to date seems to be squeaky clean. I'd even go as far as to say that Austin is your model trader.' I tell Charles how all Austin's trades settle on time despite the complexity of the way some of the deals are structured. All the Ts are crossed. All the Is are dotted. Austin Cunningham is your back-office gem. 'Yes, his strategies are complex, and very clever. Extraordinarily clever, but I can't find anything that would cast suspicion on him.'

'Interesting.' Charles stares at his napkin. The waitress delivers two double espressos.

I consider relaying the conversation I had with Melissa, but then remember something she said to me. She didn't trust anyone, not even Charles. I look at the man sitting in front of me: professional, reliable Charles. She was wrong. I'd bet my bottom dollar on it. Charles is the soul of discretion.

Isn't he?

I decide for the moment to take a different approach. 'Out of interest, have you heard of the Harvey-Bowen fund?' This is my investigation now, not Melissa's. In my mind, she is absolved of all responsibility.

He stops stirring his coffee. 'I have. Brings in a tidy sum in fees, that one. Why do you ask?'

I shrug. 'Something caught my attention that I don't like the look of.'

'What?'

'Some of the trading activity, and I had a meeting with the account manager.'

'Chris Smith, you mean?'

'That's him.'

'And?'

I shrug. 'I don't know yet. I'm on it, though.'

'Well, you know how these things work. You get some meat on the bones, and you let me know in the first instance. I want us to be watertight for the external auditors next month. And don't give up on Austin Cunningham yet. Jennifer isn't normally wrong about picking out a bad apple.'

As Charles is settling the bill, my phone beeps. I sneak a look. It's Edward.

> I'm back early. Bottle of wine waiting. Eat in or out? I picked up steaks but happy to go out. Your choice. I've missed you. E x

I quickly type a response.

> Same here. Steaks in sound perfect. How was Boston? X

> Interesting. I've so much to tell you, can't wait. E x

Charles clears his throat. 'It sounds like we need to think about you wrapping things up over here, but first I need to tell you something.'

'What?'

'It's not good.'

'Hit me with it.'

'Melissa has resigned.'

I try to inject surprise into my voice. 'Why?'

'She's found another job, she said. Big loss for us. I tried to persuade her to stay, but there was no talking her round. I got straight onto it with HR and have a few people lined up for her replacement. I want you to do the first round of interviews on Monday and put together a short list for me.'

'Crikey. That's quick.'

'When I'm back from Toronto, HR are going to arrange final interviews for me, and I'll make a decision before I return to London. By the way, Melissa's resignation isn't yet common knowledge, so keep it under wraps. Let's see how these candidates go. I'd like someone lined up before I make an announcement.'

Charles has a meeting to go to across town, so we part ways outside the restaurant. As I'm heading back to the office for the afternoon, I find Melissa's number in my phone and call her, but the line is dead. I try her mother, but her number is dead too.

The afternoon drags, and frustratingly, Jennifer collars me on a finance matter, and it's several hours before I get back to the apartment.

As soon as I put the key in the door, I somehow know things will never be the same.

It's one of those inexplicable moments, a premonition, senses acutely aware. A foreboding that accompanies the muffled cries of my daughter, whimpering like a desperate puppy. I slam the door shut, drop my bag, and rush into the lounge.

An emotional tightness contracts my chest to see Ellie on the sofa, crossed-legged in a lotus pose. Two pearl clips hold her mop of hair away from her distraught face as she uses her hands like windscreen wipers, swiping fresh tears from her naked eyes. I run over to her with open arms, ready to scoop her up. Confusing thoughts rush through my mind in the brief seconds it takes me to reach her. The speed at which they battle for priority and pose question upon question is startling. Jack has ditched her. Has he been a dick, like Toby? Like her dad? Will she want to go home now? Selfishly, those thoughts turn to me. I would have to leave Edward. I kneel at her feet and place my hands on her knees. 'Whatever's happened, Ells? It's Jack, isn't it?' I sigh. 'What've you argued about?'

She can't speak at first. Her eyes are red and puffy, her cheeks smudged with mascara-caked tears. She stares at me. A flash of light from the window shines on the end of her tiny nose and mop of messy hair. Her voice trembles. 'It's far, far worse than that.'

My pulse races. 'What is it?' Is it her dad? My stomach turns. As much as I despise him for what he did to me, I wouldn't want anything to happen to him.

'I'm so sorry, Mum.'

I can't control my voice. 'Tell me.' I'm holding her by the shoulders now.

'It's Edward.'

'Edward? What about him?'

'He's dead, Mum.'

14

At first, I laugh. 'Don't be silly.'

'It's true, Mum.'

I can't process what I'm hearing. 'You must be mistaken.'

'I saw... saw them... take him away.' Ellie's broken words, emerging through sobs and sharp intakes of breath, are difficult to digest.

'I don't understand, Ellie. Calm down and tell me exactly what you saw.' She's got it all wrong. This can't be happening. It must be a mistake. I'm panicking. My world, my life, is unravelling by the second.

An agonising silence ensues. She wipes her eyes, composing herself. Her words are clearer but still interspersed sporadically with frantic sobs. 'Jack was called into work early, so I came back here. When I was letting myself in, I heard a commotion down the hallway, and I saw a paramedic wheeling a stretcher out of Edward's door.' She pauses, snuffling loudly. 'I ran down there and asked what was going on.' Another pause, another snuffle.

I shake uncontrollably. 'Are you sure it was Edward's apartment?'

'Yes, Mum.'

I take her hand in mine, as I have so many times when she has been upset. But even when her dad left, I've never seen her so shaken. I'm still clinging to the thinning band of hope that she is wrong. Edward is going to walk in here any minute, isn't he? 'What happened next?'

She takes three deep breaths, regaining control. 'There was a body covered with a sheet. I asked if it was Edward. The paramedic said something to the other one who disappeared into the apartment. He was rude, but I guess it was a stressful situation. He said I had no business there. I think he thought I was some ghoulish thrill-seeker until I said my mum was the girlfriend of the person who lives there. He said... he said... the gentleman had suffered a heart attack.'

I gasp, incredulous. 'A heart attack?'

'I'm sorry, Mum. They said he didn't make it.'

Disbelief delivers my words in a murmur of broken babble. 'This can't be right. Edward is fit. It can't be true.'

'It is, Mum. The man told me to leave. There was nothing more to be done.'

'And it was definitely Edward? Did you see his face?'

'He's dead, Mum.'

Ripe emotions strike me deep in my stomach as the sense of unbearable loss starts to sink in. I'll never see him again. I feel like I've been beaten with a bat, the pain insufferable. All the hopes and the optimism for the future are gone. We were going to meet up this evening. He had some news for me, he said in his text. This is all too much.

I sit with my head in my hands, my daughter's arms around me until the need to do something suppresses all feelings. I have to find out exactly what has happened here. I may be in denial, but this all seems so unreal. Freeing myself from Ellie's embrace, I jump up and get my phone.

'What're you doing, Mum?'

I call Edward's number. It goes straight to voicemail. 'I'm going to his apartment.'

'Mum, you're not thinking straight. He's not there.'

Running out of the door, I head for Edward's apartment, stifling tears. This is not the time to cry. I need answers. I bang on his door. There's no answer. Praying this is some kind of horrible mistake, I bang again and again with both hands, but my prayers remain unanswered. I turn around and lean my back against his door, my head in my hands. This doesn't seem real. As if I'm in a nightmare of the worst kind.

I take the stairs down to the lobby. Surely there I will find some answers.

'Unfortunately, I'm unable to divulge any information, Ma'am,' the concierge says. A short man, what he lacks in height, he sure makes up for in width. He looks like one of the scary guys from down the gym who takes dubious substances to inflate their muscles. I swear under my breath. I've never seen this guy before. What happened to the usual friendly concierge who always seems to be here? 'But I had a personal relationship with him.'

'That may be the case, but, nevertheless, we can only deal with the next of kin. We have a strict confidentiality policy for all residents. Unless you're related, I can't help you.'

It occurs to me that I don't know who Edward's next of kin are. His parents are dead. And although he talked about his friends, I never actually met any of them. My voice breaks. 'But he's my boyfriend.'

He raises his arms. 'It's policy. My hands are tied, Ma'am.'

'But a man has died.'

'Sorry, Ma'am.'

'Where did they take the body? You must be able to tell me.'

He looks at me blankly – an empty stare of finality. In his opinion, this conversation has ended. If it ever really started!

'You must be able to tell me *something*.'

He rearranges a pen on his desk, moving it from the right-hand side of a pad of paper to the left-hand side. 'Let me see what I can find out for you.' A couple enter the building. He attempts a sympathetic smile before turning his attention to them.

I want to scream at him. How would he feel in my situation? But I know it won't make a scrap of difference. My hand bangs on the desk. A subconscious display of frustration. The couple flinches, and the concierge advises me to return to my apartment to calm down, and he'll do what he can.

I take the stairs, working out the anger tearing through me. When I get to the ninth floor, I bend over double, breathless. My legs are leaden, my spirit more so. This can't be happening. Can it? The band of hope is fraying. I don't want it to snap. Because then I really will need to accept that Edward is never coming back. I blast into the apartment. Ellie is still sitting in the same position I left her in. 'Anything?'

'Nothing. That bloody concierge was playing the confidentiality line with me. I wanted to throttle him.' I rummage around in my handbag. It's in here somewhere. The business card Edward gave me when I was at his apartment one time. I find it in my purse and attempt to call his office. What information they will or can give, I don't know. I'm acting irrationally. They won't even be aware of his death. The line rings once and clicks into a recorded message. We are not in the office; please call back or visit our website. What was I thinking? I pace around the apartment, my hands on the back of my head, elbows flung wide, trying to make sense of this dire situation.

'Come and sit down, Mum. I'll get you a drink.'

I don't want a drink. I want Edward back.

'There's some wine in the fridge. Let me pour us both a glass.'

'Maybe in a bit.' I pick up a pen from the odds and ends bowl on the small table by the front door. 'I'm going back downstairs. Get that concierge to give me a list of hospitals or morgues where he could've been taken.' The word morgue sounds so final, another hefty wave of grief pulses through me. 'I refuse to let him palm me off.'

'Why don't you look online? You'll probably find out more,' Ellie says.

I stop, staring at the items in the bowl, noticing the set of Edward's keys. The ones he enthusiastically gave me to try to persuade me to take up his offer to paint in his art room. Not that I ever have. Grabbing them, I finger the smooth surface of the fob for entry to the car park in the basement. It's clipped to the main ring via a chain. 'I'm going to have a look in Edward's apartment.' I wave the keys at her. 'See if I can find details of his next of kin. Anyone I can talk to.'

Ellie strides over to me. 'Do you think that's a good idea? It's only going to upset you more.'

Although I'm inclined to agree with her, I have to do something.

'I'll come with you. I don't want you going in there by yourself. It'll be too upsetting.'

I shake my head. This has been distressing enough for her as it is. 'You stay here. I need to do this on my own.'

15

_____

I'm driven, as focused as a laser beam. I have had to steel myself because something feels wrong. I don't know what, but I need answers. There will be time to grieve later. I leave the apartment and march down the corridor to Edward's door. My hands are shaking as I place the key in the lock. Even though I've spent many hours in here over the past three weeks – we've made love here, and shared life stories and experiences – I'm aware that I'm a trespasser about to violate someone's private property. We've talked about a future together here too. It all seemed so natural, perfect even. A real shot at happiness for both of us.

The surroundings are familiar but packed now with a sense of emptiness. As if his apartment stopped breathing the same time as him. It's excruciatingly quiet with a stillness giving the impression of time standing still. When I've been here before, jazz music has usually been playing. Edward loved his music. Last week, he took me down to the West Village to a basement jazz club. It was nestled between trendy shops that Ellie would love and cosy restaurants. Although it was small, cramped, and dark, the atmosphere was electric. Was that really only a week ago?

Creeping into the living area, I feel even more like an intruder, violating my lover's personal space. It's not right. I shouldn't be here. I peer around. Looking for what, I'm unsure. I thought it was to find his next of kin, but now I realise I want information about his previous life. His life before me. A link to someone with whom I can share the grief. The apartment is tidy. I was always impressed with how neat he was. Raw emotion consumes me, and I finally give into the realisation that the unimaginable might be true.

He is never coming back to me.

I collapse onto the sofa and let it out, crying, sobbing uncontrollably for my loss, for Edward.

Getting a grip of my emotions, I step over to the old-fashioned bureau opposite the sofa, wiping my nose and eyes. The hinged lid is open, displaying nondescript papers, bills and flyers. I rifle through them but find nothing to connect me to anyone who knew Edward. I lift the lid. There's a drawer beneath, but there's not much inside. A cupboard runs down the right-hand side of the bureau. I open it. But there's little of interest: an A4 file for domesticity, a few legal books and some brochures from New York art galleries.

I wander over to the kitchen area, the whole place eerily hushed like the occasions I've been alone at work pulling an all-nighter to satisfy one of Charles's impossible demands. A pinch of despair squeezes my stomach at the sight of a skillet on the stove and two steaks on a board covered with squares of kitchen paper, waiting to be cooked. Two knives, two forks, two plates, and two glasses waiting among a freshly prepared salad and a bottle of red.

The pain is unbearable. Have I really known him for such a short amount of time?

The two of us should be sitting down to enjoy a meal right now. Instead, I'm searching for details for the next of kin of a man I desire to know more about. I wander over to his bedroom. An unpacked carry-on bag lies open on the bed with a plastic bag on top. I open it to find a box of See's chocolate mints, a mix of milk and dark chocolates. The pinch of torment tugs at my heart. He bought them for me. I know he did. Last weekend, when he took me to dinner, we were discussing our favourite chocolates. He asked if I'd ever tried milk chocolate mints, and when I said no, he replied, 'You don't know what you're missing. I need to get you a box of See's.'

Edward's painting room catches my eye, the door wide open. I gasp as I enter. In contrast to the rest of the apartment, this room is a mess. The whole scene looks as though all of his paintings and equipment have been tossed in the air. Paint is spattered across the floor, his treasured pieces of art scattered in disarray. Was this his final resting place? It would be fitting, given his passion. But something doesn't feel right. I'm guessing the paramedics wouldn't have cared too much about the artwork. They were more intent on saving his life. Or perhaps this occurred as he fell?

I rush to a collapsed easel and stand it up. Trying to create some order, I replace the painting he had been working on, stifling sob after sob. He had been painting a piece to complement the one he gave me the day after he came out of the artist's closet. The same beautiful colours fill the canvas in a design to marry with the work of art which I hung on the wall in my bedroom in place of the Manhattan skyline that was there. I gasp. In tiny letters, he has scribed his initials next to mine in the bottom left-hand corner.

The sense of loss overcomes me again, for what must have been Edward's final paint strokes. I feel like someone has sliced me in two and stolen the better part of me. My eyes draw closer, staring until I realise that he has tried to write something on the canvas. It looks like the start of my name before the squiggle runs off the edge of the frame. Strange. His iPhone is sitting on the workbench. I tap on the screen. Damn! It has run out of battery.

I need to get into his phone. The contents will surely provide the gateway to all his personal information. How do I do that without a passcode?

I freeze, stifling a sharp intake of breath. Is that the door to the apartment opening? I can't be found in here; it would be totally inappropriate. Someone is coming in. I'm sure of it. I cover my mouth with my hand. I could kick myself. I should never have come in here. Through the open door, I see a figure enter the lounge area. A large-framed paramedic with short brown hair, wearing a surgical mask, walks calmly and confidently about the room as if he is in search of something specific.

Why don't I shout out hello? Because I soon realise something feels off. Very off. The way he moves, his countenance, is menacing, threatening somehow. Besides, what's a paramedic doing coming back here? Lumbering across to the dining table, he picks up Edward's laptop and slips it inside a black gym bag. My heartbeat pulses in my ears. This isn't right. What does he want with Edward's laptop?

The intruder rummages through the bureau. What's he looking for? He gives up and scans the apartment. I can just about see him rummaging through the kitchen cupboards before disappearing into Edward's bedroom. I contemplate making a dash for the door and getting the hell out of here but realise it's far too risky. He comes back into view. He is heading for this room. I inwardly groan and squish behind the workbench, hugging my arms around my knees, curling up as small as possible. He's in the room now, close to me. My heart is pounding. He picks up something from the floor. I strain to see what it is. A white cloth splattered with paint. He stops. Has he seen me? He stuffs the cloth in his trouser pocket and then stands at the bench. Surely he can feel my presence? He noisily moves items around the workbench before leaving the room and exiting the apartment, quietly closing the door behind him.

Tiptoeing to the door, I slowly pull it open and peer down the corridor to see him press the button to the service lift. He swipes the mask off his face and shakes his hair, glancing back down the corridor. I jerk my head backwards, praying he didn't see me. I wait. My heart is in overdrive. Beating like it's going to explode. I can't take this. I'm not cut out for this kind of crap. Finally, I hear the ping of the lift. The doors open and close. I peer around the doorframe again. He is nowhere in sight.

Returning inside, I rush to the lounge. What was Edward involved in? I hunt through the bureau again, then the kitchen drawers, bedside tables, and his wardrobe. I search inside the carry-on bag on his bed, trying to find anything the intruder may have missed. Nothing. There's no paperwork, no files or documents that might reveal more about the man with whom I fell helplessly in love with such ease. And what could be on his computer that's so important, that someone would risk coming back for it?

And I can't buy why he wouldn't have some kind of filing system here. Save for a few bills, there's nothing personal. It makes no sense. Perhaps he kept all that kind of stuff at work.

Do I really know this guy? *Did* I really know this guy?

I return to his art room to get his phone. Perhaps Ellie can help me get into it without a passcode. But when I search around his workbench, it's no longer there.

16

I barely sleep, hearing Edward's voice at regular intervals as if he is lying beside me. At one point, I think I see him, perched on the edge of the bed. The image is so intense, I sit bolt upright and reach out to him, but of course he isn't there.

When I wake up, Ellie is slumped on the sofa, drinking tea. A white mug with *I love NY* stamped on either side sits on the coffee table. Edward bought me that mug. Ellie leans forwards and slides it over to me. 'I was waiting for it to cool down, and I was going to bring it to you. How are you?'

I shrug, stifling tears, sipping my tea.

'Where will the funeral be held?'

I stare at her. How am I meant to know these kinds of things? 'I guess they'll fly his body back to the UK at some point.' I pick up the mug and sit down beside her. 'We need to talk.'

She frowns. 'What about?'

'I've been thinking. My assignment is nearly complete here. Charles told me yesterday that they're recruiting someone to take Melissa's place.'

'I know what you're going to say. We're going home, aren't we?'

'At some point soon, yes.'

'But listen, Mum. There's something I want to tell you too.'

I raise my eyebrows. Her tone tells me I'm not going to like what I'm about to hear.

'I know this is not the time. You must be so upset about Edward, but since you brought it up, I need to be honest with you. I'm not ready to go back. Not yet. I'm going to stay for a while.'

'But what about your birthday party?' I lean back in the seat. 'Ellie, you're still planning on going to uni, aren't you? Please don't tell me you might throw away everything you've worked for, for a guy you barely know.'

The innocence of youth gleans across her face. 'I do know him.'

'But you don't. Not really. You've only just met.'

'He's going to come back with me for my birthday, but we can't go just yet. He needs to wait until someone at work comes back from their holiday Then he can stay with us at home until I start uni. He can, can't he?'

I stare at her blankly.

'He needs to be back here for the start of his new college year anyway. He's going to get another shift at the bar, and I'm going to get a part-time job when I'm settled, so we can save for flights to see each other. Then next year, when I've finished my exams, I'll come back out here for the summer. We're going to stay together, Mum. Nothing can stop us.'

'I'm not trying to stop you from seeing him. I just don't want you to give up on the bright future you have ahead of you.'

'I won't, Mum. I promise. I've worked too hard to get where I am. But we are staying together.'

I can't deal with this right now.

She goes back to bed, and I email Charles, copying in Jennifer. Something I ate last night didn't agree with me. I've been up all night, I tell them. I'll log in later and deal with any outstanding matters, I add, as I snatch another tissue from the box on the arm of the sofa.

A loud knock at the door startles me. No one ever knocks here. Apart from Edward on the few occasions he dropped by. Mostly, we spent our time in his apartment. It is far more homely. I walk over to see who is there but stop, stepping backwards as another loud knock makes me jump. A key turns in the lock. I stiffen. Who else has a key to this apartment? I dart across the lounge and into my bedroom, my heart thundering. The front door opens. There's a clattering sound. Who the hell is it? I hear the squeaking of trainers crossing the wooden floor. Louder and louder, they approach the bedroom. They're coming for me.

I yelp as I come face to face with the housekeeper, a petite woman with a tired face. 'Ma'am, I'm so sorry.' She turns down the round white collar of her black dress. 'I didn't know you were here.'

It's the first time I've met her. I'm usually long gone before she turns up on a Friday. I politely tell her she won't be needed today. She tries to negotiate. She's persistent. 'You won't even notice I'm here.'

I point to Ellie's bedroom. 'My daughter is still in bed.' She gathers her bucket of belongings and tells me not to forget to water the plant in the corner of the lounge, leaving me to grab another tissue to wipe the fat tears coming thick and fast.

The tears dry into guilt. If only I'd come back earlier last night. Edward might still be alive.

Picking up Edward's business card from the table, I twirl it between my fingers. I grab my phone and redial the number of his offices. 'I need to speak to Edward Millner's secretary, please.'

'Let me check,' says the receptionist. There's a pause. I hear the clicking sound of fingers on a keyboard. 'I'm sorry, but no one by that name works here.'

She couldn't have heard me correctly. 'Sorry, you must be mistaken. Edward Millner. Millner spelt with two ls.'

She asks me to spell out the entire surname. 'Yes, that's what I thought; we don't have anyone by that name working here.'

I grit my teeth. 'Please could you check again?'

'I'm new here.' She gives a nervous giggle. 'It's only my second day. Please bear with me, and I'll ask a colleague.' The line clicks into some annoying music. It grates on me. I slide my laptop onto my lap and find Edward's company

– Pembrooke Cross International – on Google and search the Legal and Compliance department personnel for him. Like I did when he first told me where he worked. There was a striking photograph of him sitting behind a large oak desk in the company offices, the Manhattan skyline sparkling in the background. I scroll up and down the team members but can't find him. Now I'm the one who must be mistaken. I scroll through them again. But I'm not. He has been removed. They must have already updated their website.

'Yes, you are correct. Mr Millner did indeed work here, but he has left the organisation.'

There's a pause while I digest this news. 'Left? When did he leave? Why?'

The receptionist stutters, 'Let me check.' The awful music resumes. I tap my little finger on the edge of the laptop, waiting for her to tell me she is mistaken, and that she'll put me through to Edward's secretary. She returns. 'He has only recently left, but I'm unable to release any more information. I'm sorry.'

I lower the phone and stare at the screen.

'What is going on, Edward?' I say aloud.

The receptionist's voice sounds as if it's coming from another room. 'Could I take a message, and I'll see if there is a way to get it to Mr Millner.'

I consider telling her he's dead. One of their ex-employees keeled over last night and died, but I hold back. Something isn't right here. I end the call, still staring at the phone, thinking back over my time with him. He seemed so genuine. One of the kindest, most generous men I've ever met. Only last Saturday, when we were driving back from the trip to Beacon, he said we needed to think about our future. I replay our conversation in my head. He didn't want to lose me. That's what he said. The next day, he went away on business to Boston. A trip for a company he doesn't work for. Not when he died, anyway. I know he was working there when we first got together. I saw his picture on their website.

But then he died.

And I discover he lied to me. Big time. And someone enters his apartment and takes his laptop and phone.

Did I really know him?

My head is shouting at me. No, Steph, you didn't know him at all.

But the ache inside me tells me I most certainly did.

'I'm staying in with you today, Mum,' Ellie says when she surfaces an hour later.

I consider spilling my heart out to her but decide I can't let her join this drama. She'll tell Jack, and then that's another innocent person involved in whatever is going on. If there is indeed anything going on? Am I being rational here?

'No way. Don't let me ruin your plans.' Jack has taken her to some unusual places since they met: a tropical forest growing in an office building, a cat sanctuary full of feral felines, an ice cream factory in Chinatown and parks galore. Today it's a trip to a Lower Manhattan museum housed in a freight elevator, exhibiting curated artefacts of obscurity from around the world. He wants to show her the soul of New York, he told her. 'You must go out with Jack today. This is a trip of a lifetime for you.'

'Are you sure about this?' Ellie asks, hovering at the door. 'I know you didn't know Edward long, but I can only imagine how you're feeling. I'd be devastated if anything happened to Jack. I feel like I should stay in with you.'

'Go, darling. I'm no company for anyone today. Besides, no offence, but I'd prefer to be on my own.'

The door bangs shut. I sit staring into nothingness. How can a fit and healthy man have a heart attack? It doesn't sound plausible, but I know it's possible. The same happened to my friend's husband. He was forty-two when he dropped dead while watching a football match; an undetected congenital heart defect was later diagnosed. When Ellie leaves, I research where paramedics take the deceased in the concrete jungle of this city, and that's when I learn that they don't.

Paramedics don't take dead bodies anywhere when a death occurs at home. This is the responsibility of a coroner or medical examiner.

Who were those paramedics who took his body away then?

I consider calling the police. But then wonder if I want to be part of whatever trouble Edward was involved in. And when I think about what I would say, it sounds bonkers: My boyfriend had a heart attack last night. I wasn't here, but I broke into his apartment afterwards, and so did someone else who took his laptop and phone. Oh, and, by the way, he left his job at some point recently and didn't tell me. How long have you known him, did you ask, sir? Almost three weeks, sir.

Bonkers.

17

Casting aside my laptop, I go to my bedroom and throw on the jeans and T-shirt I left in a heap on the floor last night. I'll shower later. I look in the mirror, combing my fingers through my knotted hair. I look a state, my eyes puffy, my cheeks an ugly mottled red. Grabbing my keys and the keys to Edward's apartment from the blue bowl by the door, I head down the corridor.

The apartment is as I left it last night, ghostly quiet. The oaky waft of Edward's aftershave hits me like a spiritual embrace. I didn't notice that yesterday. In the kitchen, I don't know why, but I wrap the steaks in cling film. It's strange to think I should have eaten one of them last night. I finger the bottle of wine we should have shared while addressing how best to manage the complexities of being a commuter couple.

I go to the bureau and search again through Edward's belongings for any clues about what has happened here. Did he resign a while ago and not tell me? If so, why? Or was it yesterday, before he came home? Did he even go to Boston? *I've so much to tell you.* Isn't that what he said in his last text to me? I grab my phone from my pocket and check. There it is. As plain as the bottle of wine my fingers are touching: *I've so much to tell you, can't wait.* Perhaps he was going to tell me everything last night. Or am I frantically pulling at strands to try to unravel all of this?

I walk to his studio and scan the paintings hanging on the walls and resting on the easels. Absently, I start clearing up the mess. It looks at odds with the rest of the tidy apartment. Moving a paint palette, I pick up a printout of an email from the workbench. It's from a gallery in SoHo, confirming an appointment next Monday lunchtime. I read through the brief paragraph from the owner, exuding excitement about meeting Edward again and thanking him for getting in contact. They are always looking out for new talent. The owner thanks Edward for the piece he recently dropped off and says he can't wait to see more samples of his work.

Pen marks seep through the page. Flipping the piece of paper over, I see a list of four paintings. Putting two and two together, I deduce that the paintings listed are hanging on the side wall beneath two spotlights like a viewing gallery. Edward must have planned to take them there next week. Why didn't he tell me about all this? I reread the email. Perhaps he wanted to be accepted before he told me, avoiding disappointment or embarrassment if his work was rejected. So unnecessary. I would have loved to share in his new adventure. Here I go again, making excuses for his duplicity.

Walking back to my apartment, I see two figures standing at my door. As I get closer, I realise they are police officers. One is a bull-necked man, the other a woman with long blonde hair, probably older than her appearance. 'Can I help you?' I say as I approach them. The man smells oddly of cheese. Or is it onion? As if he has just eaten a cheese and onion toastie. It isn't a pleasant smell. 'Stephanie Knight?'

'Yes.' I rest a hand on the wall. My immediate thought is of Ellie.

They each present a badge and introduce themselves: Randy Tommaso is the more senior. I don't catch the name of the female officer. 'We're here concerning Mr Millner. Could we come in?' he says in a deep baritone voice.

I breathe a big sigh of relief that it's not my daughter they are here to discuss. 'Sure.' I open my door, and they follow me inside. I offer them a drink, but they decline. I feel terribly uneasy.

'There's nothing to concern yourself with, Ma'am. We're only here to ask a few questions. Then we'll be on our way.'

My anxieties revert to Edward. What could these officers want from me? I feel guarded, though I'm unsure why. It's probably because I've never had any brushes with the law before. Apart from breaking the speed limit on occasion, I'm your model citizen: on the board of governors at the primary school Ellie used to attend and a volunteer at the local food bank. Good old honest Stephanie Knight. But here I am now, face to face with NYPD's finest.

'The concierge informs me you had a relationship with Mr Millner,' Randy says.

'Yes, that is correct.' Why I answer as though I'm in a witness box, I have no idea.

'I'm so sorry for your loss. This must be a terrible time for you,' he says. The woman sitting next to him wears a sympathetic smile but doesn't speak.

If he wasn't in uniform, Randy would be intimidating. And the authority his uniform brings only adds to his unnerving appearance. But despite this, he is sincere in his condolences. He's like a big bear wanting to give you a big hug. I nod, unsure how much to divulge. My voice breaks. 'I've only been here three weeks, but we'd grown close.' Tears flow. I can't help myself.

The female officer sidles over to me and puts her arm around my shoulder. I don't resist.

'Are you OK to carry on?' Randy asks. I nod. 'Can we get you something – some water, perhaps?' I shake my head. He continues, explaining that the female officer has been in touch with Edward's place of work but was unable to obtain details of his next of kin. 'We were hoping you could give us contact details of his family in England.'

'His parents used to live in Salcombe, in Devon, but they've both passed away now. That's all I know.'

'Any other relatives you know of?'

I shake my head. 'Where is his body now? Why did paramedics take him away?'

'They took him to the medical examiner's office. There was no one with him when he died. All unattended deaths require an autopsy.'

The female officer remains silent. She is trying to be kind but seems a little distant. Maybe this work has desensitised her. Ellie's dad always says that's how the job gets you in the end. You can't help it. Having to deal with rising numbers of emotionally draining cases exhausts you.

'How long will that take?' I ask.

'I couldn't tell you. If you give me your cell number, I'll see what I can find out for you. I understand you would want to get some closure.' He gets out his phone, enters my number, and produces a business card. 'Here are my details. I'll be your point of contact. Anything you need, please feel free to call at any time, day or night.' His genuine niceness is reassuring. 'Is there anyone we can call to be with you?'

I shake my head and take the card with his details.

'If you have any further questions, please call. Again, I'm sorry for your loss.'

I'm making some coffee when Ellie turns up with Jack half an hour later.

'What're you doing back here?' I ask. I just want to be on my own.

'I can't leave you alone, Mum.' Ellie drops her leather rucksack and runs over to hug me. 'It doesn't feel right.'

Jack is standing by the sofa, his hands in the pockets of his jeans. 'I'm so sorry to hear about Edward. I couldn't believe it when Ellie told me. Is there anything I can do?'

I shake my head. 'The police have been here. They're trying to find details of his next of kin.'

'We can't leave you alone.' Ellie looks at Jack and nods. 'Jack and I thought we'd stay with you this weekend.' It feels odd to hear her refer to herself as part of a couple.

'You don't have to do that,' I say, unsure how to get out of this one. I don't want Jack here. It's not that I don't like him, far from it. The times Ellie has brought him back here, it's evident he adores her as much as she does him. They are good together. I can see that. But the last thing I need is for them to be all loved-up hanging around the apartment, however sensitive and respectful they try to be. I'd rather be alone. 'A friend from work is coming to stay.'

'Who?' Ellie asks.

'Melissa.' My face reddens. I can't remember ever lying to Ellie. But I can't have the pair of them here.

She is insistent, but after much protesting, she agrees to let me be. 'I'm going to shower before we go out,' she says to Jack. He nods and removes his denim jacket.

'Would you like some coffee?' I ask.

'Why don't you sit down, and I'll make it.'

'No, you're good.'

He runs his hands through his hair. 'I understand why you'd want to be alone, but we're happy to stay here.'

'Thanks.'

'If you change your mind any time, I'll get her back straight away.'

Ellie calls out from her bedroom. 'Jack, can you come here, please?'

'Coming,' he calls out to her. 'I'll be right back,' he says to me.

I pour the coffee, and in no mood for conversation, I

take it to my bedroom. But as I'm passing Ellie's room, I see Jack with his back to me, rummaging through her chest of drawers. I stop to watch him, curious as to his intentions. An overwhelming distrust absorbs me. I'm about to ask him what on earth he's playing at when Ellie pokes her head around the en suite door and shouts, 'Have you found it?'

'What, in this mess? Give me a break.' He laughs.

I exhale a sigh of relief as he turns and hands her a bottle of shampoo.

It's not until they've left the apartment an hour later that guilt chews me up. I shouldn't have lied to her and told her Melissa was coming over.

I don't know what to do with myself. My feelings are off the scale. A hotchpotch of frustration, anger, and grief, all mixed into a bitter-tasting cocktail of emotions. I take a long shower, but the hot water does nothing to wash away the guilt of having lied to Ellie. After I get out, I send her a text:

What about we spend Sunday together? X

Jack's taking me out for the day, but I could cancel. x

Where're you going? X

She types the emoji of a lady shrugging her shoulders, followed by:

Somewhere special, apparently. x

Don't worry. Enjoy yourself. X

He's working in the evening. I'll get him to drop me back. How about that? x

What time? X

Will text you when I'm leaving. x

Be safe. X

I'm in bits, frazzled parts. The frightened part of me wants to take the first plane out of this city and head home to familiar surroundings. Sometimes you've got to know when to cut and run. But the sensible part of me knows I can't leave Ellie. She has it all worked out if I do. She'll stay here and move in with Jack. Besides, part of me feels like I'd be abandoning Edward. It seems even the police are unable to establish his next of kin. The only other people I heard him talk about were his friend Rupert, who is yet to get in touch, a few friends around the city, and Jack. But Jack was more of an acquaintance than a friend – nothing more than his friendly barman.

Another part of me thinks about the lies Edward has told me. I question myself. Were they outright lies? Was it more deception? And the grand reveal may have been planned for when he dished up those steaks yesterday evening. That seems a lifetime ago. One thing's for certain, though, whatever he was involved in, I don't want to be a part of it.

18

After another sleepless night, I order an Uber and instruct the driver to take me to Melissa's home. Never have I felt so helpless. It's another bright but humid day, and I'm sweating when I get in the car, grateful for the air con that has been ramped up to full. But as soon as the driver pulls away, I'm shivering. I ask him to turn the air con down. He gladly obliges as he chats away about the current mayor, how taxes are crippling the middle class, and how great it would be to live in such a nice neighbourhood as the one he is taking me to. 'Visiting a friend?' he asks. I mumble a reply. Not in the mood for chitter-chatter, I turn to my phone and absently scroll through Instagram.

I feel a sense of emptiness when I press Melissa's door-bell, sad and hollow. The same feeling I had when I went back to Edward's apartment after he died. Breathing in the smell of cut grass from lawnmowers in action in the neighbouring gardens, I glance around, but nothing looks different to when I came here three weeks ago. There's no reply, so I press the bell again, listening to squeals from children playing in the vicinity, bouncing on a trampoline and splashing about in a paddling pool.

A voice startles me. The pink-haired lady who lives in the downstairs apartment is standing on the corner of the building, apron wrapped around her skinny frame, a watering can in her hand. 'No use waiting there. They've gone.'

'Gone?' I frown. 'Gone where?'

She shrugs. 'Went in the middle of the night. Woke me up. I saw her piling cases and bags into her car, and then she was gone with the kid.' She passes me and waggles like a duck along the path and through a gate in the fence.

Bewildered, I step across to a window, but the curtains are closed. I try the other windows, but the curtains are pulled too. I walk around to the back of the property where I left from the last time I was here. The garden is split into two areas. One for upstairs and one for the down-stairs apartment. Bamboo fencing divides the two. Melissa's garden looks abandoned. Weeds seep through the lawn. Flowers wilt in the containers. And several of the dried-out border plants are gasping for water. A gap between the curtains of the patio doors allows me to peep inside the kitchen. A chair is lying on its side as if it's been knocked over, and, from what I can see, the cupboard doors are mostly open. I recall the boxes when I was last here. Didn't Melissa say she was cleaning out her kitchen in preparation for decorating when she was up to it? I think she was lying. She planned this.

The neighbour passes the gate. 'Excuse me?' I hurry

over to her. 'I don't suppose you have a forwarding address; a phone number?'

She shakes her head. 'I didn't have much to do with her or the kid.'

'When did they leave?'

'Two nights ago.'

'Thank you.'

She nods and wanders off.

Disappointed, I pull out my phone and arrange for an Uber to take me back to the apartment. The app informs me that one is en route with an expected arrival in four minutes. I make my way down the short drive to the road, disorientated. I didn't expect to be walking away empty-handed. A deep-rooted fear for Melissa that started to grow inside me after my first visit is making its way to the surface. I will the Uber to hurry; I want to get away from here. A loud bang like a gunshot blasts through the air and startles me. There it is again. I shoot for cover against the trunk of the maple tree in front of the property. Only as I see a group of youths gathered around a battered old motor, do I realise that it's a car engine backfiring.

After stopping at an ATM for me, the Uber driver drops me at the contemporary gallery in SoHo which occupies the ground floor of a brownstone, between an upmarket florist and a home interior store. The large window on one side of the entrance displays an abstract painting on canvas, and a sculpture of two cuddling cats sits in the other.

A bell rings as I enter. A man in a bowler hat and jumbo, black-rimmed glasses greets me from behind a counter. Mellow music is playing, and the scent of wood moves in the air from the framing shop located at the back of the building. He announces he is the owner to me and the woman who enters directly after me. 'Pleased to answer any questions you may have.' The woman stays to chat with him while I mingle with other customers trickling in and out of the shop, viewing the various pieces of artwork on display. Edward's work would fit in well. Not that I know much about art.

When the owner is free, I approach his counter. 'I have a friend,' I say. 'Edward Millner.'

He wrinkles his thick brow. 'Yes. I know Edward.'

'You have a piece of his artwork.'

He leans backwards. 'That's right.'

'My name is Stephanie.' I put my hand in my pocket and pull out the five one hundred dollar bills I withdrew from the ATM on the way here. 'He's dead.'

His hand rushes to remove his hat which he clamps against his chest. 'I'm dreadfully sorry. What happened?'

It takes every ounce of courage to stop myself from crying. 'He had a heart attack.' My voice cracks. 'Please sell me the piece he dropped off.' I place the dollars on the table.

The owner stares at the money as if making a quick calculation of trust versus scoring a very easy, astonishingly quick, buck. 'Wait here a second.' He is gone a while. The doorbell rings. Above the calm ambience, it sounds so loud. I swing around to see a couple wander in, arms entwined. The guy picks up a gallery guide from the small desk by the door, and their heads huddle over it as the owner returns with the painting securely wrapped. 'Sorry that took so long. My assistant must've moved it.'

'Could I ask a favour?'

'Another one?' he asks, with a playful smile, quickly withdrawing it when he realises his insensitivity.

'I need to travel back to the UK soon. Could you spare me some extra bubble wrap?'

'Sure.' He wanders off and returns moments later with an armful of packaging. He places it all in a large bag and hands it over the desk.

Rushing from the gallery, I hail a yellow cab, banging my head in my haste to get inside. It's all too much. With my arms wrapped around the final piece of Edward, my body trembles the whole journey back.

What was he involved in?

After I've taken the gallery bag back to the apartment, I head out to the corner store and walk around in a daze, barely able to concentrate. Selecting some onions and peppers, I'm loading them into a basket followed by a bottle of wine, when a hefty mass of a man catches my eye. He is staring at me. Roaming up and down the aisles, I see him again. I hurry, chucking random items into the basket.

'Are you OK, Ma'am?' the cashier asks as she checks my shopping through the till. Do I really look that bad?

On the walk back to the apartment, I keep looking over my shoulder every few steps. I can't help it. But there's no one there. When I reach Bridgewood Plaza, I tell myself to get a grip, but the sense of foreboding has a vice-like grip on me. And when I get into the lift, the same man springs up like an ugly jack-in-the-box telling me my fears are for real. My heart races as he stands beside me, empty-handed, and when we reach the ninth floor, he heads in the direction of Edward's apartment. Was he following me, or is he a resident of this block? I watch as he passes Edward's door, and before going around the corner at the end of the passage, he turns, nods and carries on. I rush inside, my mind made up.

I don't want to be here any more.

I need to get out of this city.

PART TWO

19

ELLIE

'Where're you taking me?' I manage to blurt out between screams of anguish and the drumbeat of pain pounding through me. My body is writhing, trying to break free from the unrelenting pressure of Man One's hand in my back.

'Be quiet and walk,' he orders.

There must be a mistake. They've got the wrong person. My breathing has become laboured. I'm wheezing, running out of energy, and oxygen. Stay calm, Ellie. Stay calm. Otherwise, I know what could happen. I've not had an asthma attack for well over a year. Not since Mum and Dad split up when one struck me with the threat of death, and I ended up in intensive care.

A tightness creeps across my chest. I need to control it. I repeat the mantra Mum has taught me for stressful situations. Over and over like a song I can't get out of my head: I'm going to be OK. 'Why're you doing this?' My voice is wavering, struggling to emit the words I want to scream at

142

him. I'm scared I'm going to hyperventilate. 'What. Do. You. Want. From. Me?' Stay calm, Ellie. You've got this! I kick my leg, blindly aiming in the direction of this monster.

'I said, shut it.' He punches me in the centre of my back. The force of the blow knocks the remaining wind out of me. Even though I can't see him, I know this man is big. He is towering over me. The trajectory of his voice sounds like he is up a ladder. From the force of his hand, and the power of his aggressive voice, I know he means business.

The soft grassy ground turns to gravel. Are we where Jack parked his dad's car? My thoughts wander. 'I want to take you somewhere special,' Jack said the other night. 'Where I used to take my sister before she died. We'll need to drive. I'll borrow my dad's car. He won't mind.' The corners of his lips curved down. 'He won't even know.'

Is this why he brought me here? To die? No. Not Jack. We've not known each other long. Not even a month. We are boyfriend and girlfriend, lovers. He wouldn't do anything to hurt me. Would he?

A car door opens, I think. Is there another one of them? Man Three, or did Man Two open it? Heavy feet tread the gravel, crunching in my direction. One of them says, 'Open the trunk.'

There's a clunking sound. 'No. Please, no. Don't put me in there.' My entire body is shaking, my heartbeat rocketing. Is this what it's like when your body goes into shock?

Get away, that's what I need to do. I read an article

about kidnapping once in one of Mum's magazines. I'm in the critical stage. The first few hours are the most vital. You're at your strongest. You haven't been starved or dehydrated yet. You need to escape before they incapacitate you. Do anything you can to get away. Never let an assailant take you to a second place. That's my most lucid memory. Escape and run screaming, 'Fire, fire,' towards the nearest person.

I suck in a deep breath, ready to yell for help but know no one is going to hear me. Not here. When Jack pulled up earlier, I thought to myself, this isn't a place you'd want to visit on your own. Breathtakingly beautiful, but it's way too secluded. How right I was. I think of Jack returning, Teddy at his heel, to find I'm not where he left me. I imagine him looking around, wondering where I've gone. How long before he realises that I'm not coming back? Did they threaten him too? Or did he already know I wasn't coming back?

Is he part of this?

I need to get away. Now. Before it's too late. Before the next leg of this journey takes me to a place with no means of escape. I stop walking, dig my heels into the gravel. 'Keep going.' Man One pushes me. I know it's him. I'll never forget that voice. He shoves me. I stumble, face-planting into a mass of gritty stones. My nose. My nose? I whimper in agony. The smell of blood fills my nostrils. A burning pain bites into my bare shoulders as the gravel steals a layer of skin. He drags me up by my forearms. As if he is effortlessly lifting a child, not a soon-to-be adult.

Jack and I were discussing the plans we've made over

the past week as we lay on the grass staring at the photo-shopped sky. Plans for our future together and how we will remain a couple even when geography is not on our side. The ocean will separate us at some point, he said. But we will never be apart. Never. We discussed my eighteenth birthday only weeks away.

'I know where I'm going to take you,' he said in his soft enticing New York tone I've always found so sensual.

'Where? Where?' I asked.

'If I tell you, I'll have to kill you,' he said.

That's what he said.

He'll have to kill me.

I need to get away.

If I'm going to live to see my eighteenth birthday, I have to get away.

Is Jack part of this? Think. Think.

No. Jack is a good person. He wants to be a bioethicist. He is concerned with human life and doing right by people. He can't be part of why I'm here.

Can he?

My emotional state of hyperarousal enters a new phase. Go to battle. That was the advice. Fight for your life. But how do you fight Goliath when your hands are tied behind your back? Especially if he is not alone. He picks me up and tosses me over his shoulder. As if he is lifting that child again. Unprepared to give up without a fight, I wriggle, kicking my feet, trying to break free. I'm sweating, the exertion intense. Then my bladder presses against his shoulder and releases. I groan.

I mustn't let them get me in that car. Where are you,

Jack? My screams come loud and fast, so does the palm of a hand that cuffs the back of my head. The screams turn to whimpers as I buckle under the strain of another pound of a palm striking my head, the warmth between my legs completing my utter helplessness and misery.

One of them removes the bag from my head. I suck in air. Is it Man One or Man Two? I can't tell. I raise my face, catching a glimpse of him. It's Man One. He has no chin. His face merges with his neck, which is thicker than one of my thighs. And stubble covers his head and face, down to where it becomes his shoulders. He aims a cloth in my direction with his big hand which seems larger than my head. It's coming straight at me like an oncoming car on the wrong side of the road. I see and smell it simultaneously. Avoid it. I need to avoid it. But I can't. Man One stuffs it over my mouth. Hold your breath, Ellie. You mustn't inhale the fumes. His eyes are fierce, boring into me behind square-framed glasses. No breathing. Not now. Hold on. But it's too late. Another slam of a fist. This time my kidneys take the hit, forcing a sharp intake of breath. My lungs inhale the fumes from the soaked cloth. The nasty substance blasts my lungs, stealing my fight. I whimper. I'm not going to make this. Desperation grasps at the remaining resolve left in my waning muscles. But I can't fight it. I'm sinking. My body turns as limp as an overcooked strand of spaghetti, and I slide off his shoulder into the boot of the car.

I see Mum's face in the brilliant photoshopped blue sky. She smiles at me. The same reassuring smile she finds to accompany her comforting words when life is on the down. 'Things always work out for the best in the end, Ells. I promise you, darling.'

But it hasn't. Not this time, Mum. You were wrong about this one.

The trunk slams shut.

I tried, Mum. I really tried.

20

STEPH

After another sleepless night, it's noon when I wake up. Trying to summon the energy to get out of bed proves challenging. Was it only a week ago that Edward was lying here beside me on one of the rare nights we stayed in this apartment rather than his own?

When life was perfect.

It was going so well.

But then two days ago he died.

How things can change so quickly.

I stare at the ceiling, remembering the good times we had together. So many in such a short time. I recall the day we went rollerblading in Central Park. 'We have two options,' Edward said, his thumb tracing two loops, one six miles long, the other two and a half, on a map. 'When we get to the Loeb Boathouse, we can take the right-hand turn to Cat Hill or stay on the parkway, which will bring us back here. There are some tricky parts in the longer route,' he said, helping me squeeze my feet into the boots.

'I love the stone outcroppings at Cat Hill and all the squirrels.'

In fairness I didn't have the slightest idea of the difficulty posed by either of the suggested routes, but I love a challenge and six miles seemed more attractive than two and a half.

'I'm up for a six-miler,' I said, shoving out a hand for him to help me up.

'Let's do it.'

Edward was a far more proficient skater than me. We laughed so much navigating the park, weaving between walkers, joggers, and cyclists. It was a good workout, especially for a novice such as myself, taking us just over an hour to complete the six-mile loop although I'm sure Edward could have negotiated the course a lot quicker alone. 'Watch out,' he said, as we approached the ninety-foot climb of the Great Hill. 'They don't call this one Cardiac Hill for nothing.' His strong hand pulled me up that giant hill, and when we reached the top, I was red and puffing, but he looked as if he hadn't even broken a sweat.

Less than two weeks later, he had a heart attack and died.

It doesn't add up.

Tears fall down my cheeks as I roll over and hug the pillow.

I must have fallen back to sleep as the next thing I know, it's two o'clock. I pick up my phone to text Ellie and notice she sent me a message this morning. I open it. It's a selfie of her and Jack in a park somewhere having a picnic. They look so happy together, the perfect couple. Just like Edward and I were. Is this the special place Jack was taking her to? They must have set off early. I text her:

> Lovely photo. Don't forget I'm cooking fajitas tonight. What time will you be back? X

I get up, feeling odd. Part of me feels I should be doing something; the other part is lost. After taking a long shower, I clear the glass dining table of Ellie's purchases since she has been here. There's a beanie hat with a New York emblem, a tote bag with a New York harbour design, keyrings, pins – all with price tags still attached – and clothes she hasn't yet taken out of their plastic bags. I smile. She loves shopping. Her dad gave her a thousand pounds before she came out here – a leaving-school present – and told her she was only young once, and to have fun.

I set up my laptop, but when I try to fire it up, it's out of power. Damn thing is on the blink. IT were meant to sort me a new one before I came out here. I must chase it up when I get back to the UK. Going to Ellie's pigsty of a bedroom, I roll my eyes. I can't recall being this messy when I was her age. But it explains why she is a creative musician, and I'm an orderly accountant. Finding her

MacBook under a pile of her untidiness on the top of the chest of drawers, I open the lid. It used to be my MacBook, so I have my own account. The battery registers one hundred per cent.

Resuming my spot at the dining table, I log into work to answer emails I know would have mounted up from my absence on Friday. Before I left on Thursday evening, I saw an email from Charles with a job description for Melissa's replacement, his precis of the ideal candidate. A set of CVs for interviews HR has arranged was attached. I should read through them and prepare for tomorrow morning.

The system is slow. While I wait for it to load, Edward consumes my thoughts. They flit between sadness for all the untruths he told me and pondering what he could have got involved in that led him to his death. I think about being a foreigner here in New York and wonder whether I would be more forthright in dealing with the situation if I were at home.

When the MacBook comes to life, I find my email account is down. IT must be doing some maintenance. That's strange. Email is not usually affected. I log into the mainframe and start to go through all of Austin Cunningham's trades on the Harvey-Bowen account again, anything to distract my thoughts from Edward. But five minutes in, the whole system shuts down.

I concede to the technical gremlins and switch on the TV for some company, only a handful of times I've done so since I arrived here. A news program blares out the story of a new lead in the kidnapping of a five-year-old boy, captured by a doorbell camera in Harlem five months ago.

An NYPD officer gives a briefing. 'We will never give up the search.' Poor parents. I change channels.

Navigating my way to Netflix, I flick through the trending films, settling for a crime drama about a guy who spies on his victim's families by hiding cameras in their houses and hacking into their networks. Less than half an hour in, it hikes my paranoia. I switch off the TV and turn the apartment over, hunting for hidden cameras. Mirrors, smoke detectors, clothes hooks, wall sockets, the plant in the corner of the lounge area that the housekeeper reminded me to water, but I don't find anything. I try my computer again and manage to log on, frantically backing up all my files to the cloud.

I try Ellie again. Nothing. Swearing, I go to the fridge and pour a glass of wine. I down it in one and pour another, sipping it while chopping a red pepper into strips. It doesn't take long. The knife is sharper than I'm used to. I stop chopping to take another sip of wine. Nipping the skin of a yellow pepper, I dig the knife into the flesh. Chop. Chop. I play out my time in New York over and over in my head until all the ingredients for fajitas are ready to go.

Taking the bottle of wine to the armchair, I pick up my laptop again. But the systems are still down. I'm paranoid someone is hacking into my network. Or is that because of the film I watched? I turn on the TV again and flick through the channels. After such an intense time here, I feel at a loss having nothing to do. An emptiness Edward has left.

I check my phone. For God's sake, Ellie. Please message me. I hate it when she does this. I'm so annoyed with her.

How many times have I told her just to let me know if she's not going to make it back for dinner? She's done this to me before. But that's when she's been with her music buddies. They get lost in their own musical world that doesn't entertain thoughts of calling Mum to say they're going to be late. Or not come home at all, as she did after a party when she first met that cheating rat of an ex-boyfriend. Her dad says it's part of her scatty personality, or more likely her rebelling against the years of me mollycoddling her. It wouldn't be so bad if we were at home, but we're in a foreign city. Besides, I would have expected her to be a little less selfish, knowing what I've been through. But then I think back to when I was her age. Her dad was all that mattered in my sheltered world.

I close my eyes and inhale deeply, willing myself to calm down. She must still be with Jack. Only the other day, she told me how time stood still when she was with him. Anxiously, I scroll through my recent call history, searching for Jack's number. It's here somewhere; Ellie called me from his phone once when hers ran out of battery. Locating it, I go to call but stop when I hear my ex's words shouting, "Leave her alone. Let her grow up."

But this is different. I call Jack. Nothing. The phone sings a merry tune, asking me to leave a message.

Ellie, where the hell are you?

21

ELLIE

The medicinal odour of antiseptic cream overrides a lingering waft of urine. I feel as if I've been spun in a washing machine on a full cycle, my head spinning, my body beaten. Have I just woken up from an overnight sleep or a late afternoon nap? I can't tell. I lie still for a minute, curled in the foetal position. Sixty seconds of hoping that I've woken up from a nightmare. Hope dissolving into despair as the taste of vomit tells me this is no bad dream.

This is my reality.

I've been kidnapped. Or is it abducted? I don't know the difference. Is there even a difference? Not that it matters.

Visions of being in a cellar or somewhere underground cluttered with old furniture covered with dust sheets, and giant spiderwebs hanging in every corner, fill me with terror.

But then I feel super-soft cotton draped over my skin. I lick my dry lips, wanting to open my eyes, needing to know where I've ended up, but the lids are stuck together. I raise my hand to brush away the crusty discharge, but it's an effort. My arms are like lead, as though someone has strapped exercise weights around my wrists.

I try to scream but nothing comes out. My throat is raw, as if I've been screaming all night.

The door opens. Someone approaches the bed. I recoil tighter into a ball, wishing I was a baby again in Mum's arms, her holding me tightly.

'Try to sit up, girl. You sleep too long. You get up.' The accent is Far Eastern. Filipino, I think. She sounds like a girl in my class from school. I strain my eyes open. A grey-haired woman with a rounded tummy and plump hips stands over me. I snigger. I can't help it. Is it the drugs I feel have been injected into my body, or because she looks like Mrs Kwan, the babysitter from *The Cat in the Hat*? Mum and I adore that movie. It's one of our favourites. We used to watch it together all the time when I was a kid. I start whistling the soundtrack. Mrs Kwan goes all blurry. I want to sleep.

'Come on, sit.' She shuffles over to me. Her full lips are daubed a scarlet red, and she wears her clothes in layers: a pink cardigan over a gingham shirt over a vest. She hooks her forearm into my armpit and drags me up. I comply, completely numb. As if someone has flicked off my emotion switch. I'm scared, though. I know that.

Really bloody scared.

I try to scream again; this time emitting a loud piercing cry. The woman's hand flies to my mouth. 'No, girl. You no scream. Man outside kill you. Please. No scream.'

I push her hand away, coughing and spluttering. 'Who are you? What do you want from me?'

She slides my knees over the side of the bed, where my toes sink into the soft carpet. I'm wearing a T-shirt and knickers. They're not mine, but they fit me as if they were. I look down at my hands resting on my lap. Angry ligature marks have left crevices in my wrists. They throb. I touch my collarbone, wincing at the searing pain.

I look around me. No dust, no spiderwebs, it's as clean as home. Light flickers through the window shutters. Has another day passed since Jack took me for that picnic at his sister's favourite place on earth, or is it later the same day? I don't know. Time is as lost as my memory of how I got here.

'Who are you?' I ask this stranger. I want to know what I'm doing here. Where is Jack? What happened to the promises of a summer to remember that has transformed into the nightmare from hell in the blink of my ignorant eye? Do I really know the man I've been superglued to for the past three weeks? Has he set me up? But whenever I try to imagine a reason why, my mind returns a blank.

The first night he took me to the studio apartment he is flat-sitting for a friend, only a week after we met, he told me he loved me. We were lying tangled in the sheets of the futon bed, my head resting in his armpit. I was holding his wrist between my thumb and fingers as if I was taking his pulse, stroking the pink and blue tattoo inside his left wrist. I love that tattoo. He and his sister got matching ones the day they found out her cancer had got the better of her, and her body had nothing left to give. The top left-hand side morphs into pink and blue birds flying up the inside of his arm. 'They represent the removal of the shackles of pain that were imprisoning her, and her escape to freedom,' he told me, as if it was a practised statement because he gets asked a lot. The light from the large sash window was catching the smoothness of his chest. He was playing with my hair, strands slipping through his fingers. He always plays with my hair. I was staring at his bicycle leaning against the exposed brick wall next to the fireplace when he whispered, 'I love you, Ellie. You're one of a kind.'

Of course I know him.

My head drops. Maybe I don't know him at all. My hand clutches my chest. My heart hurts. Is this what it feels like when it's about to break?

'Please, girl. Remember. No scream.' The woman nods at a pile of white clothes neatly laid out at the foot of the bed the way Mum used to leave my clothes when I was a kid. Shorts and a clean T-shirt, underwear and socks wait for me. 'You shower and put clothes on.' She gestures to the open door of an ensuite. 'Come out when finished,' she says in that gentle accent. I don't hear her leave. She vanishes like a bubble. Pop.

The ensuite has a built-in vanity unit with a marble worktop which runs the length of one of the walls. I look in the mirror. My face. Just look at my face. It has been cleaned up, but it's a battered mess, covered in scratches and scrapes. My nose is swollen. It looks like an overripe pear, and my bottom lip is split down the middle like a fat sausage sliced in two.

Stepping into the walk-in shower, I turn on the taps.

The hot water burns my raw skin, but I'm past caring. It's clearing the fuzz from my head. I scrub hard to get clean, ignoring the stinging pain from my shoulder where the skin is missing. Steam fills the room as the scent of the lemon zest shower gel washes away the smell of urine. I don't want to get out. It's comforting behind these doors of glass.

I dress, watching the woman changing the bed efficiently, like a nurse. The clothes all fit. There's a pair of trainers too. White. My size exactly. An outfit I would buy myself. I perch on the edge of the bed, still dizzy from the prolonged shower. A ghost of a girl all dressed in white.

The shower has found my emotion switch and turned it back on. I want to cry. I want to laugh. I want to scream.

I want my mum.

I trudge over to the window, my legs weak. The honking of horns, the wail of sirens, and the banging and clattering of construction drones in the background. I'm back in the city, then. But am I in New York, or did they drive me to another city while I was drugged out cold in the boot of that car? I tug at the tilt rods of the shutters, but they are fixed at a downward slant; blue sky with the occasional cloud is the only sight visible. A box of a room that lets in light but doesn't allow you to see out.

This is all Toby's fault. If he hadn't cheated on me, I wouldn't even be in New York. I would have stayed in London and spent the summer with him. That's what we had planned.

But then I would never have met Jack.

The woman is waiting for me in the next room, which

has three doors leading from it. The room I was in, and what must be another bedroom, and the main door to the outside world, I guess. Where's the man who will kill me if I scream?

It's the piano I notice first. A polished white Yamaha baby grand occupying the far corner. It's exquisite. I peer around the large room. A modern open-plan living space separates the kitchen from the lounge. The same as Mum's and my apartment. Nearly everything in the room is white. All save the deep blue rug beneath the glass coffee table in front of the white sofa with matching blue scatter cushions. On the mantel sits a white vase with a bunch of fake flowers. White roses, stems hidden. Two sizeable arched windows line the far wall.

This all feels so confusing. Abducted people end up in darkened basements or abandoned warehouses, don't they? Dirty houses, sheds in gardens, encampments in woods, huts in forests, all those kinds of places – not a clinical setting like this. They are handcuffed, made to pee and poo in buckets, tied to chairs, and starved.

The woman is sitting at the head of the white gloss dining table that could comfortably sit six, reading a newspaper. She has pulled out the chair adjacent to her. An invitation to join the table set for two. It all feels so weird. As if I'm flying like a bird overlooking this confusing landscape. Yet, undoubtedly, I know this is as real as each breath leaving my lungs. I'm terrified beyond belief, but I know this one thing: if I'm going to survive this, I must hold my nerve.

'Is that today?' I ask, pointing to the date of the newspaper.

She nods. It's Monday. The day after Jack took me on the picnic. Mum knows I didn't come home last night. She wouldn't have slept a wink. I told her Jack was taking me out for the day – somewhere special – but I would come back for dinner. She was going to cook fajitas, our favourite meal. I didn't give an exact time, but I bet she started texting late afternoon, asking for an ETA, and then phoning around eight. Thoughts of her red-eyed, calling me non-stop, haunt me. I think back to when she found it in her heart to encourage me to carry on a relationship with Dad, even though he'd screwed around and wrecked her life. Despite what he did to her, he loved me and was still my dad, and always would be, she told me and made me pick up the phone. I'm so sorry, Mum. You're one of life's gems, a rare, exquisite diamond. You really don't deserve this.

I scan the room. A white carriage clock with Roman numerals takes centre stage over the fireplace. Both hands point north to XII. It must have stopped. It's not midnight, and it can't be midday. But maybe it is. I think about Mum. How long before she realises I'm missing? She must be looking for me by now.

'What time is it?' I ask.

The woman ignores me. She lifts cloth napkins printed with the American flag from two plates in front of her. Two grilled halloumi salads sit beneath. My favourite salad. Mum's too. How does this woman know this? I wonder where Mum is now. Did she go to work? I don't think she would have. When I didn't come back and didn't call, I think she would have gone to the police. I hope she went to the police. Or called Dad. He would know what to do. But my heart sinks as I remember he's away on holiday.

'Eat. You must eat,' the woman says. A wire basket filled with bread is shoved under my nose.

I want to scream at this wacko woman, tell her she's not my mother. She can't tell me what I should and shouldn't do. But instead, I do as I'm told. I finger the knife lying beside the plate. 'How do I know this food isn't drugged?'

'No. No. Good food. You drink too.' In front of me sits a can of Coke and a glass filled with ice and a wedge of orange. She hovers her fork over my plate. 'Choose a slice.' A gentle note of encouragement, not a barking order. I look at her, confused. She wigwags the fork between each slice of halloumi. 'Choose one.' I point to the middle slice. Stabbing the fork into the piece of cheese, she bites into it, leaving a curve of red lipstick along the edge. She chews several times and swallows before placing the remaining chunk in her mouth.

'Who are you?' I ask.

'My name is Nancy,' she says, as casually as if I'd just met her in a café.

I wouldn't mind betting it's not.

22

STEPH

I wake up at five o'clock the next morning still on the sofa, stiff and groggy. Feeling sick, I groan at the sight of an empty bottle of wine. That wasn't a good move. I muster the energy and slowly get up, wondering if Ellie made it home. I check my phone. Nothing. I drag myself to her room, my head pounding. She is not there. My stomach turns. I need to call the police. But what would they say? She's nearly an adult and has spent practically all her time at Jack's apartment since we've been here. They wouldn't do anything. Not yet anyway. When she turns up, I'm going to give her such a telling off.

'Give me an example of how you've dealt with a stressful situation in the workplace,' I ask the self-assured candidate in front of me. He looks so much like a younger version of Edward, it's excruciatingly painful. It's taking every ounce of my inner strength to remain seated. Wide-ranging achievements fill this man's CV, from positions in pedigree organisations to gold-medal Olympic rower. He has done his homework too. His understanding of what Crayhorne is all about is impressive; he would make an ideal replacement for Melissa. Trying to get comfortable, I cross and uncross my legs, fidgeting in my seat, troubled that this man reminds me so much of Edward. How will I feel working alongside him in the future?

Having interviewed six people today, feeling like crap, thankfully, he is the final candidate, and unless I'm mistaken, he will be the one Charles chooses as Melissa's replacement. Returning to my desk, I'm alarmed to find my computer unlocked which only fuels my annoyance. I turn to Cody. 'Who has been here while I've been away?' I say, louder and possibly more aggressively than I should.

'No one.' Glued to his computer screen, his eyes are stuck staring at a set of figures. 'Not that I've noticed. You should make sure it's locked. Company policy.'

Who is he to tell me about company policy? I never leave my computer unlocked. History is repeating itself. Have I mistaken Melissa's fears for paranoia? Or am I being paranoid now? Did I leave it unlocked? I drop down into my chair. The events of the past four days have thrown me. It's time to go back to England.

After trying Ellie again, my unease is growing. Something feels wrong. I draft a shortlist of the candidates HR are lining up for Charles to interview, before catching up on my emails. Over two hundred sit unopened in my inbox. I work my way through them, until I come to one from Rebecca Love Shield from Compliance. I sent her an email last week asking for a meeting regarding the Harvey-Bowen fund. She has replied with some attachments and says to stop by her desk when I have a chance. I glance up across the office, but she is not at her desk. I reply, asking her to call me as soon as she can.

Another email from Austin piques my interest. I sent him a list of questions before I left the office on Thursday, asking him if we could meet on Friday to go through them. My heart tightens, the pain fierce. Was Edward still alive when I sent that email?

Austin explains he came to find me on Friday to answer my questions and was sorry to hear that I was sick. He has replied to every single question with a detailed explanation. It must have taken him ages. The one thing I get from Austin Cunningham is that he respects me. I still fail to sense the vibe of a corrupt businessman. I read through his email. Everything makes sense. He ends it with a personal touch, asking me to open the attachment to an invitation to a surprise party he is holding for his sister and her friends for the opening of their new games room. It feels a little odd that he would invite me, but it goes in line with everything I have seen. He is a genuinely nice guy.

I decide to call it a day. It's earlier than I've typically left since being here, but my energy levels are depleted, as is my motivation. Besides, I want to get back to the apartment to see if Ellie is there. If she isn't, I've decided I'm going to call the police.

I'm logging off as Jennifer passes my desk. She appears agitated as she heads to her office, her usual elegance transforming into a stomp. The cause becomes apparent as I wait for the lift, gazing at the Crayhorne logo embossed on the walls. The doors ping open, and a familiar zesty scent precedes Todd, Jennifer's husband, bowling out of the lift.

He stops abruptly when he sees me, his designer sunglass perched on his head the same as they were when I met him at the barbecue. 'Hey, Steph, how're ya doing?'

I hesitate. I'm desperate to get back to the apartment. This is not the time to exchange pleasantries, but I can't help but feel a little sorry for this guy. I haven't seen him since I caught his wife cheating on him. Just like my ex-husband cheated on me. We have a lot in common. The lift doors ping shut. 'Sorry you've missed your ride.' He dives for the down button. 'These elevators are too quick.'

'No worries, I'll take the stairs.' I turn to a whooshing sound as the double glass doors leading from the main office open. His visage changes from a welcoming smile to a poorly camouflaged fury as Jennifer appears. She looks equally disenchanted at seeing her husband. It's excruciatingly uncomfortable. If looks could kill, I don't know which of them would be dead first.

Jennifer ignores me, telling her husband, 'This way.'

'Nice to see you again, Steph,' Todd says, before following his wife through the double doors.

I cringe, wondering if Todd has found out about her affair.

Leaving the building, I bump into Rhonda, and we spill into the river of the rush hour mayhem. 'Doing anything nice this evening?' I say, trying to create conversation, as her clipped tone and surly manner are making it clear she is not up for talking. It's an effort on my part as well. She's hardly said two words to me since Jennifer's barbecue. I asked her last week if something was bothering her, but she said she had some personal issues she was dealing with. I backed off, thinking it might have something to do with her IVF treatment.

She stops dead. So do I. The row of people behind steams into us. She flicks her head, looking from left to right over her shoulder. 'Look, Steph. You may as well know. I no longer work for Crayhorne.' She grabs a handful of her braided hair as if for comfort. 'I've resigned.' She resumes her stride to the subway.

The hustle and bustle of commuters disrupt my path. I quicken my pace to keep up with her. 'Can I ask why?' Frustration overcomes me. I grab her arm to bridle her, but she shakes me off and increases her pace too. I repeat my question. 'Why, Rhonda? Please answer me.'

She ignores me and rides the wave of people into the subway. Inquisitive, I continue following her. She barges through the barrier, overcoming the crowds to escape from me. Fumbling in my bag for my purse, I find my Metro-Card and chase after her. Spotting her making her way down the platform, I go after her. 'Rhonda. What's going on?' The rumblings of the oncoming train drown out my calls, already weakened by the racket of people keen to get home. The train lights reflect off the underground wall. A flash of black, a screech of wheels, the train speeds into the station. 'Rhonda. Please.'

She pulls me to the side. 'You really don't get it, do you?'

'Get what?'

A nervous unconvincing laugh escapes her mouth. 'Back off, Steph. Back off and go home. You're way out of your depth. Both of us are.'

'Rhonda!'

I stand staring at her as she tries to squash onto the train, but she doesn't make it. It's far too crowded. People push past me, knocking me from side to side and telling me to get the hell out of the way. Claustrophobia overcomes me. I'm trapped. I have to get out of here.

I leave her waiting for the next train on the heaving platform, taking a final incredulous look at her as I turn and make my way up the stairs. Halfway up, the rush of warm air and the ear-splitting grinding of wheels announces another train is approaching. I am nearing the exit when I hear a commotion from below, a cacophony of people screaming and yelling. Rush hour madness ensues as I hear what sounds like an impatient man losing his cool with a fellow passenger.

I've had enough of it here.

My mind is made up. When Charles returns from Toronto on Thursday, I'm going to tell him I'm returning to the UK. My work is virtually complete, I've identified a replacement for Melissa, and I can tie up any loose ends in the UK.

And when I see Ellie tonight, I'm going to tell her the same. She'll argue to the end with me. But the tongue of confrontation is ready.

23

ELLIE

All afternoon I've been drifting in and out of sleep, trying to cope with the persistent pain from my shoulder. It all feels so surreal as if I'm not here, but I know I am. And I'm as frightened as hell.

We've sat down to another meal that Nancy has prepared when overwhelming hysteria grips me. It's so unlike me. I'm usually a calm person. Life has gifted me an emotional language in music. It's my therapy. A subconscious maturing from a young age, learning to process any negativity with my go-to collection of tunes on the piano or saxophone. Queen's 'Bohemian Rhapsody' is my favourite at a time like this. I reach out and grab Nancy's hand. 'Please tell me what I'm doing here.'

She flinches and pulls away.

'Please.' My voice is high-pitched, a prim falsetto, the desperation in my tone difficult to disguise.

'You ask questions I have no answer.'

'Why?' I look at her as she places a forkful of pasta into

her mouth, staring ahead as she chews. Reloading her fork, she repeats. Load, chew, repeat. Confused thoughts swim frantically around my head like a shoal of frenzied fish. I know I'm sitting here. I know I'm in trouble. But I'm somewhere else too. It's like my body and mind are in two separate places.

I try to rearrange my muddled thoughts in order, but I can't. A familiar clap of rage thunders through me. It's the same as I felt the day Dad moved out. Nine days after my parents sat me at the dining table and announced they were getting divorced. My whole world was changing, and there was nothing I could do about it. I thump my clenched fist on the table. 'What're *you* doing here then?'

Nancy continues to ignore my questions, chomping on each mouthful of food like a pug dog. She stares ahead as if she is eating alone. I feel so sick, yet I know food is essential. Strength. I must build my strength if I'm going to get out of here. My right hand grips the knife, my left the fork. I stab a blood-red baby tomato from a side salad and guide it to my mouth as I repeat my question. 'Please tell me what I'm doing here.' But my efforts continue to fall on heedless ears.

She finishes her food before me and waits with her chin resting on her laced fingers. When my plate is empty, she places it on top of hers, grabs our empty glasses and carries them to the kitchen. 'Coffee?' she asks. I shake my head and watch as she stacks the dishwasher and busies herself tidying up, even though the place is immaculate.

What now?

Escape. I need to plan my way out of here. Nancy is a

large woman, at least twice my size, if not more. She must be in her fifties or sixties. It's hard to tell. Could I overcome her and run? Or am I better off trying to get her on my side? Mum always says I am good at influencing people. Not in a horrible way. Not like Dad. It's more of a subconscious thing with me, she says. I have an innocent charm that always gets me what I want in the end. It's a quality that will come in handy one day when I really need something, she has told me in the past. Maybe that time has come.

I eyeball the clinical surroundings while Nancy fusses in the kitchen. The high ceiling, the wooden floorboards painted an off-white, the fluffy rectangular footstool with spindly legs resembling a sheep's body. When I had that asthma attack last year, Mum's company's health insurance granted me a transfer to a private hospital. It was like being in a five-star hotel. That's how I feel now. Except here, there is no buzzer to press for help.

Nancy brings me a glass of water and two tablets. 'Take. Take. Help with pain.' She points to my shoulder as if she can read every feeling spiralling through me.

I've already taken tablets she gave me earlier, and they seem to have knocked me for six. What if they aren't painkillers? I'm caught between a rock of alertness and a hard place of pain, the throbbing in my shoulder intense. I swallow the tablets with a gulp of water, as I study Nancy's features: the different shades of her grey hair and the softness of her fringe. Her full brows are painted with a sharp, angled arch. The perfect shape for a round face. A girl I met at my friend's eighteenth birthday party last year told me this. We were queuing for drinks at the bar and started chatting. She told me she was a beautician, and we had an in-depth conversation about how the best brow shape is determined by face shape. For a heart-shaped face like mine, she told me as she traced her finger in the shape of a heart in the air, a soft arch balances a longer chin.

'That's a beautiful piano. Do you play?' I ask.

She shakes her head. 'Daughter play.'

At last, a breakthrough.

'How long has she been playing?'

She doesn't answer. There's a sudden softness about her, a mumsy feel. She has a daughter. She must understand what my mum is going through.

'Does she play a lot?' I ask.

Nancy stares at her drink.

'How old is she?'

Another sip of coffee.

'What does she do, your daughter?'

Still silence.

'What's her favourite piece of music to play?'

'Funeral March. Chopin.'

Her fluid answer shocks me. 'One of my favourites as well,' I lie. The solemn mood is depressing. Give me the more upbeat mood of Liszt's Hungarian Rhapsody No. 2, any day.

She sweeps an arm towards the piano. 'Go play.'

I lean back in the chair. My eyebrows crease. 'How do you know I can play?'

Not meeting my gaze, she shrugs and nods encouragement in the direction her arm is pointing. She smiles. There is a human in there somewhere.

I walk over to the piano stool. It has a polished white finish, and a leather cushioned seat. A divine piece of elegance, like the piano. I adjust the knobs for the height. At only five foot three, it's a must whenever I'm new to a piano. The last person to play must have been tall, as it takes several turns before I'm comfortable.

I start to play the Funeral March from memory. It's not difficult. I performed this piece for a school play years ago. The drugs have taken the edge off the pain. I feel more comfortable.

A phone rings. Nancy answers it. I see her nodding her head. The call ends. Nancy picks up the newspaper she was reading and walks over to me. 'We need video, girl.'

I blink, trying to focus. My eyes are still painful, my nose broken, I think. 'Video. What of?'

She unfolds the newspaper. A piece of paper is attached to the back page. 'For mother.'

'My mother?'

'Hold up and read words,' she says. 'No crying.'

Slowly, I turn the piece of paper to face me and read what's written before I speak.

The message is to the point. My voice is unsteady, the emotion audible. 'I'm OK, Mum. They're looking after me. I want to come home. Just do as they say. No police. Then we'll be together soon.'

'Good. Now I record. Speak words again when I say.' She zooms into the front page of the newspaper. I guess it's to prove the date.

When she says, 'Go,' I repeat the words. This time I add my own line. I can't stop myself. 'I love you, Mum. Please do as they say.'

Nancy stops the video and plays it. I hear my voice and shudder at the agony it will deliver to Mum. I imagine her grief when she views it for the first time and the torment it will bring as she rewatches it another hundred times.

Nancy heads to the main door. 'Keep playing.' She gives a brief smile. Do I notice a thaw in her demeanour? 'Me be back.' As she opens the door, I get a glimpse of a small lobby and another door which leads onto, I guess, the main corridor of the apartment block. Not that I know I'm in an apartment block; that's how it feels. The same as I think I'm high up, like Mum's apartment here in New York.

The image of Mum replaying that video haunts me as I move onto Brahms' Three Intermezzi, Op.117, No. 1. The piece I always choose before an exam. It calms my nerves. I can play it without even looking. I glance around the room, my fingers robotically performing as I consider my means of escape. Have they brought me here to kill me? It doesn't make sense. It's not like Mum has spare cash to pay a ransom. She's doing OK. We don't struggle like we did when she and Dad first broke up and she bought the small two-bedroomed house we live in. Joining Crayhorne was a great move for her. The quarterly bonuses alone amount to more than she received for her annual salary in her previous job. I have everything I want. But there are no spare funds for someone to demand a ransom.

Could it be Dad? As a sideline to being a police officer,

he's a second-hand watch dealer. And I'm not talking Swatch or Timex brands. His specialities are the Hublots and Omegas of the exclusive watch market. He bought and sold a very rare Rolex last Christmas, making a small mint from the transaction. But that's not the kind of money people kidnap for. Has he got mixed up in something else? A criminal that he put away at some point, perhaps?

24

ELLIE

I end the piece and turn to the large window behind me. My legs wobble as I stand up. I'm feeling fuzzy. It's those drugs; I'm sure of it. I look out of the window. On the opposite side of the road is an apartment block similar to the block I feel I am in. By my calculations, I must be about five floors up. Holding onto the ledge, I lean over the wide sill and look down at the roads jammed with yellow cabs, cars and trucks, and the pavements swarming with people. A colony of ants going about their evening business. I'm back in New York.

I crane my neck, looking down. A bright red awning with Crown Apartments inscribed along the side juts out from the entrance. Crown Apartments, so that's where I am. I run my finger down a pane of thick glass. It's translucent, I think. The kind that lets you see out, but no one can see in. Banging the glass and screaming won't attract attention. Could I smash it? I glance around the room for possible ammunition. The legs of the piano stool could do it. Then I spot a pair of candlesticks, one on either side of the marble fireplace. But there are too many unknowns. Too many what-ifs. What if the glass doesn't smash? If it does, what if no one sees me?

I return to the piano and resume playing. I could start a fire. But I don't have any matches. Perhaps there are some in the kitchen, or one of those gas firelighters like Dad uses to start the barbecue. There must be. The candles in the marble candlesticks have been burned at some point. But what if the main door is locked, and I can't escape? Besides, it could rage out of control. It could kill others. My fingers find the beat of Billy Joel's 'We Didn't Start the Fire', and I quietly sing along.

Mum loves Billy Joel.

How long before Nancy comes back? It must be about fifteen minutes at least since she left. Is this my chance to escape? Leaving the piano, I creep over to the door Nancy left from. My legs feel like they are going to buckle. From fatigue or fear, I don't know. Or Nancy's pills? I mustn't take any more. Turning my head, I glide my ear against the door but hear nothing other than my pulse beating in my ear. I place my hand over the brass knob. It creaks as I turn it. Slowly does it, Ellie. Slowly does it. My heart is thumping. Is this my chance? Gradually, I pull the door towards me. A rancid smell of old feet hits me as I step into the small lobby and let out a whimper.

I step backwards. My hand clenches the brass doorknob. No-neck – Man One from the gang that captured me – is sitting on a chair to the side of the door in the small lobby area. A laptop balances on his knees, and he is picking at what little there is of his nails with the serrated blade of a hunter's knife. The ominous look is completed with a gun sitting in a holster barely visible under the oversized girth of his stomach that rolls over the waistline of the trousers of his ill-fitting black suit. His jacket strains to contain his torso. The sleeves ride up his forearms displaying sprinkles of moles of all sizes. Dots and larger spots cover his skin. His menacing glare makes my heart race. 'Thinking of going somewhere, missy?'

'What?' I reply. A single word that sounds like the whimper from a small child, not the strong, independent woman I am. But that's how I feel. I'm a small, frightened child who wants her mum.

Thoughts of the worst kind enter my head. Flashes of her face when Mum receives the news that her daughter is dead haunt me. This is going to break her. Man One slices me up into pieces with his serrated knife and puts my dismembered body parts in black plastic rubble bags. My head in one, my torso in another, and my limbs in a third. He puts them into the boot of his car and drives them to one of New York's rivers, where he tosses them like rubbish into the water, and I sink to the bottom in pieces. Or will he remove my heart and liver, kidneys, and eyes first and harvest them for the illegal organ trade? I see Mum's crumpled face when the police knock on the door and tell her, "Your daughter didn't make it. We're so sorry."

I swallow hard. Stop it, Ellie. The drugs are playing with my head. No more drugs. I can't allow Mum to receive a visit from the police telling her that her daughter is dead. It simply can't happen. I have to get out of here alive.

'Is this an attempt to escape?' Man One glares at me like a provoked bull about to charge, waving the knife from side to side in my direction. It swings like a pendulum, and the blade glistens in the illumination of the LED ceiling light.

Fear has paralysed me. Or is it the drugs? I stare at the knife. The serrated edge resembles a saw, each serration perfect for piercing skin and slicing into tough muscle. This explains why they haven't handcuffed me. They don't need to. The threat of him is enough to contain me.

I can't help it. I start screaming. A caterwaul of shrieks makes him rush for me. I cower. Grabbing my hair, he drags me into the lounge and kicks the door shut, silencing me with his other beastly hand. He hurls me onto the sofa. I recoil into the corner, tucking my knees into my chest. He brandishes his knife. 'You scream again, I'll kill you. You hear me?' I remain silent until he roars, 'You hear me?!'

My entire body trembles and I nod as the main door to the apartment opens and slams shut. He sneers at me and turns and crosses paths with Nancy, who is holding two large brown bags. She shouts, 'What happening?!'

He dismisses her with a flick of his hand.

She plonks the bags onto the kitchen counter and hurries outside after him. They argue in hushed voices out in the lobby. She returns, rushing over to me. 'Girl, girl, no escaping. No more. Man outside dangerous.'

Is she on my side? 'Who is he? What am I doing here?'

'Very dangerous. He kill you. He no shame. He uses knife.'

'Don't leave me alone with him again.' My pulse won't calm down. I feel breathless.

'I get you pills.'

I'm a prisoner. That's what I am now. I must face it. A victim of kidnap. A hostage. There's no way out of here.

How did this happen?

How?

'Come. Come.' Nancy sidesteps me along the edge of the coffee table. Are we going out? Is this my chance to escape? A glimmer of hope ignites my dark mood. But she doesn't take me in the direction of the door. She leads me over to the piano, presses on my shoulders and lowers me onto the stool. 'We need more video.'

'Why?'

'Video no good.' She leaves me sitting there, dumbfounded. I watch her fetch the newspaper and place it on the music shelf. She steps backwards. 'Play.'

'Play what?'

'Tune. No talking. Only play. No face.' She angles her phone over the newspaper on the music shelf.

I stare at the newspaper. I've got it. They don't want Mum to see my face, but they want her to know it's me. Nancy is going to video me playing and send it to Mum. I turn to her. 'Nancy. You... or whoever... you've got it all wrong. My mum doesn't have loads of money. She can't pay a ransom.'

'Play, girl.'

I rack my brains for a tune. So unlike me, usually my fingers tell me what to play if my brain can't decide. They have a musical mind of their own. But what song do you play for a ransom video? I shuffle my bottom to the edge of the stool and arch my fingers over the keys. My thumb hovers over middle C, as I glance at Nancy and back at the keyboard. My brain is frozen, as are my fingers. What would Mum want to hear?

Nancy moves the phone towards me. 'Play favourite.'

'A Thousand Miles' is Mum's favourite song ever. I must have played it over a thousand times. She says I remind her of a young Vanessa Carlton when she recorded this song. I can't see it myself, but she insists. 'It's the long, dark hair,' she says. 'And the air of mystery.' Once, when I asked her what she meant by that, she replied, 'There's something about you that arouses curiosity.' Whatever that means. I think of Mum sitting beside me on my piano stool at home in the lounge, as we have done countless times, while I've played this song and we've sung the words together, and she's told me, "You've got such a unique voice, Ells."

And I always reply, "Don't say it, Mum."

Not that she ever takes any notice of me. "You're going to be on the big stage one day, Ellie Knight," she says with a knowing smile. "Everyone needs to hear that hauntingly beautiful voice." She can't help herself.

I can't play 'A Thousand Miles'. I'll start crying. I know I will. It'll crush Mum too.

And then it comes to me, a flash of inspiration.

My arms follow my fingers moving along the keyboard as I begin to play my favourite Queen song, 'Bohemian Rhapsody'. I adore the way this piece moves from hymn arpeggios to a jumpy operatic style. I hope Mum will notice the subtle change in the way I normally play this tune.

After thirty seconds, Nancy stops recording. I nod at the phone. 'Are you sending that straight to my mum?'

'Not me. Need one more.'

'Another video?'

She nods.

Knowing what I'm going to play, I limber up my fingers, quickly moving them up and down in turn, and break into Elton John's 'Chasing the Crown'. We did a production on 1980s rock music at school last year where I performed this song. Mum will remember it, I'm sure. I practised it for hours at home.

The same as for the first video, after thirty seconds, Nancy stops recording. 'Maybe more later.'

A sudden pain pulses through my shoulder. My head drops as I wince in agony.

Nancy touches my arm. 'I get you pills.'

We both turn to the door as it opens. Man One walks in. Nancy hands him the phone and in an instant, I picture two futures: one with me on stage playing the piano while a famous artist belts out the numerous songs I've written, and the second with Mum, weathered by years of not knowing, looking for her daughter whose dismembered body lies scattered at the bottom of one of New York City's rivers.

Anger engulfs me, unleashing a monster in my mind. Thoughts of rushing at Man One consume me. In my mind, I unbalance him. He stumbles, and his heavy body falls to the floor. He tries to grab my leg as I repeatedly stamp on his wrist to release the phone from his grip. I strike it with my foot. The screen flashes as the phone spins and skitters across the floor. I kick his knife out of his other hand. He rolls his large body over and grabs at my leg, pulling me towards him. I fantasise about kicking him like a footballer, hard and fast, to shake him off. My leg catches his face. He yells out in agony. Good, I want him to feel my pain. Good. Good. Good. I dream of grabbing the knife and stamping my foot on his face then holding the knife to his throat. "Tell me the address of this apartment, or I'll slice this into your neck," I yell at him in my head. I'm so angry right now. As mad as when Dad left us. In my thoughts Nancy is scared. But she's pleased, too. She can't disguise that smirk on her face. Man One groans and tells me the address. I run for the phone, blocking out Nancy shouting at me not to be so stupid. But I'm past caring. My hands are shaking. Her phone drops to the floor. Man One is clambering after me. My whole body aches. I click on the phone and tap in Mum's number. She answers, and I tell her where I am.

That's what plays out in my mind. And then I picture my future on the stage where Mum has always told me I deserve to be.

I will get out of here alive.

I will.

25

STEPH

I run as fast as the crowds allow, out of the subway station and along the sidewalk. I realise I no longer call it the pavement. Edward told me when I first arrived that when I'd been here for a while, I'd start to see this city differently and begin using American terms.

Oh, Edward!

Resignations are coming thick and fast. What is going on at Crayhorne? The burning late-afternoon heat and humidity are suffocating; not much of a relief from the furnace of the subway. I have a compelling desire to get back to the apartment, away from the hissing buses, honking cabs, and the hordes of rushing commuters and eager tourists in every direction I turn.

I try to hail a cab. None stop for the frantic woman waving like a maniac. Sweat is pouring off me. Wading through the crowds, I pass the glittering signs of busy restaurants and shops fluttering their invitations to come inside. Entering a gift store, I roam with tourists along the aisles, grateful for the solace of some air conditioning. We peruse the stacks of T-shirts, hoodies and mugs with *I Love NY* emblazoned on them. I bite my lip. Edward bought me one of those mugs. An elderly couple are trying to decide between a Yankees baseball cap or a Statue of Liberty sweatshirt, and I wonder what it would be like for life to be so simple.

When I've cooled down enough to brave the heat again, I walk outside and manage to secure a cab. As I get in, I catch the pocket of my trousers on the door. It rips, leaving a triangle of material flapping. I give a psychotic laugh.

All the way back to the apartment, I can't stop the turntable of my thoughts spinning the scene from the subway through my mind. When I first met her, I thought Rhonda was happy at Crayhorne. She appeared to enjoy her work. She seemed to turn funny with me at Jennifer's barbecue and has given me the silent treatment ever since. And today, she appeared genuinely frightened. When I reach Bridgewood Plaza, a man is loitering on the corner of the street opposite. Zombified, I stand and stare him out, a second of bravery in the moment of defiance. He stares back before turning in the other direction. Was he waiting for me? I don't know. I don't know anything any more.

Back at the apartment, there's still no sign of Ellie. I slump in the armchair, my hands in the prayer position resting against my chin. My pulse is racing, blood speeding through me like that train barrelling into the station. That scene with Rhonda has derailed me. First Melissa resigns and now Rhonda. Are they connected? I don't know how, or why, but was Edward involved, somehow?

I find my phone and grunt in anger to see there is still nothing from Ellie. That's it. Enough is enough. Rushing to the bedroom, I find the card that Randy Tommaso, that police officer who came to see me with his colleague after Edward died, left me. He said he would call me back with an update about Edward, but he hasn't. Sitting on the edge of the bed, I tap his number into my phone and press call. He answers almost immediately.

'Randy Tommaso.'

'Randy, it's Steph Knight here.' My voice is shaking. 'You and your colleague came to my apartment the other day regarding Edward Millner.'

'Yes. How can I be of help?'

I tell him about my predicament with Ellie. After a lengthy discussion, he says what I would expect. This is not the first time she has done this. She went willingly. She is not suffering from a mental illness. 'I'm sure she's just fine. However, leave it with me. I'll see if I can find anything. If she returns in the next few hours, call me back. I'll hopefully get you an update on Mr Millner as well.'

Reaching into my bag, I pull out my notepad and a pen. I rip out two sheets and slowly write down everything that has happened since I first got here, but whichever way I look at it, I can't work out a link between Melissa, Rhonda and Edward.

Before Jennifer's barbecue, Rhonda and Edward had never met. Not that I'm aware of. That was when Rhonda's mood changed. There was an awkwardness between us that hadn't been there before that brief encounter. It makes no sense. She had been so chatty that first week. What changed? Edward spoke to her husband but only small talk about sport, I think. He never actually spoke to Rhonda. Not to my knowledge, anyway. Had they met before and seeing him sparked a shift of mood in her?

And what about Austin? He has been nothing but helpful and friendly since I met him. There was an oddness about him at Jennifer's barbecue. Or was there? Was he simply being friendly? I sigh loudly, wondering if I'm looking for a connection that isn't there.

Then there is Jennifer, the adulteress. I think back to the time she was in London, and the gossip that was flying around the office like a falcon about her having an affair with Charles. One of the Controller's team saw them leaving a bar together in the early hours one morning. I never believed it. They weren't the type. Seems I was wrong. About her at least.

And Chris Smith. Did he give me a thinly veiled threat when I first met him or was I being over-sensitive? It's his account, the Harvey-Bowen fund, that seems to be the common denominator here.

I slump back in the chair holding the two sheets of paper in my hand, scribbled with a mess as I've tried to join the dots of confusion. Somewhere here lies the answer to this knotted web. But whichever way I look at it, I fail to find a way to untangle it all.

I try my daughter again. Still nothing. Where the hell are you, Ellie? When she gets back, I'm going to give her a few harsh words. I go through them in my head. A rant about her going AWOL last night and not being contactable. How many times do I have to tell her it's a no-go? A conversation I know I won't have. I'll hug her tightly with relief and remind her how much I fret if she doesn't reply to my messages. I find Jack's number and try him. It goes to voicemail. I toss the phone on the floor, unable to stop the two tears that spring out of my eyes as I think of Edward.

This city is destroying me.

I go to the fridge, dismayed to remember I finished off the wine last night. I don't know if I can face a trip to the store for another bottle. But I decide I need a drink. I could do with picking up a few other bits while I'm at it. There's only a slosh of milk left in the fridge.

At the store, I notice the tear of my trouser pocket, and the piece of material flapping. I should have changed before I came out. Grabbing the items I need, I spot a man who looks familiar. Was he the person who followed me the other day? I clench my jaw. Or am I imagining it? I'm going out of my mind. I continue shopping, snaking the aisles one by one, conscious the same figure is walking in my shadow as he piles groceries into his cart. As I'm making my way to the cashier, he approaches me at a pace. I turn on him. 'Who are you?!' I yell at him, unsure who I shock the most, me or him.

'What's your problem, lady?'

'You, you're my problem,' I yell again, equally as loud, bridling up to his face.

Shocked, the dark-haired man, mid-thirties, steps backwards and elevates a bank card between two fingers. My bank card. 'I think you may've dropped this.'

I stare at him, as shocked as him at my outburst. 'Thank you,' I mumble. 'I'm sorry. It's been a bad day.'

'Don't mention it.' He turns and proceeds with his shopping, mumbling and cursing about how rude the English can be. Other shoppers look on, confused. I need to get out of here.

I'm opening the apartment door when my phone beeps. My shoulders drop. Ellie at last! I place the bags of shopping on the hallway floor and rush to pluck my phone from my back pocket. I'm disheartened to see the message is not from Ellie. An unknown number has sent me a text message. I open it.

26

STEPH

I stare at the screen in horror. The message is from Ellie, but it hasn't come from her phone.

> I'm OK, Mum. They're looking after me. Do as they say. No police. Then we'll be together soon.

Confusion and panic overcome me. I reread the message, trying to make sense of it as thoughts of human trafficking and exploitation haunt me. The phone beeps again. A video attachment follows in another message. I open it to see Ellie's beautiful, delicate hands playing the piano. This can't be happening. My body jolts as another message comes in. The instructions are clear. Keep things normal. Don't talk to anyone. Go to work as usual, but back off all investigations and prepare for returning to England with my daughter. I will never see her again if I don't follow these orders. No police. Repeat, no police. We are watching you. Their words ring in my ears: don't speak to anyone. Wait for further instructions.

I pace the lounge. Rarely do I not know what to do; I'm a problem solver, always have been. Is this connected to work? To Edward? Have I dug too deep and got my daughter caught in a trap? Come on, Steph, think. Work it out. You're good at this. You solve problems all the time at work. You're a natural, that's what Charles says. I always find a way of working things out.

My beautiful daughter's life in jeopardy.

And it's all my fault.

I should have listened to Melissa and gone straight home. Then none of this would have happened. Who knows, Edward may still be alive.

I sit in the armchair and rewatch the video numerous times, torturing myself as I press play another time. It's Queen's 'Bohemian Rhapsody'. One of Ellie's all-time favourites. Her graceful hands I know so well, glide effort-lessly. Only something about it doesn't seem right. I can't put my finger on it. I put it down to the sound quality of the recording or my phone. Or perhaps they have harmed her in some way, and it's affecting her concentration. My body shudders at the bruising across the front of her hands. Why can't I see her face? I banish all negative thoughts from my mind. I need to do something here.

I google how to handle kidnappers. The advice is to go to the police. Always go to the police. Even if the kidnappers tell you not to. The police have strategies and special negotiation skills for dealing with this kind of situation. Trained officers who know what they are doing. Of course they do. But my daughter's life is at risk. I'm not reading this from an instruction manual or some online chat room.

No police. Repeat, no police. We are watching you. That's what the message said.

Frantic, I call the Irish bar. I have the number on my phone from when I made the reservation for Ellie and me that night. The night she met Jack. I've got to speak to him. He would have been the last person to see her. The phone rings and rings. Why is nobody answering? I end the call and search for Jack's number, but his phone is still switched off. Trying the bar again, I stamp my foot on the floor as the phone continues ringing. Can Jack be trusted? Does he have secrets like Edward? I run my hand through my hair. They were our friends. Lovers. And now I'm doubting both of them.

I have to call the police. Surely, that's the right thing to do? But they've made it clear. No police. And if I don't follow their orders, I'll never see my daughter again.

I jump up and pace the room, pulling on my hair. This can't be happening. I think about Ellie's father. I need to call him. Although I can't face the thought of hearing his voice, it's the right thing to do. But Ellie told me he has gone on holiday with his new woman to some exotic island in Thailand. Thousands of miles away, what can he do? Besides, I don't need him complicating matters. He'll jump straight on a plane, and I'll have him to deal with as well. And he'll insist on involving the police when there was no ambiguity in the message: no police if I want to see my daughter again.

But I find my ex's number and call him. Ellie is his daughter too. His phone is switched off, so I drop him a text, asking him to ring as soon as possible. I find Randy Tommaso's number and call him. He doesn't answer. I leave a message, asking him to call me. He can't fail to hear the desperation in my voice.

How did this happen? I think back to when I was a breath away from losing Ellie. She was five years old. I was called to her school after morning break when she had her very first asthma attack. It was the worst moment of my life. An air ambulance was descending onto the playground by the time I got there. The journey from the school to the hospital, and the following three days I spent holding her hand, are still a blur. Thinking about it still makes me well up.

I can't lose her. I can't.

I continue pacing the room until teeth marks dent the skin around my knuckle. I can't stand this any more. Changing into a pair of jeans, I slip into my trainers, grab my bag, and dash out of the apartment. I must see Jack. I need to know when he last saw her. He might not even realise she is missing but given that they've been cemented together like two semi-detached houses since they met, I can't understand why he wouldn't. Damn him. He was meant to be looking after her, protecting her. Anger rips through me as the voice of her blasted father rings in my head, telling me I must let her spread her wings.

. . .

Stairs or lift? Instinct tells me someone is sitting behind a desk watching me on a computer screen, so it doesn't matter. But that could be me overthinking things. I decide on the stairs.

Leaving Bridgewood Plaza, I run all the way to the Irish bar. The levels of adrenaline pumping through me overcome the ache in my bones from the flu-like bug I know is going to get the better of me at some point.

The bar is packed. Weaving my way through the crowds, I catch my breath, not caring about stepping on people's toes or the conversations among friends I interrupt. I'm past caring about anything other than my daughter. I spot a free seat at the end of the bar. 'I need to speak to Jack,' I shout above the din to the bartender pouring whiskey into two martini glasses. I try to smile but can't. Not even I can fake a sunny smile at a dark time like this. I hoist myself up on the stool. 'Is he around?'

Her brow furrows. She senses my desperation. 'He's here somewhere.' She peers up and down the bar. 'I'll go find him.'

A fleeting image of drinking Irish Manhattans in here with Edward enters my mind. I don't allow it to stay. I look at my phone. There are no further messages. What I'm waiting for, I don't know. A ransom? What makes them think I've got money? Everything I have is tied up in Ellie's future. I put aside my last two sizeable bonus payments to fund her education. Her uni fees are sitting in a savings account, and I've earmarked this year's bonus to support her living needs for the next three years at university. It's a nest egg, but not significant enough to kidnap her for.

This has got to do with work. My fingers tap on the bar as I will the bartender to hurry. I'm losing valuable minutes. Never have I felt so helpless. I glance at my phone again. Nothing. My fingers tap together as I watch the bartender finish serving the couple next to me and zigzag past the staff behind the busy bar. She is gone for what feels like forever. I glance at my phone. Still nothing. I look up to see Jack standing in the doorway at the end of the bar, his unshaven face as white as the painted walls. He lowers his head and whispers into the bartender's ear. They both look at me. I lift my hand and beckon him over, expecting him to navigate his way straight over to me. The woman frowns and to my incredulity, Jack catches my eye and swiftly disappears.

27

ELLIE

I wake up, confused. It's dark. I blink. No, it's light. Has another day passed? I really can't tell. I must keep track. Count the sleeps. According to the article on kidnapping I read in Mum's magazine, that's what you're meant to do. Keep track of the days by counting the nights. Sometimes that's hard if you're in the dark, so think about the change of temperature too. It's colder at night. But they come and go, the darkness and the light. I've noticed that. It's a blur.

Jack, where are you?

I stare at the ceiling.

The not knowing haunts me every waking moment in the light, and in the darkness as I drift in and out of sleep. Did *they* take Jack too? Is he in an apartment like me, with a Nancy, guarded by a Man One? Or did they silence him with fear and let him go? Or worse still... no, that's unthinkable.

Focus on staying alive. That's what that article said. It's all coming back to me. Keep physically strong. Squats and lunges. Press-ups and planks. But as each hour passes, the complexity of this situation is cracking my defences. There's a nagging doubt I can't suppress. Is everything Jack ever told me a lie? Is he party to the reason I'm here? I fight it. He can't be. He wouldn't do that to me. I can't believe he is part of all this. The gang that brought me here and locked me up like an animal in a cage with no means of escape.

You're a good person, Jack. Aren't you? The brother who nursed his dying sister. The son who visits his mum and dad every Sunday morning because his dad developed early-onset dementia seven years ago at the age of fifty-two, and his mum struggles. Really struggles. When you turn up, she heads to Walmart because she can't shop at any other time. Your dad refuses to go, and she can't leave him home alone any more. And while she's gone, you help your dad tackle all the odd jobs that have built up during the week. Not that he contributes. It's more a case of him watching you complete the tasks while he asks you the same question five or six times. And every Wednesday evening, you take him to the movie theatre. I like that term. We call them cinemas at home. Movie theatre sounds so much better. Your dad always falls asleep halfway through the film. Sometimes as soon as you get there. You don't mind. At least your mum gets a much-needed break.

That's not the behaviour of a person who seduced a stupid, gullible teenager to lead her to her death. Is it?

. . .

Nancy appears by my bedside. At first, I think I'm dreaming. An angel has come to rescue me. I'm going home. I'm finally going home.

'Sit. Sit. Take these.' She holds two pills in her extended hand and a glass of water in the other.

I follow her orders, coughing as I heave my body into a sitting position. It's an effort. As she drops the two pills into my hand, it all becomes suddenly clear. As if the halo of light shining above her head from the hallway is sending me a message. I won't get out of here if I keep taking these. No more drugs. I slip the tablets into my mouth but bury them beneath my tongue as I pretend to take a sip of water. When she goes, I spit them out and bury them in a tissue which I stuff under the mattress.

I've found my vehicle out of here.

Nancy makes more food. We eat in silence, and afterwards I play the piano. This beautiful piano is the only thing keeping me sane. Nancy enjoys it. I know she does. I'm playing the first movement of Beethoven's 'Moonlight Sonata' when I suddenly stop. What happened to my watch? I was wearing my Rolex when I was taken, wasn't I? I can't remember. That's what those drugs have done to me. Yes, I was wearing my Rolex. Jack commented on the candy pink dial. It matched my stud earrings. Small tiny pink diamonds that Mum bought me for my sixteenth birthday almost two years ago. I touch my ears. The earrings are still there, but they have taken my watch. A limited edition that Dad bought me. Every year, he sources a watch for my birthday. For a seventeen-year-old, I sure have a lot of watches. They're an investment, he says. Usually, he lets me choose. But the Rolex was a special he had picked up. When he saw the limited edition, he knew it was for me. I haven't the heart to tell him I much prefer my Apple watch I bought with last year's Christmas and birthday money which Mum topped up.

'Where's my watch?' I ask Nancy, who is sitting at the table. 'I had a watch on when they took me.' She answers the same way she answers nearly every question I ask, with a shrug of her shoulders.

I think about Dad, wondering if Mum has told him I've been taken. He'll come and find me. I know he will. He'll know what to do. But then I remember he is in Thailand with his new girlfriend. How long will it take him to get out here? Days?

I resume playing. Ten minutes later, the outburst comes out of nowhere. Man One storms into the room, waving his knife at me. 'Shut the fuck up!'

'Better than silence,' Nancy says, a hint of defiance in her tone.

He stands statue-still, staring at me, as if he has lost his mind. Pure hatred penetrates me. At a snail-slow pace, he turns his head to look at her. I sense discord, a sinister agitation from both sides of this strange partnership. 'It's driving me crazy.' He marches at me and slams the lid of the piano down. I narrowly snatch my fingers away in time. He grabs my hair and pulls my head back, resting the blade of his knife against the jugular notch of my sternum. 'No more.' He shoves my head downwards. I see my face in the shiny surface before he smashes it into the closed piano lid. 'Do you understand?'

I don't answer him. I lift my head. Stars spin in my field of vision. He's drawn blood. Drops trickle down from where his knife nicked my skin. I cower away from him. He kicks the leg of the piano stool. 'Do you understand?' he repeats. Louder this time, if that's possible.

Nancy jumps up, tugging a tissue from a packet. They argue. She tells him he mustn't hurt me. He lifts his knife to her. Fear overrides any sensation of pain he has inflicted on me. My whole body is shaking. I don't want her to argue with him. He'll turn on her next. Despite her being part of this, I don't want to see her hurt. Because then what will happen to me?

As he leaves the room, I wipe my lip. Blood stains the back of my trembling hand. I gently run my fingertip over my cheekbone, then my nose and forehead, wincing at each touch. My face has taken the full impact, and I can already feel my eye puffing up. I'm going to have a real shiner. I grit my teeth. Venom seeps through my veins, directing pure hatred at him as he slams the door.

28

ELLIE

Nancy hands me a tissue. 'I say before. He bad man. Very bad man.'

I dab my lip and the base of my neck where the knife caught me. She rushes to the kitchen, returning with a pack of ice wrapped in a towel. 'Hold against nose,' she says as if she's done this before. 'Look bad.'

It stings like hell. I can't look at her, can't be near her. She should have tried to protect me. Instead, she let it happen. I rush to my en suite and look in the mirror. What a mess. My face was starting to heal after they took me. Now fresh patches of blood mark it. I touch my neck. How dare he do this? Involuntary gasps of breath overcome me. I need to keep control. I can't risk an asthma attack. I stare in the mirror. Can I?

I didn't take A level drama for nothing.

I move the ice pack to my nose. It hurts the most. If it wasn't broken before, it is now. I cast my mind back to those terrible moments at the onset of an attack. The wheezing and tightness across my chest. The blind panic as I struggle to breathe.

I cough.

My breathing quickens.

Here we go.

I suck my lips into my mouth, and holding my chest, I start wheezing. 'Nancy, Nancy!' I shout, injecting abject panic into my voice. I hold the back of my hand to my forehead.

She comes running in. 'What's wrong, Miss Ellie?'

'Ast... Asthma.' My legs buckle as I fall to the floor, coughing and spluttering, struggling to take a breath. 'Attack. Help me.'

'Wait. I get help.' Nancy dithers, bouncing from one foot to the other. It would be comical if I wasn't in seizure mode.

'Hospital,' I gasp loudly. 'I need to go to hospital. Now.'

She turns on the tap and soaks a towel, pressing it against my forehead.

'No.' I clutch my chest. 'It's so tight.' I start coughing uncontrollably. I'm hyperventilating. 'Help.' I whisper. 'I can't. Can't. B...'

Nancy darts from the room, calling for help. I hear her open the door to the lobby. Words are exchanged. Man One appears with her in front of me. 'Holy shit.' He looks down at me in disdain, then at Nancy. 'You stay with her. I'll call the boss.'

He backs away from the doorway of my ensuite, and I see him make a call. 'We have a problem. She's down.

Asthma attack, I think. No one fucking said she has asthma. I thought we'd done our homework.'

I continue my act, struggling for breath.

He prods the arm of his glasses, eyeballing me.

'She say she need to get to hospital,' says Nancy.

'Faint.' My breathing is laboured, rattling rasps. 'Dizzy.' I tug Nancy's hand and look her directly in the eye. 'Please.' I pause for effect. 'Help me.'

I hear Man One continue his conversation. 'She seems in a bad way. I don't like it. Don't like it at all.' His accomplice barks down the phone. I can hear him from here, but I can't make out what he is saying. 'Doctor. How long? Needs to be quick.'

Nancy butts in. 'No doctor. Hospital. Now.'

'Shut up.' Man One growls at her as he hangs up the phone. 'A doctor is on his way. You.' He points at me. 'You don't die until he gets here.'

Nancy helps me up. I continue wheezing, gasping for breath, playing it out. She takes me to the bed and sits me down while she plumps up the pillows. 'Stay upright. My daughter the same. Asthma terrible. No lay down.'

I grab her. My fingers sink into the soft fat of her upper arm. 'Hospital, Nancy. Get me to hospital,' I wail with laboured breath. 'Don't let me die.'

'No, no, girl. You breathe. Slow breathing.' She encourages me to lean forwards. 'Cough when you let breath out.'

Man One's voice bellows from outside the room. 'Here.'

Nancy rubs my back. 'I get you warm drink. Helps my

daughter. You more breathing.' She hurries out of the room.

I go to the door. Nancy and Man One are oblivious to me watching them argue. 'I tell you. She had it coming,' he says.

'She need hospital.'

'A doctor is on the way.'

'How long?'

He throws his hands in the air and snarls, 'Hopefully, she'll die before he gets here. Save me a job. I've had enough of it here. Two days, they said. That music she plays, it gets right in here.' He taps his temple. 'And that singing makes me want to strangle her.'

I lay on the bed, carrying on the show. What an actress I could make one day. A knock at the front door sounds ten minutes later. I hear it open. Silence ensues as someone, I suspect the doctor, enters the apartment. I hear whispering. I intensify the coughing, wheezing like a smoker having climbed a set of stairs. A tall, lean man wearing a tweed jacket and chinos enters my room carrying the tools of his trade in a large leather bag. This is my chance. I can't fail. It may be the only one I get. Removing a stethoscope from his pocket, he sticks the air buds in his ears and places the diaphragm on my chest.

I interrupt his examination, tugging his sleeve. 'You must help me. I'm being held here against my will.' My voice is a whisper, but there's no mistaking the urgency it delivers. He can be under no illusion as to the danger I'm in.

He unlatches his bag, frowning.

I grab his arm again, gasping for breath. 'These are bad people.'

Without a flicker of emotion, he removes a rectangular package from his bag.

Doesn't he believe me? He appears to be assessing whether I am simply an overimaginative schoolgirl.

'Please, I'm not mad. I need help.'

He goes to the en suite and washes his hands, throwing me a blank stare. This isn't right. He hasn't even smiled at me. It's part of his job description. Returning to my side, he opens the package and snaps on a pair of blue rubber gloves.

What's he doing? Have I made a terrible mistake here? Is he one of them? But doctors are honest people, aren't they? 'Help me, please. Get me to hospital.'

He opens a vial of sterile water and tips the contents into one of the compartments of a small tray. I gasp and cough continuously.

'Easy does it.' He dips a swab into the water and bathes the wounds on my face.

He dries my face and applies some cream. 'Arnica,' he says.

I gulp in air. 'I need to go to hospital.'

Dismissing my pleading, he digs in the bag and produces another vial and a syringe. This is going horribly wrong. I'm feeling increasingly uncomfortable. My desperation has overridden rationality. How stupid I've been. 'What's that?' I try to sit up.

He pushes me back with a strength that belies his

frame and plunges the syringe into my arm. 'A little something to help you relax.'

I try to resist, but my efforts prove futile. I'm sinking. Falling. My body feels as if it's folding in on itself. He helps me lay comfortably. I try to speak, but the words are stuck in my jaw. Everything is fuzzy. His body is out of focus. He packs up his bag and picks it up. Stars flash around him.

He stands in the doorway with Nancy and Man One. I know there are only three of them, but it looks like there could be five or six. Maybe someone else has turned up. I feel like I'm floating, gazing at my body from above. I should be panicking, but my muscles are too relaxed.

'I've checked her over,' I hear the doctor say in an objective tone. 'Chest is clear. Heart rate acceptable given the circumstances. She's faking it.'

Man One speaks, his tone aggressive and full of contempt. 'I knew she was trouble, this one. I'm fed up with her trying to be clever.'

The doctor ignores Man One's outburst. 'I've tidied up her face. What happened to her?'

'She fell,' Man One is quick to say.

'You need to do better than that. He'll be here soon. I've given her something to settle her down. Better get your stories straight. You know what he can be like.'

29

STEPH

I glance around the bar. Why hasn't Jack come to talk to me? It's stiflingly hot in here. I step down from the stool to go after him, but the bartender is making her way along the bar, a disconcerted look on her face. The crowd seems to be getting louder, the din of raised voices deafening. My eyes are transfixed on her. She seems to move in painfully slow motion. Another bartender steals her attention. Shoving two bottles of clear spirits across her path, he lifts and lowers them as if his hands are a pair of weighing scales. She points at one of them. Hurry, hurry, don't you know this is an emergency? I want to scream at them. When she reaches me, she grabs a glass from the shelf behind her and pours a measure of whiskey. No ice. She slides it across the bar to me. 'Jack said to meet him at his apartment in half an hour. Don't take your phone.' She nods at the guy next to me. 'What can I get you?'

What the hell? Why doesn't he want me to take my phone? I neck the drink. It burns my throat. Thankful for the momentary seconds of distraction, I don't care. Slamming the glass on the counter, I weave my way through the crowds to the door.

Once on the street, I dither. Should I go to Jack's place? What if he is complicit in why I've found myself alone in the middle of Manhattan looking for my daughter? He could be trying to lure me to his apartment because I've broken the rules. I shouldn't have contacted him. But he was the only person I could turn to. And he is the only one who might hold the key to finding my daughter.

I don't have a choice.

I have to go to see him.

I check my phone, hoping Randy Tommaso has called while I've been in the bar, but he hasn't. I start walking, but I can't remember exactly where Jack lives. I wasn't paying attention when Edward and I dropped Ellie off there after Jennifer's barbecue. I can remember the building with its ornate, stone balconies and black fire escape, but I can't recall the exact address. There's no way I can find my way there. I smack my hand against my forehead. Think, Steph, think. But I can't. My mind is blank.

Two drunk men stumble out of the bar, slurring their words as they argue about which direction to take. One of them slaps his hand on the other's shoulder and leans into him, cackling, 'We need a GPS.'

Got it! Turning one-eighty, I start to run the couple of blocks back to Bridgewood Plaza. It's a struggle. I am definitely coming down with something, but I brush it aside. This is not the time to get ill. I need to get into Edward's car. If it's still there. He put Jack's address into the satnav when we were at Jennifer's house, ready for dropping Ellie off there afterwards.

Is Jack really part of this? This is the question I can't stop asking myself as my feet pound the streets. He can't be. Ellie wouldn't have been so silly as to get involved with a man who would do this to her. But then I think of Edward and what he could possibly have been up to that I was so oblivious to.

The lobby is empty. Strange, I've never known one of the concierges not to be manning the desk. I take the stairs, battling all kinds of morbid thoughts as I glance over the handrail at the drop to the bottom, which increases with each turn. My heart hammers with each step, bang, bang, bang. I stop at the fifth floor to catch my breath. Leaning on the handrail, I look down. I shudder. That would be a hell of a long way to fall.

When I get to the apartment, I find Edward's keys in the blue dish by the door. I don't know if I'm doing the right thing, but I don't see I have much choice. There's a chance his car is not even there any more. Filling a glass with water, I glug it down. I check my phone. Nothing. Why hasn't Randy Tommaso returned my call? Perhaps he's not on shift. I shiver. No police, they said. My insides are turning, the shot of whiskey from the bar repeating on me. I find Randy's number. My hand hovers over the call button. I'm always such a decisive person, but this is all beating me down. I press call, but when I hear Randy's voice asking me to leave a message, I cancel the call and slip the phone in my back pocket.

Taking the stairs, I race down to the basement and

push the button on the fob to enter the car park. I've never been down here at night. I've never needed to. Edward's Cadillac is still in his apartment's parking spot. Clicking it open, I jump inside. It smells of him. I take a deep breath, inhaling the oaky scent of his aftershave. I let out a whimper.

This is no time for emotions.

I open the glovebox and pull out the satnav. Switching it on, I find the most recent address is the Dia Beacon art museum that Edward and I visited. The memory is painful. We had such a good day; we were so happy together. I scroll through other recent addresses until I find Jack's. I glance at my watch. It must be getting on for fifteen minutes since I left the bar. I won't make it to Jack's in ten minutes by foot. I had half an hour, the bartender said, didn't she? What if I don't make it in time? Does it matter? My mind is spinning. Am I thinking rationally? I've got no choice. Taking a deep breath, I start the engine. I've never driven in New York before. But I recall Edward's words. There is always a first time for everything.

The satnav tells me it's only a twelve-minute journey to Jack's place. I study the details to internalise the route. One junction to negotiate, and then it's straight across the city through Central Park, and I'm pretty much there. At first, I'm shocked at myself – driving a car that I don't own in a foreign city, and I don't even know I'm insured to drive. Edward said he had an any-driver policy. Does someone's death make their policy invalid? Moreover, it's a left-hand drive on the *wrong* side of the road, and it's dark. I'll get arrested if I'm stopped. But I've long passed the point of caring. When it comes to my daughter, all bets are off.

I drive carefully, anticipating a car pulling out, a person running across the road. I can't run the risk of drawing attention to myself. One saving grace is that it's late. The rush-hour traffic died down hours ago, and the streets are relatively clear. Following the neon glow of the city's shops and restaurants, I regularly check the rear-view mirror, keeping a tab on the cars behind me, wondering if I'm being followed. But I don't think I am.

The route is more straightforward than I thought. The grid layout of the streets and the traffic lights working in perfect unison help. A much better layout than the roads in UK cities. As I take the turning to Jack's apartment, I remember now. The tapas bar on the corner and the Thai restaurant, both still buzzing with diners. I slow to find a parking space, edging along the road. But scaffolding is erected on the façade of three adjoining establishments in the middle of the street, and the parking spaces in front have made way for a portable toilet and building materials. I end up circling the block twice before deciding I have no choice but to leave the car in the parking garage a few buildings from Jack's place. Frustratingly, I have to download a parking app, wasting more valuable time.

I'm surprised to find Jack waiting for me at the top of the steps leading to his apartment block, huddled in the corner of the porch. I don't recognise him at first. He is puffing on a cigarette which makes me do a double take. Ellie hates smoking. Her father is a nicotine addict. Not in the house, Ellie would never allow it. He is a doorstep smoker. Even storms and hail fail to stop him. Ellie has spent a lifetime berating him for his habit. So I find it hard to believe she is in love with a smoker. Cautiously, I approach him. As I get nearer, I see his face in the porch light. He appears drawn, and his striking blue eyes seem to have faded like the old denim of the jacket he is wearing.

'I didn't think you were coming.' He flicks the cigarette on the floor and extinguishes it with his foot. 'And I didn't know if you knew which apartment I live in.'

'Where's Ellie?'

He opens the door. 'Come with me.'

I stand my ground. 'Where are we going?'

'You've got to trust me, Steph. We need to get out of sight.' The urgency in his voice packs a punch.

Panic rips through me again. It comes and goes in waves. The look on his face tells me, this man, the love of my daughter's life, is as terrified as me. Is he faking it? I'm not so sure. Knowing I have no choice, I warily follow him inside and up the stairs, feeling like he is a lion, and I'm his prey being led to his den. He keeps looking over his shoulder, telling me we're nearly there.

I can taste the rancid fear burning the back of my throat and my stomach turns when we reach the second floor. There's a whimpering sound coming from the apartment he approaches, and a scratching noise as if someone is trying to get out. At first, I think it's Ellie trying to escape. Jack senses my fleeting thought. 'That's Teddy, my dog.' He fumbles for his keys. Opening the door, he pulls me into the studio apartment which smells of unwashed men and abandoned dogs. In the kitchenette, washing-up is piled up in the sink, and a box of cereal lies on top of the over-flowing bin.

'Down, Teddy, down.' Jack gently releases his dog's paws from his thighs and ruffles his fur. 'There's a good boy.' He switches on a lamp, casting light around the place where my daughter has spent most of her time these past few weeks. A fireplace is built into the exposed brickwork, the TV above broadcasting the news. There's no sofa, only two well-worn armchairs squished around a low table in front of the fireplace. Jack drags one of the armchairs to face me, offering me a seat with his extended hands. I shake my head. 'I don't want to sit down. Where is my daughter?'

And then I see what I was hoping I would find – the forlorn weeping of a broken man. I don't intend that to sound callous. I'm not a heartless person. Far from it. But the tears from the man my daughter thought was God are a healthy sign that I'm not alone in the enormity of this city. I have someone on my side. 'I don't know, Steph. I honestly do not know.'

I slip my phone out of my pocket and, finding the message I received earlier, hand it to him. 'Read this,' I say.

'I told you not to bring your phone. They may be tracking it.' Nevertheless, he takes it. I lean over to find the video and play it.

As he watches, his bottom lip trembles. 'What the fuck!' He shakes his head and excuses himself.

Wandering through a door at the far end of the room, he disappears. And doubt resurfaces in my mind. As if it's been there all along, protesting the boundaries of my faith.

Is this man an innocent bystander in this web of wrongness? His cute dog sits at my feet, offering a paw as if he senses my sadness, frustration, anger, and fear. He senses it all.

A toilet flushes. A tap gushes. Water splashes. Jack returns composed but red-eyed, his face pink, and pulls out the other armchair. He takes a seat and tells me I must do the same. The story he has to tell isn't a feel-good tale.

30

STEPH

I perch on the end of the armchair as Jack relays the story of when Ellie was taken. The desperation of a man defeated stutters his words until he finds his rhythm. 'I went to pee, and when I got back, she was gone.'

I stare at him, stupefied. I want to tell him to shut up; I can't take any more. 'Gone where?'

He shakes his head. 'At first, I thought she'd gone to pee too. I lay back down on the blanket to wait for her, and then...' He pauses, momentarily closing his eyes. 'I heard her screaming. I thought it was coming from the direction of where I'd parked the car. I ran to look for her, and then... and then this fucking crazy freak appeared.'

He massages his temple, the pain in his eyes reliving the moment. 'He grabbed my neck from behind. All I could think about was Ellie, and what they'd done to her.'

'What did he look like?'

'I don't know. He blindfolded me and made me kneel

on the ground. He pointed a gun at the side of my head. I seriously thought I was going to die. Then he said... he said something along the lines of, if I valued my girl-friend's life, I'd go home and never say a word to anyone about what had really happened. I was to say the two of us had decided to part ways because she was returning to England.'

'Who are these people?' I ask, my voice trembling. 'What do they want?'

He shakes his head, stroking Teddy's ears. 'I have no idea, but they are crazy for sure.'

'I was scared of trafficking at first.' My voice wavers. 'Or rape. But the message they sent doesn't suggest that.'

'He made me unlock my cell phone and give it to him. He set the alarm for sixty minutes and told me if I moved from that spot before it went off, he would blow my head off.' His voice is trembling. 'Ellie's too.'

I gasp. 'This is hell.'

'I know.'

'Why didn't you come to me? You must've known how frantic I'd be.'

'I'm so, so, sorry.' He thumps his palms on his temple and slides them down his face. 'I haven't been able to think straight. You're right. I should've, for sure, but their threats have scared the hell out of me.'

'That's Ellie's bag,' I cry out, pointing to the handlebars of the bicycle leaning against the wall next to the fireplace. 'What're you doing with her bag?'

'I can explain.' He gets up and steps over to the bicycle.

Unhooking the black, soft leather backpack, he passes it to me. 'It was left there at the picnic.'

I rip open the clasp and rummage around inside, aghast. I drop onto my knees and tip the bag upside down. A jumble of items drops out. I swallow hard at the sight of my daughter's belongings falling to the floor. It feels like an invasion of her privacy. Never have I gone through her handbag. 'Her phone's not here.' I frantically spread the items out: a small spiral-bound book, a pen, a packet of tissues, a cosmetics bag, sunglasses, a tube of lip gloss. I look at Jack, now kneeling opposite me. 'And what happened to her headphones? She always has them with her.'

He reaches underneath the low table and pulls out Ellie's phone and her headphones. The screen of the phone is smashed as if someone has stamped on it. 'These were by the blanket. I've been trying to get into the phone, but I can't.'

The newsreader's solemn voice from the TV distracts me. 'An unidentified white male body was pulled from the Hudson River near Riverside Park earlier today. The cause of death has not yet been officially determined. Police are awaiting the results of the final autopsy report.'

I stand up, jabbing my forefinger in the air. 'They're connected. I don't know how, but they are.'

Jack looks from the TV to me. 'What're you talking about?'

'Ellie and Edward. And it's something to do with my work. I'm sure of it. How well did you know Edward?'

'He was a good guy. I met him at the bar when he first

started working here. I couldn't believe it when Ellie told me what happened to him. I'm sorry. You must be going through hell.'

I perch back on the armchair, biting my thumbnails. His words hurt. It would be so much easier if he'd said Edward was a creep or a nasty guy. Instead, he has confirmed what I know deep down to be true. Edward was decent.

Wasn't he?

Jacks runs his hands through his dark hair. 'You know what?'

I look at him.

'You're the only woman he ever brought to the bar. I never saw him with anyone else.'

My words spill out so easily. As if they've been restrained inside me waiting to overflow. The paramedic in Edward's apartment who took his laptop and phone. I explain the work situation with Austin, Jennifer, Melissa, and the incident with Rhonda at the subway.

He stares at me, aghast. 'You've had all this going on and haven't said anything to anyone?'

'I've been too terrified. And now the video. It's time to go to the police.'

Jack throws the palm of his hand in my direction. 'No. No police. You don't know who you're dealing with here, Steph. These are people you don't want to mess with. They're ruthless. Psychos. They'll kill her, for sure.' He points at the TV. 'And that'll be our bodies they're dragging out of a river next.' His voice falters. 'And Ellie's.'

'How did they know you would be at that park?'

He shrugs his drooped shoulders. 'They must've followed us.'

'Didn't you see anyone? Anything?'

'I would tell you, Steph.' He throws out his hands, his fingers splayed. 'I'm not keeping anything from you.' He slaps his hand on his chest. 'I promise.'

'And no one saw you at the park?'

'It's an isolated spot.' He stands and walks to the wardrobe next to the unmade bed. Squatting, he opens a drawer, grabs a bag, and returns to me, placing two boxes on the table. 'I got these for us.' He removes two phones and hands one to me. 'I don't know for sure, but my guess is they may be tracking our cell phones.'

'How can they do that?'

'These are the type of people who can do anything they want to.'

'What're we going to do?'

He bites his lip. 'I need time to think. Everything you've told me has thrown me.'

I shudder and point to the TV. 'You don't think that was Edward's body they pulled from the river, do you?'

He shrugs. 'I shouldn't think so. They're pulling bodies out of the river all the time. Go home, Steph. Act as normal as possible, and we'll speak in the morning.'

Act normal? 'I want to go there.'

'Where?'

'To the spot where she was taken.'

'I've already been back. Earlier today. To see if I could find a clue. Anything. There was nothing there.'

'The police might, though. They're specially trained for these kind of situations.'

The palm of resistance reappears. 'No police. Not yet.' He nods at my phone. 'That message says to prepare to go back to England with Ellie. We could ruin everything if we go to the police. How did you get here?'

'I drove.'

He squints.

'Edward's car. He left me a set of keys. He said I could drive it anytime.'

'Where is it?'

'In the parking garage along the road.'

'Leave it there. Take a cab. Turn right out of here and right again at the end of the street. You'll get one easily. We might need the car.' He sees me to the door. 'Take care, Steph. These people are evil. Do as they say.' The emotion in his voice is like another kick in the guts. 'I want Ellie back.'

'Me too.'

I hurry down the stairs, my daughter's backpack slung over my shoulder. The smell of Chinese food wafting from one of the apartments is nauseating. It turns my stomach. If it's possible it can turn any more. When I reach the street, I don't know what makes me turn to look up at the brick exterior of Jack's apartment block. It's unintentional. At first, I think it's a shadow, but then I see it's him, standing at the window speaking on his phone, watching me. Before he quickly turns away, I think I catch his eye.

· · ·

Sleep remains a stranger. It feels so long since I've slept for more than an hour. At five, I give up trying and take a long shower, considering my options for the day. Part of me wants to stay here, but there's a dire sense that the walls of this apartment are closing in on me. Besides, the instructions were to keep it normal. I can't bear the thought of facing anyone in the office, but I might be able to find something out there. And if I don't follow their instructions, they might harm Ellie.

I go to Ellie's bedroom. Painfully, I sift through her handbag again, hoping to find something I might have missed last night. What, I don't know. But I find nothing. I turn to her clothes, her bedside cabinet, her drawers, fear consuming me at the memories of each item. But I find nothing out of the ordinary.

All night, my phone lay on the bed next to me, plugged in to charge, as I debated whether to call Randy Tommaso again. He'd tell me what to do. But Jack's insistence and my dread of them harming Ellie has prevented me. It'd be stupid of me to go against all orders and involve the police. Won't it?

But this morning, I can't hold back.

I call Randy's number again, only to immediately regret it. What if calling him gets Ellie killed?

I don't know how, but I struggle into the office, arriving to a sombre mood. A message from the partners fuels the office gossip. There was a tragic accident at the subway last night in which Rhonda lost her life. Messages of condolence have been sent to her family. Anyone needing help in dealing with this situation is urged to speak to HR.

I'm stunned at the news. Was I the last person she knew to see her alive?

Jennifer stops at my desk, her hands hugging a cup of coffee. 'I guess you've heard about Rhonda.'

I nod, unable to speak.

She wags her head in the direction of her office. 'Could I have a word?' Her voice is shaky.

It all feels surreal. As if I've become disconnected from the body that has taken a seat in the chair opposite Jennifer's desk and I'm standing behind it, watching this nightmare unfold. Jennifer's blonde bob shines in the morning sun piercing through the windows of her office. She looks so perfect sitting there, next to a framed photo of her with Todd and their sons. How can she look at that every day knowing she is cheating on her husband, her family? Ever since I saw her in that full-bodied embrace with that catering guy at her barbecue, I've seen her in a different light. Not one that's shining so brightly. 'Are you OK, Steph? You look pale.'

'I'm not feeling my best.'

'Should you be here?'

'I'm fine.'

'I know this Rhonda situation is extremely upsetting, but we need to keep business as usual.' How can she be so calm about it all? I guess that's what makes her the professional she is.

'How is her husband?' I don't know why I ask this. I don't expect her to know.

'HR is dealing with the matter on behalf of the company.'

'Do you think she was pushed?'

Jennifer leans back in her chair. 'Pushed? I believe she took her own life. Who said she was pushed?'

I shrug.

She stares me deliberately in the eye. 'Don't listen to office gossip. Speak to HR if you have concerns.' She pushes some pieces of paper around on her desk. 'Now, where is it? Ah, here we go.' She shuffles a piece of paper from her pile. It's a printout of the email I sent her last week with a list of questions. It all feels so irrelevant now. I don't give a damn about the latest trade Austin Cunningham has fashioned. She has scribbled all over the sheet of paper. 'I've run through your questions and have some answers for you.'

How can she stay so calm, so collected? My phone beeps. I lift the screen. I recognise it straight away. The number of my daughter's captors. 'Excuse me.' I stand up. 'I must deal with this.'

Jennifer goes to speak, but I'm deaf to her words. I rush through the middle of the office where staff have started to gather in clusters, whispering among themselves. When I reach the restroom, I slip into the far end cubicle and bolt the door. I open the message.

You haven't followed instructions. We said
no police.

And then another video clip arrives.

31

ELLIE

I awake to a distorted face peering down at me, the lines and features out of focus. I blink, and the face evaporates into nothingness. My body feels like it's in a deep sleep, but I know I'm awake. I struggle to keep my eyes, as heavy as dumbbells, open. The pine tree smell of Christmas hangs around me. It's the cream; I remember the doctor applying it to my face. I touch my eyes, swollen and bruised, the pain excruciating. There's a clicking sound. I strain to open my eyes. Another blink. Slowly the room comes into focus, as do my thoughts. How could I have been so stupid? They were never going to take me to hospital. I should've known the doctor would be one of them.

Fear swarms through me, settling in my stomach. What are they going to do to me now? I should have waited. Planned my escape when they were more off-guard. I didn't think this through. I should've used the ammunition stored in the tissue under the mattress to defeat them. There must be enough tablets there now. Next time.

If there is a next time.

I ease my legs over the bed and try to sit up. The room swims. My stomach swirls. I feel like I'm on a ride at the funfair spinning round and round. I lie back down. Deep breaths. I need to get strong again. My scrambled thoughts continue to regain consciousness. A whimper escapes my mouth. No, Ellie. You must stay strong. "You're a bold, strong woman." That's what Mum always tells me. Where do I know that face from? Edward! Yes, Edward, Mum's new man. She's going to be so happy he is still alive. My senses stir, and I remember. Paramedics. Heart attack. Edward is dead.

Isn't he?

Raised voices distract me from my muddled thoughts. At first, I think it's God talking. I smile. Is he coming to get me? I giggle, a low, velvety laugh. Blinking again, I realise the voices are coming from the living room. I struggle to my feet, but dire tiredness drags me back to a semi-conscious void.

When I awake, I'm unsure how much time has passed. Seconds, minutes, perhaps, but not hours. They are still arguing. I manage to stand this time and shuffle to the closed door. Nudging up against it, I draw my ear to the wooden panel. Man One is outside. But who is he arguing with? Nancy is there. I hear her voice. I strain my ear, trying to understand what is being said, but I still struggle to make them out.

'Asset.'

'Not a punch bag.'

Man One tries to defend himself. Either the drugs that doctor gave me are wearing off, or he sounds louder. 'She's playing games with us, playing with our heads. All that singing, and that fucking piano, it's driving me insane.'

Suddenly and unexpectedly, I hear, 'Ouff.' Man One exhales. There's a groan, and a terrible thud, as if a wrecking ball has swung in and swiped him to the floor. I half cover my ears, shutting out the sound of boots in bellies. Nancy says something. I can't work out what. It's as if she is calling from the other side of the room. And then comes a voice I recognise but can't place. 'Clean yourself up. Any more nonsense, and I'll be bagging up both of you.'

I drift in and out of sleep. I feel helpless, out of control. As if I'm in one of those dreams where you are desperately trying to get somewhere, but you can't reach your destination. I recall the date on the newspaper Nancy was reading when I first arrived. It seems like weeks ago. But of course, it's not. How many days, though, I don't know any more. My hip bones are jutting out, the concave dip between them more profound, and I can circle my thumb and forefinger around my upper arm. I need to eat more. But I've lost my appetite with the constant fear cramping my stomach.

I can hear Nancy banging and clattering around in the kitchen. I get up and go to the door, but it's locked. *They* are playing with *my* head now. I'm about to knock, when I hear voices over the racket Nancy is making. I think it's Nancy, anyway. Maybe someone else is here. A discussion is going on, but I can't hear Nancy's voice. Man One is talking to someone else. It's the same person as last time. Unnerved, I press my ear to the door, straining to hear the conversation.

'How much does she know?' says Man One.

'Can't say for sure.'

'Is she getting the message?' says Man One.

'Don't know.'

At first, I think they are talking about me. I'm racking my thoughts, trying to think where I've heard the second voice before.

'She's still digging. Much more persistent than the other one,' says the second voice.

I'm sure they are talking about Mum and me until the second voice says, 'She's been looking for the boyfriend.'

Man One gives an ironic laugh.

Boyfriend? Do they mean Edward? They can't. They must be talking about someone else. Mum's boyfriend is dead.

'We need to get rid of her,' says Man One.

I stare at the door in panic. Are they discussing Mum and me? My legs give way. Sliding my back down the door, I hug my arms around my knees.

'Not a good idea. Far too risky. Anyway, we still don't know what she knows. Or who she has told,' says the second voice.

'The best solution is she disappears like the other one. Can't have her around any longer,' says Man One.

I wonder if this is all to do with Mum's work and that Austin guy she has been looking into? What has she got involved with? Or who? Was Edward part of this before he died?

The voices fade. I hear cups clanking, spoons clinking. I miss what is being said, only catching the tail end of their conversation.

'What now?' says Man One.

'The sooner we get this sorted, the better. I've had enough. We've got too much at stake. Go with plan A.'

I hear footsteps approaching the door. I scramble up and back to my bed, waiting for my destiny to enter the room.

This is not how it's meant to end.

I must do something.

Now.

32

STEPH

I hear the main door to the restroom open. Heels click-clack into the cubicle next to me. I lean into the wall as spots of light flash in my field of vision. Sitting on the toilet, I take deep breaths. I must keep calm. Playing the video in here is not an option. Whoever has walked in will hear it. I flush the toilet and exit the cubicle, shuddering at the pale sight of my sunken face in the mirror.

They must know I called Randy Tommaso. That's what the line *We said no police* must mean. Is Randy involved in all of this? Is that why he came around to my apartment the night after Edward died? To keep me quiet? Was Edward part of it too? None of it is making sense.

As I make for the office exit, I bump into people arriving. Austin appears from the revolving doors. In my haste, I drop my phone. It spins across the floor, landing at the toes of his polished Oxford brogues. 'Steph, you OK?' he asks, bending to pick it up. 'What's wrong?'

'It's Rhonda,' I lie. What has happened to Rhonda is

deeply upsetting, but when you're dealing with a stolen daughter, the death of a work colleague you've only known a short while pales in comparison. 'There's been a dreadful accident. I need some fresh air.'

'What kind of accident?'

'You haven't heard? Rhonda fell under a train. She's dead.' I desperately try to make it sound less blunt, but my mind is elsewhere.

Austin stares at me, wide-eyed. 'Do you want me to come with you?' There is such kindness in his voice, I consider saying yes for a second. But only for a split one. My head is a whirlpool of thoughts and suspicions, telling me not to trust anyone.

I leave the building, turn into the nearest side street, and open the video. At first, I can't make it out. Seven times, I watch it. Ellie is playing the piano to start with, and then the camera switches to four carrots lined up in a row. A serrated knife comes into view and chops them in half. Are they referring to Ellie losing her fingers because I called Randy Tommaso? I'm going to be sick. My gag reflex makes me bend in two, but nothing comes up.

I march to the park. It's the only place I can think of to go. It's so hot again today, but a soft breeze brings a light relief. I find the bench under the giant elm tree where Rhonda and I ate those jumbo shrimp salads, and she told me about the drunken bridesmaid at her cousin's wedding and her journey with IVF.

Little did she know what was coming.

I rewatch the video. That song. I know it, but I can't remember the name of the piece. What have I done? Ellie's music is her life. She can't lose her fingers. My forearms are on my knees holding my head, as I think back to when Randy and his colleague knocked at my apartment door. I should never have made that call to him. My phone beeps.

> You are to make an excuse for work. Family issues. Book two tickets. JFK to Heathrow. American Airlines. Tomorrow 6.20pm. Your daughter will meet you at the airport. She is safe as long as you do not talk to anyone again.

I reread the text. Hope. There is hope. If I'm to believe what I'm reading, then I will soon be reunited with my daughter. All I must do is follow their instructions. But how can I trust people who one minute allude to maiming my beautiful girl, and the next are offering me a ticket out of here?

I look around me. I'm shaking like the leaves on the trees in the gentle breeze, stifling the tears that would be flowing if I were at home alone. Am I really being watched? It's impossible to tell. Too many people are meandering through the park going about their daily business. I dig the phone Jack gave me out of my bag and call him with the latest update.

He is emphatic. 'Do as they say, Steph. Just do as they say.'

I throw my phone in my bag and panic. I shouldn't

have called Jack. The text said not to talk to anyone again. I let out a long, low groan.

'I'm sorry about earlier,' I say to Jennifer. 'Can I have a word?'

Jennifer glances up from the document she is reading. Her face is pale. She clears her throat. 'I'm busy at the moment. I need to read this before my ten o'clock meeting. Could you catch me after lunch?' She turns her attention back to the document.

I close the door to her office louder than intended. 'It can't wait, I'm afraid. Something has come up.'

Her body stiffens. She frowns, adjusting the collar of her cream silk blouse.

I speak before she has the chance to. 'I need to go home. My sister is sick.' I will myself not to blush. I never was any good at lying.

'I'm so sorry to hear that,' she says, looking genuinely concerned. 'Of course, you must go. Family always comes first. Your work here is pretty much done, anyways. You've given me comfort that everything is above board with Austin. Any loose ends you can tie up from London.'

'Thanks for your understanding. I'll spend today wrapping things up here, and I'm going to book flights for tomorrow evening, if I can.' It suddenly dawns on me. What if I can't get us on the flight tomorrow?

'Don't worry. I'll get my PA to sort them. She might be able to get you on a flight today if that's what you want?'

'No. I want to go on the American Airlines flight tomorrow night.'

'Sure. Drop her an email with the details and copy me in.'

'Thanks. And Jennifer?'

'Yes?' She looks up from her document again.

'If it's all right by you, I'd like to duck out of here quietly. What with all that has happened to Rhonda, I think it's for the best.'

'Understood.'

Returning to my desk, I alternate between emailing screen grabs of what I am certain is fraudulent activity on the Harvey-Bowen fund and all the associated accounts to my personal account and sitting staring at my screen.

'I didn't know you had a sister,' Charles says when he calls later. 'I thought you only had a brother.'

He's right, but I can't lie and say my brother's sick. It's not right. I relay the story I fabricated on the way back from the park. 'She's older than me, lives up north. She got diagnosed with cancer at Easter. Pancreatic. She's deteriorated rapidly these past few weeks. She's not got long.'

You tell one lie, and they come like breaths to keep you alive.

'I'll spend today finishing up here, and Jennifer's PA is arranging flights back for tomorrow. I'd like to take next week off if that's OK?'

'Sure. Take as much time as you need. Anything I can get on with while you're out of the office?'

'No. I'll prepare a full report while I'm off and send it to you.'

My phone rings when I get back to the apartment. I dig it out of my bag, hoping it's news of Ellie. But I quickly realise it's not my phone, but the one Jack gave me.

'Have you heard anything more?' Jack asks.

'Nothing. Flights are booked.'

'Good. I don't want anything to go wrong.'

'Funny that, Jack. Neither do I.' There is silence. I sigh. 'I'm sorry for the sarcasm. I'm going out of my mind here.'

'Not long, and you'll be out of here.'

In the hallway, I drag out the two large suitcases I arrived with from the cupboard. Placing them on the bed, I unzip them. I had hoped to do lots of shopping while I was here. A whole new wardrobe of clothes... that never transpired. Packing my belongings takes no more than an hour. Even then, half of that time is taken up with me sitting on the floor at the end of the bed, sobbing after taking Edward's painting down from the wall and wrapping it in the packaging the gallery owner gave me.

Ellie's room is another matter. Despite the mess of her things, the emptiness echoes around me. What if they kill her? I couldn't live with never seeing her again. As soon as these thoughts enter my head, I banish them. There's no vacancy at the hotel of thoughts for any negativity at a time like this. With tears streaming down my face, I open her wardrobe. A few items hang on the rail, but most of her belongings are scattered across the floor. I throw everything in her two suitcases as they are, scrunched up, some dirty: a nightshirt with a *Let Me Sleep* slogan, and a star-covered T-shirt, and the short floral dress she wore the night she met Jack. I start crying. Why did I ever agree to this trip? Silly ambition. An ego trip. I can beat myself up until the end of time, but no one could ever have predicted this outcome.

I now know how Melissa felt when she said, "If only I hadn't gone out that night." If only I hadn't taken this stupid bloody assignment.

33

STEPH

Every waking moment is torture, and there's no relief from sleep. I dropped off in the early hours only to be hounded by nightmares of being at Ellie's funeral. The constant headache isn't helping. I cling to my phone, desperate for some news, wishing this nightmare would go away. I check I've got our passports for the tenth time. Jennifer's PA has emailed the tickets. I'm making a second cup of coffee when my phone rings its distinctive and familiar tune, an explosion of sound in the quietness of the apartment. In my desperation to answer it, hoping for news of Ellie, it drops to the floor. I squat to pick it up. A number I don't recognise flashes across the screen. I answer it, cautiously.

The cheery male voice at the other end of the line is not what I expect. 'Is that Steph Knight?'

I don't know who he is, but there's one thing I'm pretty certain of. This terribly well-spoken gentleman is not connected to Ellie's disappearance. I grit my teeth. Not another salesman. Resisting the temptation to hang up, I reply, 'Who is this?'

'Rupert Hughes, Edward's friend. Is this a good time to talk?'

'Sure,' I say, although I'm torn. A thousand thoughts are muddling their way through my head. I wonder if I should be speaking to this guy. What if my phone is being tapped? It could jeopardise everything. My daughter's release, her safety. But then again, I'm putting all my faith in these monsters who have taken my daughter, and expecting them to be true to their word. I realise I have no insurance policy, no means of bartering.

I sit back on my heels, my rounded back heavy with the baggage of the situation I've been dumped in. He's taken his time to get back to me. I've been wondering if he had forgotten me.

'As instructed by our good friend, I've been doing some digging for you. I think you're going to be interested in my findings.'

I lean back against a kitchen cabinet. 'Carry on.'

'Sorry it's taken a while,' he says, as if he has read my mind. 'I've been away, and then I was waiting for the opportune moment. I've not gone through the usual channels, pretty old school, actually. Friends with yachts come in handy.' He gives a hearty chuckle. 'I managed to get a few drinks down one of the chaps in the know. Those after-work sunset cruises always come up trumps. Plied him with a few more, and he started jabbering. They always do with a few of my rum punches inside their bellies. Couldn't stop the old chap in the end. All turned frightfully mucky.'

I can understand why it has taken so long for this guy to get the information, but I'm not in need of a full glossary of events. 'Please explain,' I say, wanting him to get to the point.

'The Harvey-Bowen business.' He pauses. 'Hang on, can you? I've got another call.'

I frantically bang my knuckles on the tiled floor. Come on, I want to scream into the phone. It sounds like he has some news I need to hear.

'Sorry about that. Wifey chasing me. I'm late for lunch.'

Come on, please. Get on with it.

'Anyway, where was I? Yes, Harvey-Bowen. It appears to have started off legit until some of the nasties got their teeth into it.'

'The details please, Rupert.'

'Of course. The shortened version. They've been pumping dirty money through accounts with a number of the smaller banks. You name it, and they're involved in it. They've been keeping it low-key. Lots of layering going down, but they've started to ramp things up in the past few months. It's got pretty serious; I can tell you. The person you're interested in goes by the name TP. Owns a host of IT companies under the Power Housing Services umbrella. Brilliant mind, shame about the scruples. Or lack of, should I say. The chap I spoke to implied he was close to the host. The person on the ground in New York.'

'What does TP stand for?'

'Todd Penderson, you heard of him?'

I gasp loudly. 'He's the husband of one the partners at the company I work for.' I frown. So Jennifer is involved in all of this? I can't believe it. Is Charles as well? Are other partners?

'Are you still there?'

'Yes. Sorry, I was thinking.'

'I hope it helps you.'

'I think it will.'

'I'll send you the bar bill.' He gives another hearty chuckle. 'Only joking. You take care, Steph. This is a very small cog in a huge global wheel of corruption. A multibillion-dollar enterprise. These people wouldn't think twice about extinguishing lives to keep their operation ticking over.'

'I didn't know it was on that kind of scale.'

'Sure sounds like it. Send my regards to Edward. Tell him I'll be in town at the end of the month. I'll give him a shout.'

'Rupert. I have some terrible news.'

'I don't know you, but I don't like the sound of this.' The light-hearted tone vanishes as if he was half-expecting what I'm about to tell him.

'Edward is dead. He died last week of a heart attack. I think. Oh, I don't know for sure.'

I'm not sure why I have opened up to this well-to-do gentleman, but between wiping my tears and snotty nose, I find myself relaying the events of Edward's death and everything that has happened with Ellie.

He chokes on his words. 'Do as they say and take your

daughter back to England. These are not people you want to meddle with.'

'Rupert?'

'Yes?'

'Edward wouldn't get himself involved in any of this, would he?'

'I don't follow.'

'The Harvey-Bowen fund, everything I've told you. He couldn't have played any part in it, could he?'

'I've known Edward for many years, Steph, and no. No, he most definitely wouldn't.' Why do I detect a slight thread of doubt in his answer? Or is it my paranoia?

He continues. 'When I last spoke to Edward, he told me all about you. How smitten he was with you. Quite a thing for him to admit, I tell you. Said he was going to make some lifestyle changes he would tell me about when he next saw me. All sounded a bit hush-hush: cloak and dagger kind of thing.' He pauses. A void I can't fill. I don't trust myself to speak. 'Look, he wouldn't have asked me to do some digging into this Harvey-Bowen fund if he was somehow involved, now, would he?'

'Unless he wanted to make sure the corruption was watertight.'

'Oh, come on.'

'Sorry, but my mind is racing at the moment.'

'Do as they say, and you'll get your daughter back. Stay in touch. I'll see what I can find out on my end.'

I spend the next hour googling Todd Penderson. Searching through various social media channels, from what I can make out he was hugely popular at university, and by the end of his freshman year he had set up a website design business with a college friend. The company went from strength to strength and when he left university, he sold his share and invested in various other businesses in the IT sector.

I log into work and look at the paperwork Compliance sent me on the Harvey-Bowen fund. Why didn't I see this before? Jennifer introduced the fund to Crayhorne. What has she got me messed up in? I find her number in my phone and go to call her, but stop.

First, I need to get my daughter back safely. Then I can deal with her.

A chill settles around me as I reflect on my earlier thoughts, realising I need an insurance policy. I have all the data in my notebook and emails: trade flows, money movements, cash injections, dates. I just need to keep it safe. So if anything happens to Ellie, or me, then Jennifer and Todd Penderson's world will come crashing down with a big bang.

Once I've composed myself, I find my first aid travel kit and pop a couple of paracetamol. That should ward off the fever I feel coming on. I finish making that coffee, dig out my iPad from my handbag and set to work.

34

ELLIE

Time drags like a series of never-ending maths lessons. I hated maths at school. It was my worst subject. How Mum works with numbers all the time, I just don't know. I've asked Nancy to bring me a pair of headphones or some books, but all I get is trashy magazines and more clothes: jeans and T-shirts, joggers and a sweatshirt. I keep telling myself to stay strong, but my hopes of ever escaping this place alive are slowly fading each time I fall asleep.

In a moment of positivity, last night, I slipped a teaspoon up the sleeve of my sweatshirt, and this morning, while the shower is running, I take the tablets I've stored in a tissue under the mattress and crush them. Carefully, I wrap the fine powder back in the tissue and slip it into the little watch pocket of my jeans. Don't forget to act appropriately, Ellie. Carry on the pretence. You don't want to give the game away. You're meant to be taking the drugs Nancy gives you, I tell myself as I lather shampoo into my hair.

I sense a shift in the moods of both Nancy and Man

One. Now that I'm no longer taking the tablets, I feel more sensitive to the most minor of their actions. The things they say make me think this situation is coming to a head. Man One has taken to spending more time in the kitchen. Something is being planned. Every time Man One's phone rings, which has become more frequent, I try to decipher the one-sided conversation.

'That can be arranged.'

'What time will the car be here?'

I sense they are planning to take me somewhere. And the fear that place is to my death is crippling me. Death has never scared me. Mum has always told me life is a journey with a destination shared by all. We simply have a different route of getting there. But in my darkest moments here, when I think my life might end at the hands of these monsters, it puts a different perspective on the dying process. And, I wonder, how will it change me if I survive this?

The infinite hours stretch painfully as I lie on the bed, softly singing, thinking about Jack, as I do most of my waking hours. I quietly sing his favourite song, 'I Never Told You' by Colbie Caillat. I'd never heard it before I met him. A knock at the door quietens me. I know it's Nancy. Man One never knocks. I gaze up at the ceiling when she enters. 'I make coffee, girl. You want some?'

'That's kind of you, Nancy.' I try to be as charming as possible with her. There's still a human being in here. Can't she see that? If I'm going to be murdered, I want her to feel the enormity of her crime. Man One, too, but I know he won't give a toss.

She leaves the door open. 'Nancy,' I call out, going after her. Careful, Ellie, slow down. You're meant to be sedated. 'Are they going to kill me?'

She turns to me. 'No,' she says. But the look of sadness on her face tells me she is lying, because she simply doesn't know the answer to that question. There's a pull in my stomach. Another yank reminding me of the possibility of how this could end.

I follow her, stopping at the sofa, telling her I'm extra tired this morning. Man One barges into the room. He looks at me with disdain and heads to the toilet. I can't resist flipping him the bird behind his back. Nancy spots me from the kitchen. She suppresses a smile, I'm sure, as she prepares three cups. I lie down on the sofa, pretending to rest. Man One emerges from the toilet and barks an order at Nancy to bring his coffee outside.

Opening one eye, I glance at Nancy removing a carton of milk from the fridge. 'Nancy,' I call out. 'I've changed my mind. I won't have a cup of coffee. Can I have some water instead, please?'

Discarding one cup to the side, she takes a clean glass from the drainer and fills it with water before pouring coffee into the two cups with a drop of milk to follow.

I'm at the point of hyperarousal as she wanders off to the toilet.

Patience is a virtue. That's what Mum has always taught me.

This is my chance.

I spring up from the sofa and dash to the kitchen. Taking the tissue out of my pocket, I distribute the powder evenly between the two cups. I dare not think about the consequences if this doesn't turn out as I've planned. Stuffing the tissue back into my pocket, I grab a spoon from the worktop and stir the drinks. I'm shaking so badly, I drop the spoon. Bending down, I pick it up from the floor and replace it where I found it, knowing if I get caught, my life is over.

Nancy returns as I'm resuming my horizontal position on the sofa. Through a squinted eye, I see her sip her coffee before taking the other cup to Man One outside. I hear him grunt. Returning to sit at the dining table, she quietly sips her coffee. She removes one of her trashy magazines from her bag, and I watch her browse through it, shifting in her seat, until her head flumps on the table like a piece of frozen meat.

The door bursts open, smashing against the wall before rebounding back into Man One's face. He stumbles into the room, unsteady on his feet. 'What have... have you... done?' He hasn't consumed enough to render him unconscious, but he falls to his knees.

Patience is a virtue.

I scoot around him and dive for the door. My escape route is in sight. I run along the carpeted corridor, Man One in pursuit, calling after me. 'You stupid girl. You don't understand.' I feel feeble, my legs like leaden posts, but the fear of death impels me to keep moving. I look back. He is bouncing off each side of the corridor like a drunken bum. I reach the lift. The door to the stairs is on its right. I dither.

Life or death presents itself. I look behind me again. Man One is gaining on me. I shoot for the stairs; I can't risk the lift.

My muscles are weak, the days of inactivity taking their toll. I mutter to myself. The words I know Mum would use if she could. 'Keep going, Ells. You've got this.' Adrenaline kicks in and delivers in spades, and I imagine myself as an Olympic athlete, taking three stairs at a time to gold. I hear him behind me – the grunts and groans of a monster defeated. I blast through the double doors expelling me to freedom, and I gasp a lungful of wonderful New York air.

I'm standing between two buildings, disorientated and sweating. It's so hot out here in the sunshine. Such a contrast to the air-conditioned prison I've managed to escape. I run to the sidewalk, the need to be among people intense. I look to my left and then to my right, dithering again. Matters of life and death can't be taken recklessly. I chance turning left, stumbling along the street without looking back. Stopping an elderly couple strolling along arm-in-arm, I beg for help, but they look at me, then at each other, and skirt around me in haste.

I spot an entrance to Central Park. From the walks Jack and I have taken together, I know police patrol inside. I look behind me. Man One is not in sight. I run along the sidewalk and am about to cross the road when I hear someone call.

'Ellie!'

My cry of relief vibrates in the New York sky. I vaguely recognise him as the man from that barbecue I went to with Mum, although he's wearing a baseball cap. The man who listened so intently to me playing the piano and singing. His name escapes me. The man who complimented me to such an extent it was embarrassing. I remember now. 'What a remarkable talent you have,' he said.

Muffled cries whimper out of me, and my hand motions a gleeful wave as I run for safety. But I look right when, of course, I should look left. Only when I hear the screech of brakes do I turn to my left and glimpse the bumper of a yellow cab hurtling towards me. Time stops. A complex series of images blaze in my field of vision like a comforting fire on a winter's day. It's true. Your life does flash before you in slow motion in the moments leading up to your death. A suited man passes me a microphone as I climb the stairs in a flowing black dress to accept my Brit award. Mum is holding the baby Jack and I haven't yet had. Dad walks me down the aisle.

I feel a dull thud, and then I'm flying.

35

STEPH

Our four suitcases are lined up by the front door. I glance around the apartment, saying a silent farewell as I think about everything that has happened since Ellie and I arrived in this city and wonder what could have been. What could have been a positive, career-defining period in my life, with a soulmate thrown in for good measure, has turned out to be the horror movie from hell.

There's a knock at the door. I open it to a young man dressed in a smart suit, his hand wrapped around the brass tubing of a bell cart. 'Your car is waiting downstairs. Let me help you with your luggage.'

I take one final look and shut the door.

I arrive at JFK far too early, a little after three. But I couldn't have stuck another moment in that apartment. The driver drops me off at terminal eight. The smell of jet fuel hits me as I get out of the car. Our American Airlines flight is not until six-twenty, but Jennifer's PA told me to get here in plenty of time. I'm praying Ellie will turn up early too.

I consider getting a bite to eat. I've not eaten all day. But I don't think my stomach could handle it. I feel nauseous, and I may have a slight temperature, so I hang around the check-in desk. I glance at my phone. Nothing. I haven't heard anything since the message last night confirming the plans to meet my daughter.

I desperately scan the crowds, trying to pick out Ellie. An hour passes as I watch people funnel through. Some walking aimlessly, others rushing because they are late. They bump into each other, necks crooked in the air, trying to get a glimpse of their flight information on the boards above them.

Oh, my goodness.

Here she is.

Relief sweeps through me, brushing away the aches and pains that have started to cripple me. I've been terrified this moment would never come. My hand slams over my mouth to contain uncontrollable whimpers as my daughter's slim body strides confidently between a man with green hair and a mother pulling on the hand of her stroppy toddler. I glance at the security gate, with lines of passengers ebbing and flowing, and I imagine freedom beyond. Soon we will be through there and safely on the way to the UK, and this whole sorry episode will be behind us. My shaking hand moves from my mouth and waves, and I bounce up and down like a school child, unable to stop screaming her name. 'Ells, Ells!'

But as rapidly as jubilation exalts me, abject misery strikes as if the woman walking towards me has kicked out a foot and tripped me up. She looks nothing like my Ellie. I stifle a cry of disappointment as I start to scan the crowds again. I look at my watch. She should be here by now. Where is she? I call the number that has been messaging me about her, only to be put straight through to voicemail. I send a text asking them where my daughter is.

I continue looking out for her, trying to control my breathing, but my chest is tightening. Something is wrong. Something has happened. I can feel it bone deep. Why isn't she here? I keep scanning the crowds. Every minute seems like an hour. Time is running out, and I still need to check these suitcases in. Waves of passengers pass me, and my heart beats hopefully at the sight of every dark-haired young woman. 'Are you OK?' an elderly woman standing next to me asks. 'Waiting for someone special?' I give her a polite nod. When the flight information board displays the final boarding call, I go to the American Airlines desk and join the queue of people. I don't know why. What're they going to do? I unleash another text to Ellie's captors.

I kept my end of the bargain. Where is my daughter?

The reply is instant.

> She was a silly, silly girl. Take the flight.
> She will follow.

I glare at the screen. How can she follow? I've got her passport. And you think I'm going to leave her here? The flight details disappear from the board, and another one takes its place.

What do I do now? Who can I trust? No one. I consider Jack. Can I even trust him? I close my eyes, clenching my fists around the cold handle of the metal trolley. How did I find myself here? Alone in the capital of capitals, with a stolen daughter. I suck in streams of air, slowly puffing them out as I give myself a talking to. Dig deep, Steph. For the sake of your daughter, you must steel yourself and tackle this head on. You need a plan.

There is only one person who can give me answers. I stare blankly at the four suitcases. I can't go about finding my daughter with all this baggage. Tracking down the information desk, I find there is a luggage storage facility in the arrivals area. I steer the trolley there. The bags piled precariously seem to have a mind of their own, and I need to keep stopping to prevent the top one from sliding off. When I get there, I open one of my suitcases and rummage around for my small backpack, stuffing a few essentials inside.

As I offload the luggage, I wonder if I will ever see it all again. Then I remember Edward's paintings and know I'll be back for them at some point.

I take a cab back to New York City, directing the sullen driver to the tapas bar on the corner of the street where Jack lives and the garage where I left Edward's car, silently praying it's still there, and relieved I kept the keys. I zone out from the loud advertisement blasting from the screen in the back of the cab as the driver pulls into the corkscrewing queue of traffic departing the airport.

Every muscle and bone in my body aches. I'm not sure if it's the flu-like symptoms I've been feeling for the past few days coming to a head, or the enormity of the situation I've found myself in taking its toll. Most likely a bit of both. I wonder if they are tracking my phone. Not wanting to take any chances, I switch it off. I keep turning to look out of the back window, suspecting that I'm being followed at every juncture, but nothing piques my attention to suggest I am.

It's gone eight o'clock by the time I reach the parking garage. I make my way down to where I left Edward's car and exhale a pit-of-the-stomach sigh of relief to see it's still where I left it. Putting my plan into action, I check the boot. It's empty. Frustrated, I climb into the car and lean over to open the glovebox. I rummage around, pulling out an old Swiss army knife. This will have to do. Scanning for surveillance cameras, I pick a blind spot and move the Cadillac. Incredulous at my actions, I proceed to swap over the number plates with the vehicle in the next bay. Like I saw them do on a film I once watched. If I am being followed, and they have Edward's car on their radar, it may buy some valuable time. I can't believe what they have driven me to. This is not my style. Before I came to this city,

I was an average woman living an ordinary life. Sensible, law-abiding Steph, that was me. Compliant and respectable in everything I did.

And now look at me. I'm a bloody criminal.

Before I leave the car park, I turn on my phone, kidding myself, for a moment, that there will be a message waiting for me. *It was all a big mistake. Go back to the airport, collect your luggage. Your daughter is waiting for you.* Instead, when I click into my voicemail, I find three panic-stricken messages from Jack asking why we haven't called. We should be through check-in by now. I delete them and turn the phone off. I'm on my own.

I drive carefully. The roads are pretty clear. I keep checking to see if I'm being followed. They must be wondering what I did after Ellie's no-show. But there's nothing suspicious. Halfway there, I turn the air conditioning off. I'm freezing, despite the stifling heat of the summer evening.

It takes me fifty minutes to navigate the twenty miles to Jennifer's place. Her car is not in the driveway. It's all going to plan. So far. I park up in the adjacent street and walk back to her house. When I step foot on her winding driveway, a security light flashes on. I dash between two juniper trees that line the path, where I falter, doubting what I think I'm going to achieve here. But then I see my daughter's face and tell myself I don't have a choice. When the security light clicks off, I crouch down and follow the path of the trees, until I'm about halfway up, where I sit on the ground, and wait.

I know Jennifer usually leaves the office around

eight, so she should be home very soon. Unless she has decided to join members of staff for a drink, which she occasionally does. I doubt it though. Not with what's happened to Rhonda. I hug my backpack to my chest, not quite believing what I'm doing here. Rewind the hands of time several weeks, and I wouldn't have dared to be so brave. But then again, who knows how you're going to react in a situation like this. Apart from the occasional rumbling of a passing car or the chittering of scavenging raccoons, it's as quiet as a graveyard out here. Such a contrast to the babel and reverberation of the city.

After an hour, my anxiety levels rise even higher. What if Jennifer doesn't come home? I haven't got a plan B. I can't stay here all night. I shiver. I'm still cold, even though the night is warm.

Finally, I hear an approaching car slow to turn into the drive. My heart races. It's her. Jennifer is back at last. I pull my iPad out of my bag. When Jennifer switches off the engine, I run to her BMW convertible and try to open the passenger door, but it's locked. I hear a faint scream. She switches the light on. I knock on the window. 'Open up, Jennifer.' Overcome with shock, I think, she makes it easy for me and unlocks the door. I jump into the car, which smells of expensive leather and her perfume.

'Jeez, Steph. You scared me. I thought you were on a plane back to England.'

I stay composed. I don't want to frighten her. I imagine reaching over and clasping my hands around her throat, pressing harder and harder until I squeeze the dying breath out of her. Yes, I'd like nothing more. But for now, I want her to stay calm. 'Where's Todd?'

'What?'

'Where is your husband?'

'In Seattle with work. Why?'

Good. That's one thing less to worry about. If she is telling me the truth, that is. 'Where's my daughter?'

'Ellie?' She looks at me blankly. 'Why are you asking me?'

I stare at her. I could murder her. 'Don't play the innocent with me. You know she has been taken. She was meant to meet me at the airport, but she didn't turn up.'

She looks over to the house. 'Why don't you come inside? You look terrible.'

She is taking me for a fool. I unlock my iPad. 'Before you watch this, I want you to know my solicitor in London has a copy. So have two of my friends, with instructions to go straight to the police if anything happens to me, or my daughter.'

Her healthy, rosy cheeks pale, and her nostrils flare as she clenches her teeth, looking from me to the iPad.

I press play.

The clip is of me explaining what has been going on here in the New York offices of Crayhorne. The corruption and the people I think are involved.

All she can say is, 'It's not what you think.'

I laugh. I actually laugh at her. 'What do you take me for? I'm not some employee you can boss around any more, Jennifer. I have the proof.'

Her usual composed demeanour falters. She rubs her

hand over her mouth, as if she knows she can't slip up and needs to choose her next words carefully. 'Look, Steph. Todd is away. Let's go inside. Get a drink. Talk this through.'

'Stop taking me for a fool. I'm not going anywhere with you until you tell me where my daughter is.'

She slaps her hand on her chest. 'Hand on heart. I honestly don't know.'

36

ELLIE

'Ambulance!' a frantic voice shouts.

Another joins in. 'I'm on it.'

Silhouettes of faceless people are gathering around me, bending over, and snuffing out the daylight. I drift in and out of consciousness. Someone shoves them aside and leans over me. They swoop me up while talking to the individuals who have gathered around us. 'It's OK. She's going to be OK. I've got this.'

Except I'm not OK. In the slightest. At all. I'm numb, as if I'm levitating, having an out-of-body experience and watching this mayhem unfold around me from above. And as they lift my limp body, I feel as though I'm floating like a kite up in the sky.

Another bystander joins in. 'The girl needs a hospital. That was a nasty bump. I saw it happen, man. Flew through the air like a shot bird.'

'I said I've got this.' The man continues reassuring people as he walks past them, his arms holding me tightly against his muscular chest. For a moment, I feel safe. Then it comes flooding back in a wave of hopelessness and despair as his voice registers. 'She's my daughter. I'm going to take real good care of her. No. No need to go to hospital. She'll be OK.'

I know him. He is the man from the barbecue I went to with Mum. The person who heaped praise on my piano playing and "angelic voice", as he put it.

'She's in shock, that's all. I'm taking her home. We live on the next block,' he says in his smooth-talking manner.

No, I'm not, I try to scream. But my words are buried somewhere in the shock of the ordeal.

'I'm telling you, man. If that was a girl of mine, I'd be getting her straight to the emergency room.'

'If you don't mind, I need to get her home. Thank you.'

Effortlessly, he carries me away from the bystanders and rubberneckers babbling amongst themselves. All I can hear are muffled objections on how I belong in hospital.

Memories of when I was first taken resurface as I try hard to stop myself from drifting into unconsciousness. I missed the critical time – before they put me in the boot of that car. I can't miss this one. I need to shout, scream, kick my legs. But they won't move, and my words won't work. My body is failing me. I try to yell, 'Fire! Fire!' It's the merest of whispers as I fall. Down, down, down.

The smell of laundry stirs me. I open my eyes, unsure how long I've been out cold. Crisp white cotton sheets come into focus, whiteness everywhere. Am I dreaming? Am I dead? The orchestra of pain is killing me, high and low notes of agony moving through me. I wiggle my toes. My leg, what has happened to my leg?

I move my hands and turn my head. They hurt, everything hurts, but my goddamn leg is screaming with agony on another level.

I hear running water and hands rubbing together from the en suite. A man wearing a familiar tweed jacket appears like a film on replay. I groan as he enters the room, not bothering to engage him in conversation as he examines me. 'Quite a resourceful young lady, aren't you?' he sneers as he opens my mouth and places two tablets on my tongue. He hands me a glass of water and barks, 'Let me see you swallow.'

I surrender. The pain from my leg is too unbearable. Another person enters the room.

The doctor turns to him. 'Nothing broken. Some notable bruising, trauma to the thigh. Mostly cuts and abrasions. She'll live. For as long as you need her to.' He gives me a wry smile. 'I've given her a sedative. She's all yours. I'd appreciate you not calling me again.' The doctor loads his bag, nods to the man and leaves.

Closing the door, the man leans over me, meeting my fearful gaze. 'What do you think you were doing, you stupid girl? You were going home. Now...'

At first, I don't recognise him, my vision blurry as the sound of his voice rouses me from a deep sleep. My head is pounding. This man is talking to me, but I can't make out his words. I rest my eyes. I'm so tired. He slaps my face. My eyes pop open and stare at him. His bald head shines like a light in the darkness. He doesn't belong here.

Another slap comes my way. Terror cripples me. I want to cower away from him, but there's nowhere for me to go. His large frame looms over me, his tone menacing. 'Silly girl.' His voice registers. He came to the apartment when I fabricated the asthma attack. It's all coming back to me now. He was the one who beat up Man One. What is his name? I can't remember.

'You should be on a plane with your mom right now. We were going to drop you at the airport to meet her. But your games have ruined you. Silly, silly girl.' His face contorts with belligerence. 'The question is, what're we going to do with you now?'

Hopelessness consumes me as I remember who he is. The large house, the fancy cars, the lemony smell of after-shave. This man belongs at that barbecue I went to with Mum, telling me what a beautiful voice I have. Todd.

This is all tied up with Mum's work. What has she got involved in? Fear creeps through me like a terminal disease. They're never going to let me go. Why would they? I've seen their faces. I'm just collateral damage to them. My reality sinks in.

I'm not getting out of here alive.

37

STEPH

I hit her. I don't mean to. I've never hit anyone in my life, but I find myself twisting in the seat as the hand of subconsciousness strikes Jennifer's shoulder. 'I'm warning you. Unless you tell me where Ellie is, I will expose you and every lowlife involved in this corruption. I have all the evidence I need to blow this wide open.' My assertiveness shocks me. 'Where is Ellie?'

She clasps her shoulder and looks at me. 'You've got it all wrong.'

'I don't think I have.'

'You're dealing with dangerous people. You have no idea. You can't win. They are unbeatable.'

'It's nothing to do with winning. This is my daughter's life I'm talking about.' I want to hit her again but stop myself. 'Tell me where Ellie is. Now, Jennifer.'

She starts sobbing. Cool, calm and composed, Jennifer – one of the most unflappable people I've ever met – is sitting next to me with a river of tears cascading down her face. 'I honestly don't know where Ellie is. It isn't my fault. Any of this. He played me.'

'Who played you?'

'Todd.'

'How?'

She digs in her bag for a tissue and wipes her eyes. I don't know what I expected. Not really. But it certainly wasn't to see Jennifer cry. She stares ahead. 'I'm leaving him.'

'What?'

'My marriage is a sham. He has played me for many years.'

Isn't it the other way around? I scoff, 'A smart woman like you? Never.'

'It's the smart ones who have further to fall, Steph.'

I fold my arms, staring at her. 'Carry on.'

She wipes her face and composes herself. Shuffling in her seat, she turns to face me. 'I want you to understand. I never knew at the start what he was really like. From when we first met at college, I always knew Todd was obsessively ambitious. He was one of those men who had everything going for him.'

I don't have the time for a sob story and her pathetic lies, but I force myself to listen. If it leads me to Ellie, then I'm all ears.

She stops to blow her nose. 'You know the type. He had the looks, the personality, the brains, and to top it all, he was a really nice guy: kind, considerate, loving. Everyone knew *the* Todd Penderson, and he knew everyone. Everyone loved him. Everyone wanted to be him. He used his business degree to get him what he wanted in life. Success. We were the perfect couple in many respects.'

'But you cheated on him.'

Her head turns sharply to look at me. 'What?'

'I saw you with that catering guy at your barbecue. Todd directed me upstairs as the downstairs bathroom was in use, and I saw you two in the bedroom.'

She ignores me. 'But then Todd got mixed up with the wrong crowd. The sad thing is, he didn't need to. But greed got the better of him. Todd was the one who suggested I get the Harvey-Bowen account on board. An up-and-coming client, that's how he sold it to me. Be good for the company profile. It was all legitimate, at the start. Passed all our reg checks. And then bit by bit, they started to pump their filth through it. I want you to understand, Steph. I've only recently found out about everything Todd is involved in. That's when Cody joined the company.'

'Cody? What's he got to do with it?'

'Todd planned it all. Our post-trade senior resigned – family issues. Todd told me there was this brilliant guy he knew who would make an ideal replacement. He told me Cody had been working for one of his business associates' firms in their London office but was relocating to New York. He came highly recommended.' She shakes her head. 'Of course, he did. I believed him. Why wouldn't I? He was my husband. But it was all part of the setting up phase. Rebecca from Compliance...'

I interrupt. 'Rebecca Love Shield? Don't tell me she's involved too.'

'They bought her.'

'Bought her?'

'In more ways than one. They bought her silence, and they bought her to fake documents when needed.'

My wide eyes stare at her.

'Chris Smith is part of all this too.'

'That doesn't surprise me.'

'More business came our way because we won the Harvey-Bowen account. Other partners were applauding my success in securing the account. It was an ego trip. I admit it. I made partner. The activity slowly started ramping up this year.'

'I've certainly seen that.'

'A select few at Crayhorne contributed to the collusion keeping everything running smoothly. That's when I found out about Todd's involvement in it all. Believe me, he has gotten in way over his head.'

'Who are these people?'

'A faceless organisation pulling the strings of corruption. I'm not even sure Todd knows who the crime bosses are. If he does, he's never told me. I found out he was involved from some papers I found in his office at home. He came clean about it all and started threatening me. Telling me I had to play along otherwise I'd never see my boys again. He's a very persuasive man when he wants to be. That's when one of the controllers started making noises. We had to get rid of her.'

'Rid of her?'

She shakes her head. 'Not like you think. He made me orchestrate her leaving the company. The worst thing is...' She wipes her nose again. 'Todd thought I'd go along with it, but I told him I wanted out. He warned me these weren't the type of people you said this to. They'd stop at nothing. I'm not perfect. Yes, I've had affairs. And I can only imagine what you must've thought of me, seeing me with the catering guy. But I'm a good person, Steph.'

Is she? I don't know. I've read her so wrong. Jennifer has always come across as so level-headed and composed. A swan elegantly and calmly swimming the Crayhorne river of corruption when all this time she has been frantically kicking her feet, struggling to keep up.

'I don't know if you remember when I came to London at the beginning of this year, and we went out to dinner to that Indian restaurant in Covent Garden?'

'I do remember.'

'You told me all about your divorce. You were the motivation for me to decide, enough was enough, I was leaving him.'

Me? The motivation for her? I do recall when she came to London. She was commanding the limelight in a meeting, and I remember thinking, it's time for change, Stephanie Knight. I wanted to be like her. How strange we were both aspiring to be like each other.

'When I came back from that trip, I told Todd I was leaving him. He threatened me. Told me I'd never see my boys again if I didn't play by his rules. And I'd spend the rest of my life looking over my shoulder. I've been doing my own investigations, gathering data on them. The same detail as you have on your iPad. I'm just waiting for the right time to expose the lot of them. I have my boys to think about.'

I listen intently, wondering how much truth her eloquent words hold. 'You still haven't answered my question.'

She turns to me, frowning.

'Ellie. Where is Ellie?'

'I told you. I don't know.'

My voice wavers. I'm no closer to finding Ellie than when she was taken. 'And what about Melissa?'

'Let's just say, she started meddling. Like you. They found a means to get her out of the way.'

'So why haven't I ended up in a car crash or worse still, under a train, like Rhonda? That was their doing too, wasn't it?'

She nods. 'She was onto Cody. Threatening to expose him.'

'Todd murdered her?'

'Not Todd himself, no. They have a team of men who do their dirty work. Vicious psychopaths, all of them. Rhonda refused all offers to keep quiet. They coerced people to say they saw her jump. Funny how CCTV never caught any of it.' She shrugs. 'They know a source for every job and for all occasions. I'm telling you, they're ruthless.'

'How come I'm still alive?'

'My guess is, they knew doing anything to you was going one step too far. And they weren't sure what infor-mation you have in your possession. What you have on them. That's what I think, anyway. Taking Ellie was meant to frighten you away, I guess. Make you take off like Melissa.'

I'm incredulous.

'Plans are afoot. One way or other, I'm getting out. I'm ready for whatever the law has in store for me. So long as my boys are safe.' She is shaking, I notice, but I still don't know if I trust her. This could be one magnificent act. I could be wrong, but it's as if calculations are running through her head, working out how much to tell me.

My mind is made up. Once I get my daughter back, I'm going to expose every single one of these ruthless bastards.

If I get my daughter back.

'So why didn't Ellie turn up at the airport?'

'I don't know. I know nothing about her being taken.'

'Where was she being held before she was meant to be taken to the airport?'

She looks at me blankly. 'You've got to believe me. I know nothing about Ellie's disappearance.'

'What about Austin? How does he fit into all of this? And Edward? Is he connected?'

She leans her elbows on the steering wheel of her car and drops her head in her hands.

'Jennifer. What happened to Edward?'

A car pulls into the driveway. 'Shit.'

Headlights flash. I glance behind me.

'That's Todd,' she says.

'I thought you said he was in Seattle.'

'I thought he was.' She looks at me. I can't decide if it's terror in her eyes I see, or contempt. 'I swear.'

38

STEPH

My stomach sinks. And so do I – into the leather seat of Jennifer's BMW.

'Stay here. I'll distract him.' There's panic in her voice I've never noticed before. 'I doubt it, but I might be able to find out what has happened to Ellie. I'll pretend I've left something in the car and come back as soon as I can.'

She leaves me slumped in the seat, listening to her and Todd argue their way to the door. Try as I may, I can't work out what is being said. Edging my body up in the seat, I strain my neck until they come into view. I'm tense as I watch them. Todd appears agitated, seemingly in a rush, waving his hands in the air. He opens the door and pushes her inside.

I don't trust her. She was too quick to devise a plan to exit the car and get to her husband. The tears, the pretend anger, it's all part of her self-serving bullshit. She knows where my daughter is.

I shiver, despite being inside a car without the air

conditioning on in this heat. The leathery smell is making me nauseous. I need to get out of here before I throw up. I touch my forehead and then both cheeks; they are hot. This is not the time to be ill.

I'm not thinking straight. Jennifer could be relaying our conversation to Todd right now. They could be out of that door any second. I can't take any chances. Grabbing my backpack, I slowly open the door and climb out of the car, keeping below window height. Crouching, I slink into the camouflage of the juniper trees and follow the line of them down to the road.

There's no relief from the night air, still so heavy with heat and humidity even at this time. When I've almost reached the end of the drive, I hear the front door open. I turn my head to see Jennifer hurrying to her car. Maybe she has found out where Ellie is and is coming to tell me. I clench my fists to my temple and press them down my face. That's a chance I can't afford to take. I scramble into the depths of the trees until I'm squashed against the fence.

Todd appears, shouting at his wife. I can see her through the branches. She opens the car door, and I hear her swearing. Climbing into the car, she starts the engine and reverses out of the drive with Todd running after her.

Todd passes me, racing to the road. I drop my head in my hands. It feels so heavy and hot. I'm burning up, and my body feels like I've run a marathon. Every muscle aches. I need to rest. There's no way I can go anywhere else at the moment. Todd does a U-turn and comes marching back past me muttering to himself. I hear the front door slam, the noise reverberating around the neighbourhood.

I take a chance and continue wading through the trees until I reach the end, where I attempt to make a break for it. My efforts are feeble. I'm too ill. My legs can barely carry me along the street. I hear a car approaching. Knowing it could be Jennifer, I dart into a row of bushes in front of a house a few along from theirs. The car passes. It's her. She must be looking for me. She turns into her drive. I'm surprised she is going back to Todd with him so angry. I stay put for a while until I've mustered the strength to struggle back to Edward's car, where I start the engine and drive off with no clue where I'm going.

I will myself to keep driving. To where, I don't know. I'm burning up. Damn my body for failing me at such a vital time. Then a road sign makes me realise where I'm driving: Hastings, where Austin lives with his sister. I turn into an avenue and pull over. Jennifer didn't admit Austin was part of this, but then again, she didn't say he wasn't. But why did she instruct me to look specifically into him, if he was? She was bluffing. She knows he's clean. When Charles sent me over here, she needed to direct my attention away from the other illegal activity. She had no choice. Jennifer has no power over Charles. She couldn't have opposed him sending me here. I shudder. Or is Charles part of all this as well? Surely not. Charles is the epitome of integrity. Isn't he? Besides, why would he have sent me here?

I find Austin's address in my phone. He gave it to me in that email when he invited Edward and me to the party for his sister. When he thought Edward was still alive. I type it into the satnav. It's less than five minutes away.

Desperate measures in desperate times. I don't know if I'm doing the right thing, but this is the last throw of the dice. Knowing I need someone to help me, I take the risk and gamble on Austin Cunningham. Because at this moment, he seems my only someone. Nothing he has said or done during my time here has led me to think he is part of the corruption. Yes, he has executed trades on behalf of the Harvey-Bowen account, but he trades for many funds. He made me feel uncomfortable at Jennifer's barbecue. But I was on edge that day. Most people were making me feel the same way.

Pulling up opposite the weatherboarded house, I recognise the swing on the front lawn from his sister's Facebook page. I think of all those posts. The evident love between brother and sister, and everything Austin does for Polly. I can't be wrong about him. Can I?

The house is in darkness, which is hardly surprising given it's now late. I switch the engine off. My breathing is laboured. My fever has intensified. I roll my tongue around my lips. They feel dry and cracked, and my head is pounding like never before. I need some water. The desire to lie down is intense. Five minutes, that's all I need. But I can't afford it. Ellie needs me.

I get out of the car, miss my footing and stumble. My whole body feels like it's on fire. Steadying myself, I stagger like a drunk up the path to the porch. I look at the steps. It's going to take every sinew of effort to negotiate them. I achieve the first step, then trip.

. . .

I awaken to a stream of light shining in my face through half-closed shutters. I'm disorientated. My eyes are heavy, and my thoughts fuzzy, but the headache has gone. I'm in a bed I don't recognise with no recollection of how I got here. My mind is blank. The last thing I remember is leaving Jennifer's house.

White cotton sheets cover my body; there's a faint waft of freshness about them, but I can smell antiseptic cream too. And body odour. I pull the sheet down. It's coming from me. I stink. If fear has a smell, this is it: a chemical combination of excessive sweat and urine.

A half-empty bottle of water sits beside a full glass on the bedside cabinet. My mouth is so dry. I reach out for the glass, but my arm is like lead. It flops against the side of the bed. I call out, but my words are lost in the low moans escaping with each hot breath. I try to keep my eyes open, but it's impossible. They are as heavy as my arm. I drift in and out of sleep. Someone is talking, but I can't work out if I'm dreaming or not. It carries on. A voice I recognise, but my eyes struggle to open to see the face.

'Want to tell me what's going on, Steph?'

39

STEPH

'Austin.' I shield my eyes from the light, slowly regaining consciousness.

'How are you?' Austin stands at the side of the bed with a look of concern etched on his face.

I'm confused, disorientated. 'Where am I?'

'At my house; well, my sister's house. I found you passed out on the porch when I got home last night. What the hell has happened? What are you doing here?'

'No one else knows I'm here, do they?'

'Only one of my sister's caregivers. She helped me carry you in. You were delirious, begging me not to let anyone know you were here, not even your daughter. I've never seen anyone so scared.' He passes me the glass of water from the bedside cabinet. 'Plus, I thought you'd gone back to London.'

I heave myself up into a sitting position. 'What time is it?'

He pulls up the cuff of his shirt. 'Eight am. The

overnight caregiver has been looking after you. She has been feeding you Tylenol to bring your temperature down. We're well equipped for illness in this house.' He passes me a thermometer. 'Here, take your temperature again.'

'Thanks. I feel better than I did yesterday.' Holding the thermometer in my ear, I press the button on the side. I suddenly feel vulnerable. Last night, I came here when my defences were at rock bottom. I feel better than I did, but they are still down in the depths of despair. What if I got it wrong, and Austin is not a man to trust?

The thermometer beeps. He takes it from me and studies the display. 'It's still raised. Not as high as last night, though.' He passes me a packet of tablets. 'You last had two of these around four o'clock, so you could have another dose. You cut your face at some point. Probably from when you fell on the steps. We put antiseptic cream on it.' He sits down on the end of the bed. 'Do you want to tell me what you're doing here?'

I pop two more pills, swallowing them with a sip of water. 'It's a long story.'

'I'm listening.'

I'm silent, staring into the glass of water. I can't control all the thoughts flashing through my mind. They are making me dizzy. I shouldn't have come here. Now I think about it, I should've found a motel.

'You know you can trust me,' he says. His voice is so incredibly gentle, I feel his words in my heart. He sounds sincere. But then, so did Jennifer when she was talking to me last night. I'm not sure if it's my frailty or pure desperation, but I proceed to tell him everything and my mandate for coming out to New York, and that I was encouraged to focus my attention on him.

To the latter, he laughs, before turning serious. 'Me?' He shakes his head. 'I had my own suspicions, which I took to Jennifer only last week. She said matters were in hand. Where are these videos of Ellie?'

'On my phone. But I don't want to switch it on.'

'Why?'

'I'm scared they're tracking it.'

'Is it your work cell?'

I shake my head. 'My personal one.'

'Can they even do that?'

I shrug.

'Where is it?'

'What?'

'Your cell.'

'In my bag. What happened to my bag?' I start to panic. I need my phone. It's the only means of communicating with Ellie's kidnappers.

'I put it in there.' He nods to the bottom drawer of the bedside cabinet. 'If I'm going to help you, I'm going to need to know everything.' He reaches for my backpack.

I find my phone and navigate to the first video. 'That's her favourite Queen song.' My eyes well up at the sound of my daughter playing. The thought of never seeing her again is unbearable.

Austin nods and gives a straight-lipped smile. 'I remember her playing at Jennifer's barbecue.'

'I don't know what they've done to her, but she doesn't seem to be playing like she normally does. I can't put my finger on it. It may be the speaker, or the phone.' I play him the second video. 'I think the carrots represent her fingers.' I let out a low cry. 'If I don't follow their orders.'

He replays the second video.

'I can't place the song,' I say.

'It's Elton John, 'Chasing the Crown'.'

'That's it. I remember her practising it a while back for a production she was doing at school.'

'It's not one of his popular songs. Not sure why, it's a great track.' Austin replays both videos several times. 'It's the key.'

'What?'

'The first video.'

'You mean she's playing in the wrong key?'

'Not necessarily the wrong key, simply a different one to what we're used to hearing that song played in.'

'Sounds like the wrong key to me.'

He plays the videos again, chewing his lip, deep in thought. 'Is there a clue here?'

'What do you mean?'

'A clue in the songs she is playing.'

'I hadn't thought about it like that.'

'Or the artists? Queen and Elton John. 'Bohemian Rhapsody' and 'Chasing the Crown'.'

'Is that why she was playing in the wrong key? To divert attention to it?'

His phone rings, breaking his trance. He hands my phone back to me and takes his phone out of his pocket. 'I'll explain,' he says to the caller and ends the call. He turns to me. 'I need to deal with something. I'll be back in ten minutes. Then I'll help you all I can.'

When he leaves, I will myself to get out of bed. I'm in a plain white T-shirt, which is clinging to me. The dampness makes me shiver. My neatly folded clothes rest on the top of a chest of drawers. I walk over to the window, unsteady on my feet, and look into the garden. The woman I recognise from Facebook as his sister is outside with another woman playing ball with a dog. Austin is walking along a paved path towards an outbuilding, talking on his phone. It must be the games room he was telling me about at Jennifer's barbecue. The one he was painting for his sister. He turns to look at the house. I move to the side of the window. He is animated as he speaks on the phone. It could be a client, another trader, he is talking to, or anyone for that matter, but he keeps looking at the house. And suddenly, justified or not, I feel very afraid.

40

STEPH

I stand with my back against the wall. I don't think he saw me. Irrational or not, I question my actions again. Can I trust this man? He was one of the reasons Charles sent me to this city in the first place. I shouldn't have come here. What was I thinking?

A fresh surge of adrenaline drives me forwards. Ellie. My daughter is all that matters now. Discarding the white T-shirt, I slip into my jeans and top from yesterday, ignoring how rotten I feel. And how disgusting I smell. I gather my things and leave the room. As I descend the stairs, I hear people in the kitchen talking over each other loudly amongst a melody of crashing crockery and clinking cutlery. I head for the door and slip out of the house, hopefully unnoticed by Austin who I can see still striding around the garden on his phone.

Edward's Cadillac remains parked opposite the house where I left it last night. I find the keys, climb in and drive off. I don't know where I'm going. I've never felt so lost and alone in my life. My phone rings. 'Shit,' I call out. I should've switched it off. Jennifer's number flashes on the screen. I pull up on the side of the road to answer it.

'Steph, it's Jennifer. Where did you get to last night? I've found out what's happened to Ellie.'

I gasp loudly. 'Where is she?'

'She tried to escape, which is why she never turned up at the airport. It's all a mess, but I can take you to her.'

'No. I don't trust you. Tell me where she is.'

'She's being held in one of our corporate apartments on the Upper West Side. The Crown Apartments. They're mainly used for staff who live outside the city and are working late. Where are you?'

'How do I know you're telling me the truth?'

She sighs loudly. 'Because I want to help you. These bastards keep ruining lives. It's not going to stop unless people like you and me do something about it. I'll text you the full address. I'm going there now. Meet me in the lobby, and I'll take you to her.'

My voice wavers. 'Is she OK?'

'She stepped in front of a car. She's hurt her leg, but she's OK. I've brokered you a deal. I'm going to get you on a flight back to the UK today. How long will you be?'

Is this it? Am I finally going to be reunited with my daughter? 'How do I know you're not lying to me?'

'You must trust me, Steph. I never wanted to be mixed up in all this. I want you to get Ellie back safely. We must go now, though. They won't think twice about killing her. I can tell you that for sure.'

'What happened to Edward? And Austin?' My voice breaks. 'And Jack? Are they involved in all of this?'

'We haven't time. I'll tell you everything I know when I see you. For now, I need to get you and your daughter on this flight.'

Jennifer ends the call and texts me the details of the address of the Crown Apartment block where I'm to meet her. I enter the details into the satnav and go to switch my phone off, but I needn't have bothered. It's run out of battery. Jack enters my thoughts. I should have called him. Shouldn't I? I simply don't know. I find the phone he gave me and switch it on to find twenty-seven texts he has sent since yesterday. As I scroll through them, I swallow the lump in my throat for the acute desperation in every single one of his messages. Unless he is a very good actor, he has played no part in any of this.

The phone rings. It's Jack. I don't know whether to answer it. The fever is muddling my thoughts.

I pull onto the road, praying I'm going to find my daughter alive. I'm aware of the acute danger I'm putting myself in, but I have no other choice. As any mother would, I'm willing to lay down my life to save my daughter.

The traffic is busier than when I've driven before, escalating my stress levels, which were already off the scale. Ellie consumes my thoughts the entire journey. I wonder if it's time to call the police. But then I think of the possible consequences. Look what happened when I called Randy Tommaso.

I abandon the car near the apartment block. Although

I don't feel as bad as I did last night, and despite being drugged up with paracetamol, I still feel like hell.

The Crown Apartments are nowhere near as plush as Bridgewood Plaza, and there's no concierge. Jennifer is waiting for me by the lifts, looking as if she never went to bed last night.

She nods at me and jabs the lift button several times. 'These elevators are always so damn slow in this place. Where did you go last night?' she asks. 'Why did you run away?'

I fold my arms across my chest. 'I was scared. I slept in my car.'

Her blonde hair, usually so shiny, hangs limp. 'It's going to be OK. I will get you out of here. I promise you.'

The lift is stuck on the twelfth floor, and the one opposite is out of order, so we take the stairs. Each step is a struggle, but I refuse to let her see or feel my weakness. When we reach the fifth floor, she turns to me. 'You were right not to involve the police, you know. They wouldn't have thought twice about getting rid of her.' She boldly guides me along the corridor.

'What's a piano doing in a corporate apartment?' I ask.

'It was left by the previous owners. Why do you ask?'

'Never mind.'

We stop at number five-seventy-two, and she raps on the door. 'Remember, they think I'm part of them.' I lean against the wall behind us, wondering if coming here was the right thing to do.

The door opens. The smell of cheese makes me gag.

Jennifer beckons me to follow her into a small lobby where I can't make sense of what I'm seeing.

Randy Tommaso greets us, brandishing a handgun.

I step backwards. What did I expect? 'You!' The immense anger I feel for this brute is palpable. 'You're a police officer.'

He smirks at me. The cavalier manner in which Jennifer dismisses him astounds me. I pause. This is not how I expected it to play out.

Thoughts rush around my head. I've been a fool. Jennifer has delivered me straight into the mouth of the lion, and I have gone willingly. Or is she acting, like she said, pretending she is still a big part of this? My head tells me to run for my life, but if Ellie is inside this apartment, abandoning her could see her dead. I have no choice but to follow this woman.

I look around the large open-plan room, stunned to see Todd jump up from a sofa. He sneers at me. What happened to the friendly guy from the barbecue? An older Asian woman who appears strangely out of place is also present, along with Randy, clenching his gun.

'Ah, here we have her.' Todd nods at me. 'I've heard you've been trying to blackmail us.'

I glance at Jennifer. Is that fear I see in her tired eyes and furrowed brow, or contempt? Is she throwing me to the wolves? I'm confused. 'Where's my daughter?'

The older woman ducks behind the kitchen cabinets as Todd speaks as calmly as if he was negotiating an everyday business transaction.

'You'll have your daughter. But first, we need to agree on a few things.'

'What things?'

'You can take your daughter, get the hell out of this city and never say a word about what has happened. This has all got out of hand, I must admit, but you've compromised our operation, and my associates are none too pleased that you're still walking on this planet. If they find out you've ever breathed a word about your time in New York to anyone, you and your daughter are dead. You're lucky you've got me looking out for you. These are not people you want to cross. You'll be forever on their radar.'

I'm having difficulty processing his threat. Why would these uncompromising monsters risk letting Ellie and me go? Unless, of course, the information I have safely stored away has more power than I thought. Or is Jennifer fighting our corner? I'm too consumed by the thought of seeing my daughter to contemplate the alternative. 'Where is she?'

He nods to a door on the other side of the lounge. I run towards it. I'm going to see my girl. But when I get to the door, I stop. Is this a trap? Are they trying to corner me? I'm going to die. My head pounds. The room is spinning. What have I done? There's a click, and the door opens.

41

STEPH

I duck, expecting a bullet. But it doesn't come. Instead, there stands my daughter at the entrance to the bedroom, looking like a ghost in white. 'Ells.'

'Mum.' She tries to hobble towards me, but there's something wrong with her leg. Tripping forward, she throws her arms open. Mine open wider, catching her fall, and I wrap myself around her frail body, pulling her close. We cling to each other tightly, sobbing tears of relief and joy. I don't think I'll ever let her go again.

'It's OK, darling. I'm here.' Drawing away, I grab her hands and check her fingers. They are all there. I touch her beautiful face, scarred by the brutality of these despicable creatures. I brush my fingers over her cheeks and rest them on her dimples. The indentations seem more pronounced, her weight loss evident in her sunken eyes and the prominence of her shoulder bones. 'What have they done to you, darling?'

She winces. 'I'm fine. Honestly, I am. Where's Jack?'

I want to tell her he is at his apartment, but I'm still half-expecting to see him mixed up with these brutes. Or is that my distrust in everyone I've met since I've been here? 'I don't know. He's OK though. We can see him when we get out of here.'

If we get out of here.

Jennifer is approaching us. 'Come on. Let's go.'

From the other side of the room, Randy speaks for the first time. 'Hey, now. Let's hold on a minute.'

I hesitate. There seems to be a change in the mood. Or is my anxiety turning the wheels of doubt? The order of command has not been quite clear to me, the hierarchy muddled somehow. But I sense it has definitely shifted in the worst way imaginable. And the hope of us getting out of here alive is evaporating by the second.

Ellie cowers against me. She fears this animal. What has he done to her?

'This is all very civilised, I'm sure, but do you honestly think they are gonna be happy with these two strolling out of here now? Ain't gonna happen.' He taps his revolver on the side of his thigh.

Jennifer stands in front of us. 'Look, Randy. This has gotten way out of control.'

I back Ellie into the bedroom.

'We've got enough blood on our hands,' Todd says. 'These two can't disappear in this city. Not now. We'll have the UK and US authorities all over us. We won't get away with it.'

Randy gives a malevolent sneer as his hand reaches into his pocket and pulls out a silencer. He walks over to

Todd. 'I've already had one beating from you, and I took it. I knew I'd get my chance sooner or later to repay the favour. You're too weak. People way above you call my shots and I have authority to tidy up this "situation". Make it all go away.'

Jennifer addresses Randy. 'But what's changed? If Ellie hadn't messed up, they would've been well out of the way by now.'

'Don't you see? It's easy for us two to disappear.' Randy nods across to the older woman. 'We'd never be found. And a little accident was being arranged when they arrived back over there.'

'Over where?'

'England, of course.'

I cover Ellie's ears. She doesn't need to hear this.

He continues, 'But now your cover is blown, it causes us a great deal of inconvenience. If you know what I mean. We need to protect our investment. There's too much riding on this.'

I hear a whimper from the older woman behind the kitchen counter.

As Randy goes to attach the silencer to the handgun, Todd launches himself at him, knocking the hollow metal tube from his hand across the room. A struggle ensues as both men fight over the weapon, pulling it this way and that, grunting and groaning with the exertion. I stare, numb, until I come to my senses and manage to push Ellie, manhandling her through the threshold of her bedroom door.

The piercing sound of a gunshot reverberates around

the apartment. I instinctively cower, holding my hands to my ears, and see the two of them drop to the floor.

In an instance the world changes.

Bedlam ensues as the room appears to implode.

Or rather the entrance to the apartment disintegrates. I can't see, but I can hear a muffled eruption, deafened from the momentary damage to my ear drums. It has the desired effect of shock and awe. 'Police! Don't move!'

Standing at the entrance to the bedroom, I stare on as four NYPD officers charge into the room, fanning out. Their weapons are trained on each of us. 'No one move!' comes the authoritative yell of one of the officers, as they seek to handcuff each of us. 'No one move!' repeats another officer.

An officer charges towards me. 'But I'm a victim, and so is my daughter.' I motion to Ellie in the corner curled in a ball, her hands protecting her head 'She's been through enough.'

His response is uncompromising. 'It's procedure.'

Todd lays motionless, while Jennifer and the older woman, in shock, stare at the scene. From where I'm standing, I manage to glance into the bedroom to see the officer attending to Ellie.

Randy, if this is indeed his name, looks on in disdain. He has thrown his weapon across the floor. Confusion ensues as more armed officers appear and assess the scene. How did they know we were here? Is this nightmare finally coming to an end?

When the officers are satisfied the scene is secure, paramedics file in.

Help is finally here. A thought flashes through my mind. No. These are real paramedics. Aren't they?

Someone puts a covering around Ellie's shoulders and then mine. I'm transfixed by Jennifer. She is staring blankly at her husband, who is face-planted on the floor in a pool of blood as the emergency services try to revive him. 'Come on,' the gentle voice of a paramedic says to me, 'Best if we close the door on this.'

'What about Edward?' I call out to Jennifer.

She is emotionless, backing away as paramedics fail to revive her husband.

'What happened to Edward?' I repeat.

She turns to me. 'He's dead, of course, Steph. You know that.'

'I just thought, maybe...'

'I'm sorry, Steph. I'm so sorry. It was only meant to be a warning, I was told.' Her voice is shaking. 'Todd heard him say something at the barbecue about the Harvey-Bowen account.' She shakes her head. Two tears roll down her pale cheeks. 'They went to find out what he knew and to warn him off. He fought back. From what I can make out, they didn't intend to kill him. It was an accident. Things got out of hand. There was an altercation, and he hit his head. The last I heard, they had dumped his body in the Hudson.' Her voice breaks. 'I'm so sorry.'

It's like he has died all over again.

And it's all my fault.

42

STEPH

Sixteen months later

'You've done so well, Mum.' Ellie leans her head on my shoulder. 'I'm so proud of you.'

Her words wrap around me like a cosy winter coat. I kiss her hair, staring out of the window of the eighteenth-century building. A blanket of snow covers the cobbled street: an atmosphere of serene tranquillity only achievable this time of year. It's as if a celestial being is smiling down from above, inspiring a picture postcard scene with falling snow. 'I'm nervous,' I say.

'Me too.'

'You'll be fine.'

She lifts her head. The light catches one of her dimples. 'I dreamt about Nancy last night.'

'You haven't done that for a while.'

'I dreamt they let her out of prison early and sent her home to her family.'

'I doubt that's going to happen.'

'I get waves of sympathy for her, you know. Ever since her daughter wrote me that letter. How poor they must be for her to do what she did.'

'Poverty is no excuse.'

She sits up straight. 'I know. She was never horrible to me, though. She never wanted me to get hurt.'

'I'm sorry, Ells. You'll never get me to feel sorry for her.'

She nudges my arm. 'I need to warm up.'

'And I need to get Edward. He was with Jack.'

Ellie laces her fingers and stretches her arms up to the ceiling, where the track lighting emits a soft, warm glow. 'Give them both a kiss from me.'

I leave my daughter limbering up playing a selection of scales and walk around, ensuring the LED spotlights award each piece of art the lambency it deserves. I've learned so much about lighting since securing these perfect premises in Greenwich Village, London earlier this year.

I can see Jack talking to Edward, alongside several artists who are unpacking boxes of glasses I rented that turned up last minute. The artists are joking amongst themselves. Probably to steady their nerves. They have their work displayed on the brick walls and glass plinths. For many, this is the first time they've had their paintings and sculptures on show professionally. But that's the spirit of the Edward Millner Charitable Foundation Gallery. It's exactly what Edward wanted. It's why he resigned from his job. A means for struggling up-and-coming artists whose talents would otherwise stay buried in their poverty.

Jack and Edward wave to me as Ellie begins to play 'Silent Night'. I wave back and look to the far end of the room where Edward's canvases adorn the walls. They look spectacular. I swallow the lump that still pops up now and again to remind me of those tumultuous weeks in New York.

Ellie's ethereal voice fills the room with her angelic musical presence, as the polished brass bell rings, and Charles enters with a bouquet of winter flowers. A show-stopping mix of ruby red and white roses and anemones dotted among sprigs of pine and eucalyptus. I hurry over to him. He stamps his feet and brushes snowflakes from his bald head. 'Congratulations.' He hands me the flowers and kisses my cheek. 'I'm half an hour early, but I thought I might be able to nab five minutes with you before the party begins.' He waves to Ellie at the piano. 'This is magnificent.' One of the artists comes over and takes his coat and the flowers from me, and another brings us glasses of champagne. Charles slips his arm through mine, and I take him on a guided tour.

'Ellie's sounding as exquisite as always,' he says. 'How's she coping?'

'She's made her first term at uni. Finished last week. She and Jack are moving in together. He starts his new job here in January. And how's your new job?'

He shrugs. 'Not quite Crayhorne, but it'll do me for a few years until I retire. And yours?'

'Better. You know how it is when you join a new company; there's lots to learn.' After taking a year out, going back to work was hard at first, especially after the heartache and stress I'd been through. 'It's good to be back in the city. I missed London.'

'You've done well for yourself. I always knew you'd make VP one day. But nothing less than you deserve, given the number of people you put behind bars.'

'Not single-handedly.'

'Almost,' he jokes.

'I have Austin to thank. If he hadn't cracked Ellie's code and called the police that day, God knows what would've happened to us.'

'Your daughter is a very clever girl.' He laughs, his head bobbing up and down. 'The Crown Apartments. Queen played in the wrong key and Elton John's, 'Chasing the Crown'.'

'Not the wrong key. Just a different key than we're used to.'

'Same thing to me. I never was musical.'

'She can't play those songs any more.'

'Maybe she will one day. Have you heard from Austin?'

'He's started a new job at United,' I say. 'Melissa contacted me too. She's living with her mum. She was still too scared to tell me exactly where, but she wanted me to know she's doing OK. I don't think I'll ever hear from her again. Even with all those Crayhorne crooks put away.'

'I still can't get over it. All those years I worked with Jennifer.'

'She wasn't all bad. Just married the wrong person.' I shrug. 'It can happen to the best of us.'

He laughs. 'You never know anyone, hey? Not really.'

I lean into him and laugh too. 'I like to think I know you and vice versa.'

'You do,' he says.

'Greed, Steph. It always catches up with you in the end.' He squeezes my arm. 'And how are you coping?'

'I'm getting there. Working through the guilt that I caused the death of the love of my life.'

'You can't think like that.'

I raise my eyebrows at him. 'You sound like my therapist.'

'Perhaps your therapist is right?'

We turn to the babble of Jack walking over to us with Edward. I throw out an arm, and Jack passes my son to me. I jiggle him on my hip, kissing his baby blonde hair.

Charles digs a present out of his pocket. 'Happy Christmas, little fella.' He hands Edward a teddy bear. My stomach flutters as Edward smiles. He looks so much like his dad.

Charles turns and raises his glass to me. 'Here's to Edward senior. You've done him proud.'

I clink my glass against his. 'To Edward senior.'

ACKNOWLEDGMENTS

Writing is a lonely pursuit. Publishing is the opposite. It's a crowded space full of the best people I'm lucky to have on my side. Thank you to my brilliant editor, Louise Walters, for once again wading through the muddled first draft of this story to help me get to this version, and to Tim Barber for another cracking cover. Mr and Mrs Wills, my fellow AJs, thank you for your proofreading skills and continued support. To Tony Shaw, thank you for all the Zoom calls and talking through the financial aspects of the story. And to Monica Walls for promptly answering all my texts about how an American would phrase certain words.

To my shrewd beta readers – Mr C, Christine Henderson, Maddie Standen, John Black, Mel Vout and Sally Riordan – thank you for helping me turn *The Wrong Key* into the finished version. And to Dawn Harland for all your help with New York.

To my ARC team, most of who have been with me since my debut novel, thank you for believing in me and continuing this crazy ride. I'm blessed to have you. And thank you to all the fantastic book bloggers and media people for supporting my work. Your endless support means the world to me.

A special thank you to Christine Henderson for your unwavering support in championing my work.

To my readers, thank you a million for choosing my books. Without you, I couldn't carry on writing and publishing my work. Your reviews, emails and comments on my social media pages keep me company and always make my day.

And thank you to Rebecca Love Shield from Book Swap Central, who won a competition to have a character named after her in this novel. What a great name to use!

Mr C, thank you for your ongoing encouragement and for making me kick the imposter syndrome on the days it shows up. And last, but always first, to my boys, my everything.

AJx

PLEASE LEAVE A REVIEW

As for all authors, reviews are the key to raising awareness of my work. If you have enjoyed this book, please do consider leaving a review on Amazon and Goodreads to help others find it too.

All my novels undergo a rigorous editing process, but sometimes mistakes do happen. If you have spotted an error, please contact me here, so I can promptly get it corrected.

www.ajcampbellauthor.com/contact

Thank you for choosing to read my books.

AJx

A FREE GIFT FOR YOU

For me, building a relationship with my readers is one of the joys of writing. I set up the AJ Campbell Readers Club to keep in contact with you all. As a member of my community, you will receive reading inspiration via my monthly newsletter, plus details of giveaways to win book-related gifts. You will always be the first to know about my upcoming book launch promotions and ongoing special discounts. Plus, I'll ensure that you are the first to receive sneak previews of my book covers and exclusive free downloads of my work. Click here to join, and I will send your free copy of my short story Choices. I look forward to welcoming you personally.

Warning signs presented themselves from the start. Flashing like the neon displays in Piccadilly Circus, they couldn't have advertised things more clearly. But Abbie was too troubled to see clearly. Too damaged to see the dangers Tony Sharpe brought into her life. Until the day he pushed her too far.

Visit my website get your copy:
authorajcampbellauthor.com

ALSO BY AJ CAMPBELL

I hope you enjoyed reading my fifth published book *The Wrong Key* as much as I adored writing it. If you haven't read my other novels, check them in the following pages.

All my books are available from Amazon.

ALSO BY AJ CAMPBELL

A single phone call can destroy your life.

Joey Clarke was just fifteen when his dad died, leaving him to raise his much younger siblings as his mum dealt with the trauma of bereavement and her failing health. Ten years on, Joey's only pleasure is spending time with his friend Becca, the love of his life. It's the one escape from his dead-end job, his ever-increasing debts and the fear that enforcement agents will knock on his front door any day.

So when a phone call brings Joey the chance to ease the burdens of his life, he grabs the opportunity, even though he knows things are not entirely as they should be. He justifies it to himself as a way to get back on his feet. But when he finds himself party to a crime linked to Becca, he panics.

As catastrophic events unfold, Joey becomes further embroiled in a web of secrets, lies and deceit. He is now faced with the impossible. Should he confess to the police? Tell Becca? Or should he keep quiet and say nothing?

And when the next job comes in, Joey wants out.

But this time, Joey's in way too deep to say no...

ALSO BY AJ CAMPBELL

A broken family.

Skeletons in the closet.

Lives in danger.

How far would you go to protect your family?

When Eva's brother Ben announces he has found their mother, Eva is determined to have nothing to do with the woman who abandoned them eighteen years ago to a traumatic childhood in foster care. Eva is happy now, in a loving relationship with rich and dependable Jim, and she is pregnant.

Nothing can change Eva's mind. Her eyes are firmly on the future. But when her baby is born with a serious hereditary illness, she is forced to confront both her mother and her past. Eva begins to find forgiveness. But as old secrets and layers of deceit emerge, she makes a shocking discovery, leaving her fearing for her baby's, Jim's, and her own life.

ALSO BY AJ CAMPBELL

A missing man.

A desperate friend.

A circle of deceit.

Would you refuse your best friend's plea for help?

Marc O'Sullivan has disappeared.

His wife Sasha is frantic, and Eva is baffled.

They were blissfully married with three kids. The perfect couple... or so everybody thought.

Sasha begs Eva to help her find Marc. But he has given a written statement at the police station where Eva works. It's on record – when his family report him missing, Marc does not want to be found. But why?

Ultimately, friendship and loyalty override Eva's professional integrity, and she is compelled to use her resources to delve into Marc's life, even if it means breaking the police Code of Conduct and jeopardising her career.

As each day passes, the mystery deepens. Murky goings-on from Marc and Sasha's neighbours heighten the tension. What dark secrets are they hiding? And what drove Marc's inexplicable actions in the weeks leading up to his disappearance? Behaviour so out of character, Eva struggles to tell Sasha.

Will Eva uncover the truth before it's too late and lives are destroyed forever?

ALSO BY AJ CAMPBELL

Family secrets can kill.

Cara De Rosa is the heart of her large family and community in London. Her restaurant business is booming. She's found a second chance at love, and an impending marriage is on the horizon. But there's no such thing as a perfect life. And the good times never last forever.

When Cara's health suddenly falters, her family's world turns upside down in the blink of an eye. In a bed-ridden haze, she confides in Sienna, her favourite grandchild, that her rapid decline may be at the hands of one of her own.

Sienna, a young, single mother, is reeling in the wake of her husband's unsolved death. She is haunted by crippling anxiety and misplaced guilt, heightened by suddenly finding herself in a race against time to save Cara's life. As she begins to pull at the strings of a tangled family web, she'll reveal disturbing secrets, decades of deceit and shockingly serious crimes.

ABOUT THE AUTHOR

AJ CAMPBELL is an Amazon bestselling author of psychological suspense and promises stories full of twists, turns and torment. Her fifth book *The Wrong Key* was released in January 2023. AJ draws inspiration for her novels from seemingly unbelievable situations in which ordinary people find themselves. She creates compelling characters that resonate with her readers. AJ lives in the UK on the Essex / Hertfordshire border with her husband, sons, and cocker spaniel, Max. A dog lover, Netflix junkie, wine and Asian food enthusiast, either reading or writing, AJ enjoys nothing more than getting stuck into a twisty book!

ELLIE'S PLAYLIST

Don't Stop Me Now: Queen
What a Wonderful World: Louis Armstrong
Funeral March: Chopin
Hungarian Rhapsody No.2: Liszt
Intermezzi, Op.117: No. 1 in E -Flat Major: Brahms
We Didn't Start the Fire: Billy Joel
A Thousand Miles: Vanessa Carlton
Bohemian Rhapsody: Queen
Moonlight Sonata: Beethoven
Chasing The Crown: Elton John
I Never Told You: Colbie Caillat
Silent Night: Franz Xaver Gruber